*A Golden Gi*

# MURDER
## BY
# CHEESECAKE

## RACHEL EKSTROM COURAGE

**HYPERION AVENUE**
LOS ANGELES • NEW YORK

*Murder by Cheesecake* is an original novel inspired by the television show *The Golden Girls*. Any similarities to actual persons, places, and events are purely coincidental.

For information address Hyperion Avenue, 7 Hudson Square, New York, New York 10013.

First Paperback Edition, April 2025
1 3 5 7 9 10 8 6 4 2
FAC-029261-25030
Printed in the United States of America

Library of Congress Cataloging-in-Publication Data

Names: Ekstrom Courage, Rachel, author.
Title: Murder by cheesecake: a Golden Girls cozy mystery / Rachel
   Ekstrom Courage.
Description: New York : Hyperion Avenue, 2025. | Series: The Golden Girls
   cozy mystery series; vol 1 | Summary: "When Dorothy's obnoxious date is
   found dead in a hotel freezer, it not only ruins a gorgeous cheesecake
   but threatens the elaborate St. Olaf–themed wedding Rose is hosting."—
   Provided by publisher.
Identifiers: LCCN 2024045441 | ISBN 9781368102988 (paperback) | ISBN
   9781368102971 (ebook)
Subjects: LCGFT: Cozy mysteries.
Classification: LCC PS3605.K84 M87 2025 | DDC 813/.6—dc23/eng/20241001
LC record available at https://lccn.loc.gov/202404

www.HyperionAvenueBooks.com

SUSTAINABLE FORESTRY INITIATIVE

Certified Sourcing

www.forests.org
SFI-01681

Logo Applies to Text Stock Only

FOR BEA ARTHUR, BETTY WHITE, RUE
McCLANAHAN, AND ESTELLE GETTY—
THANK YOU FOR BEING A FRIEND TO SO MANY.

# COFFEE AND CATASTROPHE

············ **1** ············

*R*ose Nylund whispered into the lemon-yellow telephone receiver, twisting the cord tightly between her fingers, her words obscured by the gurgling of the coffee percolator. The aroma of toast and melting butter filled the kitchen as the early Florida sunlight filtered through the ruffled curtains above the sink.

"Who's that you're talking to, Rose?" Blanche called in her languid Southern drawl as she poured herself a cup of coffee. "A new beau?"

Rose hung up the handset with a clatter and smoothed her floral robe. "Oh, it was just one of those prank calls."

"For *twenty minutes*?" Sophia piped up from the breakfast table, her small face framed by the scalloped collar of her nightgown. "I've had dates that ended quicker than that."

Blanche stifled a giggle as she carried her mug over to the table, seating herself with a swirl of chiffon on a white bamboo chair.

"When was that, back in the 1800s?" Dorothy said as she swept into the kitchen, already dressed for the day in a flowing cream blazer, beige slacks, and chunky gold earrings.

"Exactly. Right after you were born," Sophia said, her sharp tone softened by the twinkle behind her large bifocal lenses.

Dorothy reached for a banana from the fruit bowl on the kitchen island, ignoring her mother's barb. She leaned against the oak cabinets, noticing Rose's worried expression.

"What's the problem, Rose?" she said kindly.

"Well, I'd rather not say," Rose said, dipping her head.

"Don't worry honey, we won't pry," Blanche said. She leaned forward and peered over the rim of her coffee cup, as if she very much wanted to pry.

"Well . . . if you're going to drag it out of me . . ." Rose said, settling herself at the table between Sophia and Blanche. "I can't keep it all cooped up inside for much longer."

"That's never a good idea," Sophia said sagely. "Just ask my gastroenterologist."

"It's clear something is bothering you," Blanche purred,

tilting her head to one side. "*I always feel better after I unburden myself.*"

Dorothy opened her mouth, ready to make a wisecrack. She thought better of it and poured herself some coffee before joining the others at the table.

"You know how I was going to fly to St. Olaf for a wedding next week? Well, something terrible has happened there," Rose said. She fidgeted with the edge of the tablecloth, wrinkling the abstract leaf pattern between her fingers.

"On no! Is everything all right with your niece, sweet pea? Nettie, was it?" Blanche asked, her voice full of concern. She passed a plate of buttered toast to Rose, who usually felt better once she had a snack, especially one involving dairy products.

"No, everything is not okay," Rose said. "And technically, Nettie is my cousin. Since I'm closer to her mother's age, she's always called me Aunt Rose. Her mother is my aunt Greta, and I have a few choice words to say about *her*, believe me!" She released the edge of the tablecloth, leaving it in crumpled pleats.

Blanche and Sophia exchanged a knowing glance. In their experience, Rose hardly ever spoke ill of anyone—and when she did, the words were lengthy, guttural, and vaguely Norwegian. Dorothy took a fortifying sip of coffee as Rose cleared her throat.

"So Nettie's mother is your aunt, but her daughter thinks you're her aunt," Sophia said. "Got it."

"It's more of a term of respect," Rose said. "Especially

because I helped raise her after her parents ran off to follow their dreams of starting a poodle circus in Pittsburgh. Ever since I've lived in Miami, I've been more like a long-distance surrogate mother to Nettie."

"Poor girl," Dorothy said. "She's lucky to have you in her life."

"She hasn't had it easy," Rose said, shaking her head. "When my aunt Greta was pregnant with her, there were terrible rumors that she was actually carrying the Sturgeon General's baby. But when The Amazing Shapiro delivered her, it was clear that Nettie was a Lindstrom through and through." Saying that last bit in a voice full of pride, she paused to make sure her friends understood.

"Dare I ask?" Dorothy said as she joined the others at the table.

"Which part did you find confusing?" Sophia said, lifting her hands in the air. "The Sturgeon General or The Amazing Shapiro?"

"They're two *completely different* people!" Rose said, exasperated. "The point is, Nettie just told me there's a problem with holding the wedding in St. Olaf and they're going to elope instead!"

"That's young love for you," Blanche said, raising her eyebrows. "Elopements are so romantic. Sneaking out of your window, running away with a handsome man, and pledging your love in a secret gazebo overgrown with wisteria with only moonlight as your witness . . ."

Rose took a sip of coffee, then placed her mug on the table with a clank, jolting Blanche out of her reverie. "Well, that's not what I had in mind for Nettie. It's been years since we've had such a joyous occasion in the family, and since Nettie is a direct descendant of Heinrich von Anderdonnen, we have a *lot* of serious St. Olaf traditions to uphold. We must have a real wedding, and there can't be a herring out of place!"

"But, Rose," Dorothy said, reaching across the table to pat her on the arm. "Certainly you can convince her."

"That's not the whole story," Rose said sadly. "Just this week I read something dreadful in the *Courier-Dispatch*." She hid her head in her hands for a long moment. The three other women exchanged worried glances over Rose's pale cloud of platinum curls.

"I knew something was wrong when she forgot to put mayonnaise in her tuna fish salad yesterday," Sophia muttered under her breath.

"I did?" Rose gasped, putting a hand to her chest. Traditionally, mayonnaise was the first ingredient in every dish she made.

"I thought maybe it was a butter incident!" Sophia quipped, and Dorothy shot her a silencing look.

Rose slowly lifted her head. "Not *every* injustice in St. Olaf is butter related, Sophia," she said, her voice quivering. "Apparently, the Storslagen Hotel hosted a particularly aggressive Grand S'mores Challenge this year. . . ."

"And?" Sophia said. "C'mon, I don't have much time!"

"Don't be so dramatic, Ma," Dorothy said, shaking her head. Her mother seemed to bring up her own mortality more and more these days. "You know I hate it when you talk that way."

"*What?!* I mean I have a busy schedule today. I have the podiatrist, the optometrist . . ."

"I'll just take a regular old tryst," Blanche joked, trying to lighten the mood.

"As I was saying," Rose continued. "The Storslagen burned down! It's the only hotel in St. Olaf and it'll be impossible to hold a big family wedding without a venue or place for everyone to stay."

"So that's why you've been so worried lately," Dorothy said, remembering that her dear friend had been acting a bit odd recently—not finishing her cheesecake the other night, muttering to herself when she thought no one was listening, and bringing up wild St. Olaf stories. However, that last part was pretty normal for Rose, Dorothy had to admit.

"Now Nettie feels her only choice is to elope," Rose said. "And she told me she's never been enamored with St. Olaf's vaunted traditions." She bit her lip, staring morosely down at her untouched toast. The women fell silent, and Dorothy stirred her coffee pensively.

"That is a predicament," Blanche said. "Is there a motel in town?"

"Ah! Your favorite subject." Sophia peered over her glasses at Blanche. "But aren't you the expert? I assume you're intimately

6

acquainted with every motel from here to Tuscaloosa."

"Very funny," Blanche said, lifting her chin and adjusting the shoulder pads in her chiffon robe.

"What about the town next door, can't you find a hotel there?" Dorothy asked, ever practical.

"In the rival hamlet of St. Gustav?" Rose said, voice rising in disbelief. "I may be desperate, but I'm not foolhardy." She shook her head and looked down at her hands again.

Dorothy paused to stifle a smile. Now wasn't the time to bring up Rose's many foolhardy ideas. She was her friend, and Rose was clearly upset. "I'm sure there's a solution," she said. "Together, we can figure it out."

Rose lifted her head, her eyes wide with gratitude. "You'll really help me?"

Sophia held out her hands, palms up. "What are friends for?"

She then got up from the table and headed slowly for the door. "Unfortunately, I'm not that kind of friend—see you all later!"

After breakfast, Rose paced in front of the coral-upholstered rattan sofa in the living room, now dressed in a silky teal blouse and skirt. Dorothy and Blanche sat in matching fan-armed chairs on either side, watching with anxious expressions as Rose practically wore a path through the cream-colored carpet with her low-heeled pumps.

"So, we can't have the wedding in St. Olaf, but we still have to rigorously adhere to all of the St. Olaf traditions," Rose said, clasping her hands together in intense concentration. After a moment she unclasped them. "I'm drawing a blank."

"Is it really necessary to be that strict?" Dorothy asked, in a matter-of-fact tone. "It's the twentieth century. People get married all sorts of ways." She thought back to her own shotgun wedding to Stan decades ago and frowned. It hadn't exactly been a fairy-tale experience, she had to admit. At least she had gotten her two children out of it, she thought with a bittersweet sigh.

"First of all, Nettie's fiancé is . . . well, he's . . ." Rose covered her mouth with her hand, as if the truth was too terrible to speak aloud. Her silence allowed Blanche and Dorothy's minds to run wild with exactly what *could* be wrong with Nettie's fiancé. A secret family in Canada? A history of petty crime? A pet chinchilla for whom he'd built an elaborate habitat? All would be cause for concern.

"Spit it out, Rose," Dorothy said, using her intimidating teacher voice.

"He's—he's an *outsider*, okay?" Rose said, with a little bow of her head. "He's not from St. Olaf. . . . He's not even from the Midwest!"

Blanche and Dorothy let out relieved chuckles.

"Surely the people of St. Olaf aren't that closed-minded and provincial anymore," Blanche said.

Both Dorothy and Rose gave her a pointed look.

Blanche cocked her head to one side. "Well, maybe they are. But what's so bad about this young man?"

"He's originally from southern Florida, from Coconut Grove," Rose said. "But that's not the issue. Apparently he *loves* St. Olaf and wants to move back there with Nettie. But his rather tepid throwing of the hay during the last annual Hay Day—that *really* disappointed the elders." She placed a delicate hand on her stomach, as if the very thought made her a bit queasy.

"I can see how that would be a problem," Dorothy deadpanned. "But if he's from the area, why can't you host the wedding right here in Miami?"

Rose stopped in her tracks. Dorothy thought she could literally see the gears—or gear, in Rose's case—turning slowly.

"Now that's an idea," Rose said, pointing to Dorothy as if she'd just gotten the correct answer on *The Price Is Right*. "As long as the wedding follows the weeklong guidelines to a T, there's nothing in the town bylaws that says the event must take place there. And if you all help me, I just know I can make it *perfect*." Rose let out a little squeal, then grabbed a turquoise throw pillow from the sofa, squeezing it to her chest with palpable excitement.

"There, you've found a solution, Rose," Blanche drawled. "A destination wedding! There are plenty of hotels here, and you could rent out a banquet hall for the reception."

Rose took a deep breath and straightened her shoulders. "It'll be a great chance to prove that even though I live a fast-paced, glamorous Miami lifestyle, I'm still a St. Olaf girl through and through."

"Oh, I think they'll be able to tell somehow," Dorothy said, grinning. "You'll do a wonderful job, I'm sure. And if the wedding's here and we're all going to attend, I for one will need something to wear. Who's up for a trip to Aventura Mall?"

"Ladies, first things first! Before we decide on our outfits, we need to find dates," Blanche added, pushing up her seafoam-green blazer sleeves. "I met a charming doctor the other day—maybe I'll telephone and ask him to be my plus-one."

Dorothy leaned across the arm of her chair to Blanche and put a hand on her knee. "I just don't understand how you stumble into eligible men everywhere you go. Now, where did you meet a doctor—and more importantly, does he have a brother?"

Just recently Dorothy had admitted to herself that she had begun to dread attending events alone. It would be nice to have someone new—and male—to spend time with, other than the fellow residents of 6151 Richmond Street. Preferably someone handsome, educated, and interesting. Heck, she'd take two out of three. Or maybe even just one.

"I suppose you could make an appointment to meet one, but I met this one in an elevator," Blanche said. "You just have to put yourself out there. Go where the doctors are!"

"I'm not going to hang around hospitals and emergency rooms just to meet a man, but thank you for the advice," Dorothy said. "Maybe I'll try that VHS dating service my daughter is always going on about. She sent me this yesterday." She grabbed a plastic-wrapped video cassette and trifold brochure from the rattan coffee table and placed them on her lap.

"That sounds very technical," Rose said, furrowing her brow as she seated herself on the sofa. "I'm not so sure that humans can fall in love with machines."

"Oh, Rose, you don't date the video player." Dorothy laughed. "You watch recordings of men talking about their interests, their personalities, and what they're looking for in a partner. Then you pick the ones you like, and the service connects the two of you and you go on a date." Dorothy fanned through the brochure, which featured photos of happy couples playing tennis, smiling over piña coladas, and walking along a beach silhouetted by a candy-colored Florida sunset.

"Very sensible," Blanche said, nodding at the pictures. "Kind of like browsing the JCPenney catalog."

"Just make sure you meet in a public place, and don't get in his car, or go to his apartment," Rose said, putting a hand over the brochure and looking at Dorothy with earnest intensity. "You can't be too careful these days."

"I'll be careful, Rose. If I find anyone suitable, I'll be sure to suggest lunch or coffee in a public place."

Dorothy smiled. Though Rose was overcautious, one of the many benefits of living with her girlfriends was that they all kept an eye out for each other. They'd helped each other time and again, dealing with problems large and small. On good days it was like having a bunch of close-knit sisters. On bad days it was like having a fleet of nosy neighbors right inside your own home.

"See that you do. I need your help to plan this wedding, and I can't have you getting kidnapped. We simply have too much to do, starting now! I need to scout some wedding venues and find out their pricing." Rose stood up and gathered her purse. "A Miami wedding is sure to be much more expensive than a St. Olaf one, and I'll need to find a place for the St. Olafians to stay."

"Good idea," Blanche said, also getting up and pulling her purse from the hall closet. "I'll come with you. Maybe I can sweet-talk some of those venues into giving you a discount."

"Wonderful! We have no time to waste!" Rose said, picking up her purse from an end table and heading toward the front door. As Blanche rose to join her, she waved at Dorothy. "Enjoy sitting here alone watching videos of single men!"

Dorothy laughed. "You make it sound so tawdry. It's simply a more modern way of dating."

Rose stopped before opening the front door and turned back to Dorothy somberly. "Just don't bring a man back to the house, not until you're sure about him."

"Unless he's really good-looking," Blanche added, lifting her eyebrows and wiggling her shoulders. "Then *absolutely* bring him over."

"You think I'm being silly," Rose said, her forehead creasing in worry. "But what if this man is the next Ted Bunderson!"

"Don't you mean Ted Bundy?" Dorothy chuckled, leaning back in her chair.

"No, I mean Ted Bunderson. He dated my best friend Ingrid back in St. Olaf. After every date, he'd ask to come inside for a glass of water or to use the bathroom."

"That's not a crime," Blanche said. "What if he really liked her and didn't want the date to end?"

Rose leaned conspiratorially toward Blanche. Her voice fell into a whisper. "Well, every time she let him inside, she'd notice something missing from her curio cabinet the next day. It turned out, he was stealing her miniature ceramic cow figurines!"

"Not the cow figurines!" Dorothy said, clasping her hands together in mock horror. She softened her expression into a comforting smile for Rose. "I promise, I won't bring anyone like that into our house. Plus, everyone using these tapes has been screened by the dating company." She tapped a section of small print at the back of the brochure. "It says here, right under the money-back guarantee, that each user will get at least one compatible match from using this service and that all applicants are vetted."

Rose peered over Dorothy's shoulder and squinted at the fine print. "Well, if they've all been to the vet at least they have all their shots. . . ."

Somewhat placated, Rose nodded silently. After Rose and

Blanche left, Dorothy placed the brochure back in her lap and thought about that money-back guarantee. She wished finding love were really as simple as picking out a new television set. If it broke, you could get it repaired, or get a brand-new one to replace it. It hadn't worked out that way for her in her relationships at all.

But if she didn't find Prince Charming from these videos, Dorothy thought to herself, maybe that would be okay. She wouldn't let hope run away with her. She'd readjust her expectations and use this service to look for Mr. Pleasant Enough to be a decent wedding date.

# FAST-FORWARD TO ROMANCE

## ............. 2 .............

*A*fter two hours of watching grainy video compilations of men of all ages sharing their interests (scuba diving, trading stocks, building miniature railroads) and their laundry lists for a female partner (great legs, sense of humor, Daryl Hannah's look-alike), Dorothy rubbed her eyes and stood up from the armchair as the words LUCKY CHANCES DATING SERVICE faded from the TV screen. She needed to stretch her legs—or, better yet, pour herself a stiff drink.

The videos were like watching a first date mixed with a job

interview. They all boiled down to just a few awkward minutes set against a plain off-white backdrop that made everyone look a little bit like they were getting photos taken for their passports—or their mugshots.

But Dorothy persisted, looking past the unflattering setting and too-strong lighting, though several of the men seemed far too young for her. She'd fast-forwarded past anyone under fifty, those with too much facial hair, or any man who reminded her of Stanley, her ex-husband. She'd stop the tape and press play when men in their fifties and sixties appeared, most of whom seemed normal enough.

One man in particular, Henry Pattinson, had salt-and-pepper hair and a not-insignificant resemblance to Tom Selleck, minus the mustache. His interests were French cuisine and playing the saxophone—respectable, even sophisticated pastimes for a potential beau, and he lived in nearby Coral Gables. He wanted to date "an educated and experienced woman" and added that "no airheads need apply" with a chuckle at the end of his video. Dorothy sat up a little straighter. As an avowed bookworm with experience as a teacher, she felt that she fit the bill and that maybe, just maybe, she'd found a match. His eyes glinted behind light gold aviator frames, and Dorothy watched his video again, and then once more. She took a deep breath and seated herself by the ivory touch-tone phone next to the sofa and dialed the number in the brochure. After spending several minutes being shuffled from operator to operator, giving and repeating information several times, including her shoe size, astrological sign, previous relationship history, top three pet peeves, and favorite dessert (cheesecake), Dorothy was finally connected to Henry's phone line.

She felt a flutter of nervousness as she waited, half hoping that Rose and Blanche—or even her mother—would barge in and interrupt the call. When that didn't happen, she almost hung up the phone herself, just to end the anxious anticipation.

*You'll never change things in your life if you're not willing to get uncomfortable*, she told herself. After all, she was so tired of attending events alone, and she really wanted a man on her arm for Nettie's wedding. She couldn't take any more comments about always going stag to important events, or pitying looks from everyone else who was sure to be there with a spouse or date. It wasn't just about appearances, either. She wanted someone to dance with. To talk to during the long reception, to share jokes with. Someone to tell her she looked nice. Someone to pull out a chair for her. Even her octogenarian mother had more romantic suitors than she did, and Dorothy was a woman still in her prime.

A man's deep voice answered, with a slight Brooklyn accent, just like in the video, and Dorothy immediately felt more comfortable. After a few minutes of introductions, Henry and Dorothy made small talk by discussing their favorite authors (Tom Clancy for him, Dorothy Parker for her), local museums they enjoyed, and their ideal first dates. He wanted someone he could converse with, cook for, and maybe take out on his boat. Dorothy asked Henry lots of questions and got the highlights of his childhood in Brooklyn, how much he loved his rat terrier (named after Jayne Mansfield), and the fact that he had a brother, though they weren't close. Soon Dorothy felt comfortable opening up about her living arrangements, her divorce, and wanting to get back on the dating scene after an admitted dry spell. Finally she mentioned that she was hoping to find someone to bring to a wedding in about a week.

"I love weddings!" Henry said. "As long as the food's decent, I can talk to anyone—boring in-laws, sullen teenagers, snot-nosed toddlers. And I'm no expert, but I become a dancing fool whenever a Whitney Houston song comes on."

Dorothy laughed, imagining this handsome man twirling her to "I Wanna Dance with Somebody" on a dance floor under a crystal chandelier, the rest of the wedding party fading into a hazy background. The warm feeling spreading throughout her body almost seemed too good to be true. *I'm just looking for a date*, she reminded herself. *It doesn't have to turn into happily ever after.*

Dorothy and Henry stayed on the phone for over half an hour, the conversation flowing easily. After some tentative hinting around, Dorothy finally came out and officially asked Henry if he was free the day of Nettie's nuptials. He said he loved when women made the first move, and that he'd be delighted to go with her. They exchanged phone numbers and made a date to meet in person for lunch in Miami Beach in two days' time.

Dorothy hung up the phone with a grin, feeling a giddiness inside that she hadn't felt in years. Henry was so charming and the conversation so smooth. Not like the combative exchanges she'd had with Stanley, or the awkward pauses over sundried tomatoes and Beaujolais on countless lukewarm blind dates. Maybe it was because they were speaking by phone, without the pressures of being in person. Or maybe because Henry was something special.

With a smile, Dorothy retreated to her room to take stock of her options before determining if she needed to buy a new outfit, or two—one for the wedding, and one for the lunch date. She pawed through a closet full of blazers, pleated trousers, and high-necked blouses, not finding anything that felt right. She needed something that felt like her, but maybe a little more soft and romantic. She'd been told by other men she'd dated (and her mother) that she could come off as aloof or intimidating. For Henry, she'd make the effort to put her best foot forward.

Over the course of the following morning, Rose made dozens of phone calls to airline carriers, local hotels, and taxi services, rerouting Nettie's entire wedding party and everyone on the guest list from St. Olaf, Minnesota, to Miami, Florida. She sent a letter to Nettie's parents' last known address inviting them to the wedding in Miami, noting that the venue was "TBD." She didn't think she'd hear from them, but she wanted to try, for Nettie's sake. Then she covered the pink wallpaper in her bedroom and much of the living room in Post-it notes and checklists, scurrying around with at least one (though usually several) pencils tucked behind her ears, a clipboard full of to-do items, and a harried expression. After a tense interlude where she'd explained why exactly the groom's donkey riding was nonnegotiable, and the culturally significant role of tuna in the traditional Welcome Tuna Tea, Rose made a chart on poster-board that explained each St. Olaf wedding tradition for her roommates, complete with cartoon illustrations, and propped it up on the white baker's rack in the kitchen for easy reference.

She'd handed a phone to Blanche, roping her into selecting potential venues for all the events in the lead-up to the wedding, plus the ceremony, the reception, and the post-wedding brunch.

Rose conscripted Sophia into planning the bachelorette party, insisting that having a Roman Catholic in charge would keep things kosher. Sophia grumbled and threatened to move to Shady Pines Retirement Home just to avoid the incessant wedding talk, and yet she couldn't help but offer her two cents when it came to floral arrangements ("White roses are more virginal!" she asserted) and appetizers ("I know your people are Scandinavian, but you can't get married without caponata").

Rose pressed Dorothy and her brilliant mind into streamlining the logistics of moving people and the various items needed for the St. Olaf ceremonies into the least amount of schlepping around the city. A welcome benefit of having Dorothy in this role was her composed competence. Her clear head was instrumental in calming Rose down when she got overwhelmed, especially when it came to seating charts and livestock rentals.

Then Rose spent the afternoon making enough cheesecake to feed an army. She'd invented a new recipe infused with the traditional flavors of her beloved hometown to celebrate the lovebirds. St. Olaf's Kiss was a creamy vanilla cheesecake surrounded by an almond-and-graham-cracker crust and topped with a sweet lingonberry drizzle. It was hard work, making sure the cream cheese wasn't too cold or too warm, crushing up all the graham crackers, making sure not to overmix the ingredients, and timing everything out, since she only had one oven and limited counter and fridge space. She wished her frie..ds could lend her a hand, but they were already off doing all the wedding tasks she'd assigned to them.

By the time several cakes were cooling on the counter, progress had been made on the hasty wedding planning and Sophia, Dorothy, and Blanche had finally retreated to the terra-cotta-tiled lanai. A magenta bougainvillea cascaded over a low stucco wall as palm fronds and potted ferns waved in the warm Miami breeze. The three women kicked off their shoes to put their feet up on the chaise longues, groaning with exhaustion.

"In Sicily, we had a word for this kind of treatment . . ." Sophia began, shaking a finger.

Rose came out in her pastel apron, pushing a wheeled cart bearing a tray of lemonade and a fresh-baked Vanskapkaka cake covered in a rich layer of creamy icing.

"Just a little token of my appreciation," she said, setting the tray down on a wrought-iron table. "You all have been working so hard helping me get this wedding underway." She had circles under her eyes but wore a cheerful smile. Her friends didn't need to know that the frosting was made from a cheesecake that had come out of the oven riddled with deep cracks. Instead of throwing it out, she'd scooped out the center and blended it with some extra whipping cream and sugar, making her own version of cream-cheese frosting. She'd always learned to make do with whatever life threw at her and knew better than to cry over split cheesecake.

Dorothy and Blanche gratefully reached for glasses of lemonade as a tiny lizard ran across the terra-cotta tiles. Rose began to cut the cake, the aroma of vanilla and almond perfuming the late-afternoon air.

"This is lovely," Dorothy said, pointedly looking at Sophia. "Rose is trying to do right by her family, and helping her out is the least we can do."

"Her heart's in the right place," Blanche added, taking a long sip of lemonade.

"But about her brain?" Sophia quipped, reaching for a generous slice of cake. "Doesn't she know we're too old to be running ourselves ragged like this?"

"Speak for yourself," Blanche said, patting her short caramel curls. "I feel as young as I look. And this cake makes all the hard work worth it. I probably burned three hundred calories from hefting that phone book around."

"You *all* are beautiful, inside and out," Rose said, finally sitting down herself with a small sigh. "Though I was thinking of gifting you all makeovers from St. Olaf's leading beautician. She's Nettie's maid of honor and she's arriving tonight on the same flight as Nettie and the rest of the bridal party."

"I shudder to think about the latest beauty trends in St. Olaf," Sophia muttered through a mouthful of cake. "I don't want to be slathered in butter at this stage of life."

"Oh, hush," Blanche said. She licked a dab of icing from her pinkie. "This is exciting. We're only a week away from the wedding!"

"I'd go with you to the airport, Rose," said Dorothy, setting down her now-empty glass. "But I need my beauty sleep. Tomorrow, I have a date."

"A date!" Blanche gasped. "Do tell."

Dorothy paused, not sure how much to tell the other girls. On one hand, she didn't want to jinx the good feeling she had about Henry; on the other, she knew she couldn't keep secrets from this group for long.

"I actually found someone from that video service I mentioned," she admitted.

Blanche and Rose leaned forward in excitement and Sophia paused in her chewing, watching Dorothy carefully.

"We've been talking on the phone," Dorothy continued. "He's an excellent conversationalist, I must say. A perfect escort for this wedding. We're going to meet in person for the first time over lunch." Dorothy didn't add that she'd watched the video of Henry a few more times than was strictly necessary. Or that she had daydreamed about their perfect first date, sharing erudite conversation—perhaps with their hands brushing each other's across the table. He was easy on the eyes, she thought, and she could only hope he'd feel the same way about her.

Sophia gave Dorothy a long look over the rim of her glasses. "It's about time you got back out there," she said. "I'm proud of you. Now don't screw it up!"

Dorothy bristled, ready to knock the half-eaten slice of cake from Sophia's hands. She could always rely on her mother to poke at her tender spots, even when she was saying something positive.

"It's *just lunch*, Ma," Dorothy snapped, aggressively digging into her own serving of cake with a knife and fork, as if she were annoyed at it, too. "What could go wrong?"

# LOVEBIRDS ON A WIRE

············· **3** ·············

*B*lanche at her side, Rose stood at a terminal in the Miami International Airport in a pale pink shirtdress, holding a sign that said NETTIE in swirling calligraphy, and waited for the first members of the wedding party to arrive. She bounced on her feet, excited to see her cousin again after two long years. The last time she'd seen her had been at the girl's graduation from the University of Wisconsin–Madison, near where Nettie had been working as an assistant teacher ever since.

Rose suspected that it had been hard on Nettie when her parents sold her childhood home in St. Olaf, but Nettie never said anything about it. She'd loved college and her work as a teacher, and her letters to Rose over the years had been filled with funny stories about her students and dotted with exclamation points.

Still, Rose felt that she had to make up for Nettie's wayward parents and give her a proper wedding with all the St. Olaf bells and whistles. *And all the horns*, Rose thought. They couldn't forget the Blugelhorn, the ceremonial goat horn that would be blown before the wedding night. Rose frowned, wondering how they'd obtain such a thing in Miami. Maybe she could get one in South Beach.

After dozens of passengers disembarked the plane from Minneapolis, Rose finally spotted a group led by a freckled brunette in her twenties. She was wearing high-waisted stonewashed jeans, a poet's blouse, and a huge smile as she pulled along a nervous-looking young man in a striped rugby shirt.

Rose hugged Nettie for a long moment, breathing in the scent of Love's Baby Soft and the apple fragrance of her Salon Selectives shampoo. It felt so good to hug her again, but Rose eventually pulled back and looked at Nettie from an arm's length away. Nettie wasn't a little schoolgirl with oversize glasses and a mouth full of braces anymore. She was all grown up, Rose thought a little sadly. But when Nettie smiled, Rose saw the familiar dimples she'd had since babyhood.

Rose cast a longer glance at Nettie's fiancé. Jason had a wide smile and a mop of hair the color of brown sugar that he kept flicking out of his eyes. He gripped Rose's hand in a slightly sweaty handshake.

"I'm so glad to meet you, Mrs. Nylund," he said politely, shaking her hand. "Nettie has told me the most wonderful things about you."

"Oh, isn't that sweet," Rose said, noticing that Jason was still nervously shaking her hand. She gently pulled it back and wiped her palm on her dress. "I can't wait to get to know you better." She meant it. If this boy was going to marry the girl she'd helped raise, he'd better be something special. From the way Nettie was looking at him through her long bangs, it seemed like she certainly thought he was.

"May I call you Aunt Rose, Mrs. Nylund?" Jason asked shyly.

"Of course, Jason," Rose said, smiling indulgently at the newcomer. He was making a good first impression as a sweet, polite boy, she thought. Maybe his hay-throwing skills could be worked on. They could practice on the lanai. It was something she'd speak to him about when the time was right, she decided. "Welcome to the family," she added warmly.

Rose turned to introduce Blanche to the young couple, and then Nettie brought another young woman forward and introduced Rose and Blanche to the maid of honor, a bubbly redhead named Bess. The next member of the wedding party to greet them was a strikingly attractive young man with intense green eyes and honey-blond hair.

"Jorgen!" Rose cried. She recognized him as the son of her childhood friend Ingrid. In a lilting Scandinavian accent, Jorgen explained that he'd gone to college with Nettie, and they'd all become friends when Nettie met Jason their senior year.

Rose hugged each one, and Blanche offered her hand to Jorgen, letting it linger in his for several extra seconds. She batted her lashes at him as they proceeded down the terminal toward the baggage claim area while Rose peppered Nettie with questions about the flight, the airplane food, and, of course, some last-minute wedding plans.

"Oh, thank goodness!" Nettie said when a hard-sided plaid suitcase appeared on the carousel. "That one has my wedding dress in it!"

"I can't wait to see it," said Rose. "I can have it steamed for you, if you like."

"Wonderful," Nettie said. "I had to save up for it, and I admit, showing off this dress to everyone is one reason why I'm happy we're not eloping after all."

"I'm glad you're not, either," said Rose.

Nettie smiled, leaning against Jason as they walked through the airport, full of people of all walks of life coming and going from up north and to and from the Caribbean and South America. The sounds of people speaking in English and Spanish and even Portuguese swirled around them in between flight announcements over the airport loudspeakers.

Once they got to the airport parking lot, Rose turned and

looked at everyone with a smile. "We can drop the others off at the SeaBreeze Motel. It's not fancy, I'm afraid, and they don't have color TV, but I got a pretty good deal for a block of rooms. Then I'll bring you back to our house and make some Ovaltine so we can go over the itinerary for this week!"

"Aunt Rose, I'm just beat from the trip. After two connecting flights I just want to take my shoes off and sleep!" Nettie rubbed her eyes, which were looking exhausted and a bit pink around the edges.

"Oh, Nettie, I know it's a long journey, but we have so much to discuss. And just think, if you still lived in St. Olaf, you'd have to add the train and donkey rides to that itinerary." Rose pulled Nettie aside, trying to get a word with her outside of Jason's earshot. "We have a lot to coordinate, and we still need to discuss potential venues for the ceremony. Not to toot my own Vertubenflugen, but my friends and I have been working around the clock to make sure that your wedding will not only be the best wedding ever, but will include every single authentic St. Olaf tradition."

"But I don't want every St. Olaf tradition," Nettie said, shaking her head. "They are so . . . *unique*, and a bit old-fashioned. It's all too much."

"Nonsense, sweetheart," Rose said, thinking of how important each practice was. Even if some of them were silly—like the Bridal Ribbon Ballet, or the Sharing of the Soup—she couldn't help but feel that each one had somehow contributed to the happiness of her own marriage to Charlie. Nothing could have been better than what they shared, and they'd put up with the nuptial sunrise cold plunge and the Blessing of the Pajamas.

Rose wanted a lifetime of happiness for her cousin and would settle for nothing less. She'd just have to explain things to her, one-on-one, woman-to-woman. But for now, she'd keep things light so that Nettie wouldn't get spooked by the daunting list of traditions and try to elope again. Rose pasted a big smile on her face and looked up at the youngster with shining blue eyes. They'd finally reached the baggage-claim area, and the warm early-evening air blew in through the automatic doors. Jason and Jorgen stood with Blanche and Bess at the conveyer belt, waiting for everyone's suitcases to roll by.

"We're going to have a down-home, old-fashioned midwestern wedding, right here among the high-rises and turquoise waters of Miami," Rose said, her voice full of excitement. "It's going to be so special, and we'll make sure it's what you and Jason want. You'll see—this will be a week no one will ever forget!"

All six adults squeezed into Blanche's car. Blanche had flirtatiously offered Jorgen her keys, then scooted across the bench seat to be near him as the others piled in.

"Where to?" Jorgen said, after making sure everyone had their seat belts on securely.

"The SeaBreeze Motel," Rose said as he drove out of the airport parking lot. "I'll direct you."

Jason cleared his throat. Nettie glanced at him, then back to Rose.

"Aunt Rose," Nettie said slowly. "Jason has something to tell you."

Jason cleared his throat again. "I should have mentioned this earlier by telephone." His voice was a bit strained, as if he were about to deliver bad news.

*Oh no*, Rose thought. *They're going to back out of the wedding. They're going to elope after all!* Her heart sank, but she would just have to try to change their minds. They were already here in Miami, after all.

"My family . . ." Jason started. "They, uh . . ." He swallowed, then paused to roll down the car window, filling the sedan with fresh evening air.

"What Jason is trying to say," Nettie chimed in, "is that his family owns a hotel in Miami Beach and has offered a block of rooms free of charge to the wedding party, and any guests who are coming in from St. Olaf. They're expecting us to arrive any minute."

Rose exhaled and slapped her knees. She almost squealed with joy. "Why didn't you say so! This is wonderful news!" she cried. "Blanche, did you hear that? We've got free hotel rooms for everyone!" Rose's mind ran wild with what they could do with the money they were saving—they could put it toward renting a hall for the reception, or for the food, or flowers . . .

"But there's a catch," Jason added. "My family . . . wants to *host* the entire wedding. The ceremony, the reception . . ." He sighed, staring out at the palm trees whizzing past on the side of the road, as if he were being driven to some terrible fate, instead of toward the neon lights of Miami Beach.

"That's wonderful," Rose said. "That's so generous—and lucky! You two must be over the moon! I know I am."

Nettie and Jason looked at each other with tense expressions.

"Well, Aunt Rose," Nettie said, "I'm afraid it's not that easy."

"My family is very particular," said Jason. "They tend to . . . take things over. And there are always strings attached. If we take them up on their offer, they'll insist on their way for *everything*—the guest list, the food, even the song for our first dance. We won't get *any* say in the matter."

Nettie grasped Jason's hand and squeezed it. "That's why we wanted to elope," she said. "After our wedding venue burned down, we were ready to find a justice of the peace in Minneapolis and not involve our families, before you convinced us to come to Miami. Jason's parents want to throw a big flashy Miami wedding and invite hundreds of people we don't know. We want something more *us*."

Rose pressed her lips together, thinking. A fancy wedding that was practically all bankrolled by the groom's family would solve a host of issues—they wouldn't have to cut corners, and they'd have everything a wedding needed and the big-ticket items covered—a venue, the catering, possibly a full bar, and a place for people to stay.

"I hear you two," Rose said, choosing her words carefully. "I understand that sometimes what your family wants isn't the same as what a young couple in love has in mind. But a big wedding is a chance for the whole family to connect and celebrate together. Surely there can be some sort of compromise?"

Jason shook his head. "You don't understand my family. Compromise isn't their way. They have strong opinions on *every*thing. It's why I went to college so far away—and stayed there. I love them, but I don't want to be bossed around by them anymore."

"You understand, don't you, Aunt Rose?" Nettie said, giving Rose the same puppy-dog eyes she'd given her when she begged for a Nancy Drew Madame Alexander doll for her tenth birthday. "It's not that we're not grateful. But Jason has worked hard to become his own person outside of his family's shadow, and we want to get married without the stress of them controlling everything."

Rose nodded. If the Bryant family was really that opinionated and controlling, it didn't bode well for integrating the dozens of St. Olaf traditions that were necessary, none of which she was willing to compromise on. For a second, Rose wished that Nettie could get married without a groom—or at least the groom's family—before she realized how ridiculous an idea that was.

"Let me think about this," Rose said, patting Nettie's hand. "Why don't we have everyone stay at the hotel to start, and I'll speak with Jason's family? Your aunt Rose just may have a few tricks up her skivomslags." She'd never been very strong when faced with Nettie's puppy-dog eyes, and Rose knew she'd have to proceed carefully. Nettie didn't employ them gratuitously, but she had unwrapped that doll on her birthday.

"Oh, will you?" Nettie said. "I've only met them by phone, and I want to make a good impression. I don't want them to think I'm a demanding bride, or not a good daughter-in-law. But I don't want to do anything Jason doesn't want."

Jason gave Nettie a light kiss on the cheek. "You're a wonderful bride, and they're lucky to have you as a daughter-in-law."

The rest of the car let out a collective *Oooh* at their sweetness, and Rose noticed Jorgen making goo-goo eyes at Blanche, who was pretending not to notice while studiously powdering her nose.

Bess turned around to grin at the couple. "Rose, if you need any backup talking to the Bryants, I'm here. I need these two to get married so I can catch the bouquet!"

"Thank you, Bess," Rose said. "But I'm sure it'll be okay. Everyone wants the same thing: a lovely wedding for our happy couple."

*How hard could it be?* she told herself as a knot of worry twisted in her stomach. She'd meet the in-laws, and she'd convince them to listen to Jason and Nettie's wishes—and all her own as well. And if she didn't convince them right away, she could always lean on Blanche, Dorothy, and Sophia to help her.

They pulled up to the front entrance of the Cabana Sun Hotel behind a red Ferrari Testarossa. Night had fallen, but the portico was ablaze with lights, and a thirtyish man with dark, leonine hair nodded to the driver of the sports car before it roared away. He wore an open-necked pink shirt and white blazer and greeted their car with a dazzling smile.

"Oh no," Jason groaned, slumping deeper into the car seat. "My brother-in-law. He's the kind of guy who wears loafers without socks and about a gallon of cologne."

The smiling man helped open the sedan doors as bellhops took Nettie, Jason, and Bess's luggage from the trunk. "Welcome, welcome!" he said jovially. "I'm Chip, VP of Guest Relations, husband to Patricia, Jason's sister."

As Rose stepped out of the car to greet him, he offered his hand to her and she noticed that he did, in fact, smell good. Like a Macy's perfume counter in the middle of a pine forest. Jorgen remained at the wheel, eyeing Chip warily when he did the same to Blanche.

"So nice to meet you," Rose said. "We'll be family soon!" She smiled up at Chip, noticing a little gold pin on his jacket lapel winking in the sunlight.

"Assuming Jason here doesn't choke!" Chip joked, slugging Jason on the shoulder. Jason did not look amused, Rose noticed. Neither did Nettie. Jason reluctantly shook Chip's hand and introduced him to Nettie. Chip went right in for a cheek kiss, which Nettie endured with a tight smile.

"And is Patricia here? And Jason's parents?" Rose asked, looking around. She was eager to meet them in person to start talking shop.

"They've all turned in for the night," he said. "Long day with finance meetings for our renovations and forthcoming expansion, and we've had a lot of VIPs to take care of. But let me help everyone get settled." He directed the bellhops to take the luggage inside the gleaming revolving doors, which shot out spurts of icy air-conditioning as they spun. "We'll put the wedding party on a high floor. And don't worry, we've got Nettie and Jason in separate rooms that don't adjoin." He snickered with a salacious wink.

Rose huffed. Of course Nettie and Jason would stay in separate rooms. They weren't even married yet, for goodness' sake! She and her dear Charlie had waited until their wedding night, though they had gotten a *little* frisky before they were legally wed, she remembered. Her cheeks flushed slightly.

"I need to speak with the Bryants," she said. "There are some wedding matters we need to discuss, especially the Welcome Tuna Teatime, the first official event."

"I'll ask them to call you first thing tomorrow," Chip said.

"Please do," she said. "I'll leave a copy of the wedding itinerary with you. Will you make sure they get it?" She handed Chip a sheet of lined paper filled with lists and diagrams, a timeline, and a family tree. He glanced at it and raised his eyebrows, then neatly folded it into thirds and tucked it into his blazer pocket.

"Of course," he said smoothly. He turned to Jason, Nettie, and Bess, who were waiting on the steps of the hotel. "Shall we?"

Rose nodded and hugged Nettie. As Jorgen drove her and Blanche back to 6151 Richmond Street, she mentally applauded herself for stopping the elopement and moving the wedding to Miami—and in a free hotel, to boot! She wished that Charlie could see her now. She'd love to have him at her side this week, to hold his hand during the ceremony and dance with him at the reception. She missed him, and she hoped he'd be proud of her for pulling off a multipronged matrimonial extravaganza with barely a week's notice. She knew she could get overwhelmed with the details and the rigid, often confusing rules for a St. Olaf wedding. But, really, she had thought of everything. With her careful planning and the support of her best friends, nothing at all could ruin this perfect week.

# PICKLE MY FANCY

............ 4 ............

*T*he next morning, Dorothy dressed in a long skirt, a flowing cowl-neck blouse, and a gorgeous burnt-sienna scarf that her daughter had given her for her birthday. She spent extra time on her makeup, adding a pearly eye shadow, a little extra blush, and some elegant dangly earrings. She brushed through her silvery curls and took one last look in the mirror before braving the gauntlet of opinions she'd face while leaving the house.

But when she stepped out of her bedroom, Rose, Blanche,

and Sophia paid her no mind, as they were busy ferrying cheesecakes and platters of sandwiches from the kitchen out the open door to Blanche's car.

Rose was red-cheeked, perspiration and Florida humidity already flattening her hairdo. "We'll be hosting the Teatime at Jason's family's hotel tomorrow," Rose wheezed. "They said we can store these in their industrial-size refrigerator overnight. We only have three more to go!"

"Are you sure you have enough cheesecake?" Dorothy joked.

Rose stopped in her tracks, her face stricken. She began counting on her fingers.

"I'm just kidding, Rose," Dorothy added quickly. "You've got this under control."

"I do?"

Dorothy grasped her friend's hands. "I know you do."

"Thank you," Rose said. "I swear, if I don't write every little detail down, I'll forget it—ah!" She grabbed a legal pad from the coffee table and jotted down *LOOFAHS*. She underlined it twice.

"And I'll help as much as I can after this lunch date, I promise," Dorothy continued. "As a matter of fact, you can write down Henry's name on the guest list. I've already asked him to be my plus-one. Henry Pattinson, with two *T*s."

Rose nodded and peered up at Dorothy, her face sincere. "I will, but you haven't even met this man in person yet. Please be careful—remember Ted Bunderson!"

"Thanks for the vote of confidence," Dorothy said, rolling her eyes.

*With friends like these*, she thought.

She decided to hurry out the back door before her mother saw her and added any other less-than-helpful words of encouragement.

Wolfie's was a Miami institution, more of a boisterous deli than a romantic hot spot, with a huge neon sign above the entrance. But Henry and Dorothy had found out during their phone call that it was a favorite of both of theirs, and they'd decided it was an ideal place to meet, since they both loved sandwiches and sour pickles and it was equidistant from where they both lived.

Dorothy walked into the busy restaurant, scanning the crammed booths and talkative crowd for the man from the video she'd watched a handful of (all right, a dozen) times. The air smelled like fresh-baked bread, Danish, and pastrami. Dorothy hoped her stomach wouldn't growl before their lunch arrived.

She spotted a handsome, mature gentleman in a baby-blue button-down shirt a few booths away. She tamped down the nerves that bubbled up at the sight of his only slightly thinning salt-and-pepper hair and broad shoulders and walked toward him with a friendly smile on her face.

*Be approachable*, she reminded herself. *Not intimidating.*

He was poring over the menu and didn't notice Dorothy until she stood right in front of him.

"Hello, Henry," she said, offering her hand to shake. In person, she could see the crinkles at the sides of his eyes, his weathered suntan, and the deep brown of his eyes behind his glasses. He was much more handsome than he'd come across in the video.

"Hello," he said, blinking up at her. "Do I know you?"

"I'm your date," Dorothy said, "Dorothy Zbornak, from Lucky Chances Dating Service?"

"Dorothy!" Henry said, looking her up and down. "I'd pull out a chair for you, but we're in a booth."

"Aren't you a charmer." Dorothy chuckled, seating herself across from Henry. This seemed to be going well. "So nice to meet you in person."

"Dorothy," he repeated. "You're the one with the wedding coming up, right?"

"Yes," Dorothy said. "And are you the one who makes excellent chicken cordon bleu?"

"That's me," he said, with a touch of pride. "I'm working on my side dishes now. Can't have the green beans too soggy, you know what I mean?"

"I certainly do," she said, smiling. "And how's that boat trip you're planning to Sanibel Island coming along?"

Blanche had told her that men loved it when a woman showed interest in *their* interests, so she'd thought up a few conversation topics ahead of time, based on what he'd said in his video and on the phone. Blanche also said that men loved it when you showed a little cleavage, but Dorothy wasn't going to take that advice just yet; it was only lunchtime.

Henry sucked at his teeth and reached for his ice water. "I've been patching leaks. My brother borrowed my boat for the weekend, and he doesn't take as good care of her as I do."

"That's too bad," Dorothy said. "I hope you get her seaworthy soon."

"I just have a little bit more to do. Then I'd love to take you on the boat for dinner sometime."

"What a lovely idea," Dorothy said, grinning to herself. *He must like what he sees, too*, she thought, *otherwise he wouldn't bring up a romantic dinner on his boat so soon.* She was about to ask what one should bring to a dinner on a boat when something seemed to catch Henry's eye somewhere behind her.

He quickly bent his head to the laminated menu. "So, ah—what do you think you're going to get?"

Dorothy stared down at the large yellow-and-orange menu, trying to decide what would be easy to eat and still carry on a conversation. Her regular order of a pastrami sandwich with extra pickles might be messy and hard to manage.

"You're the gourmet," Dorothy said, looking back up at Henry. "I'm curious to see what you're getting."

But Henry wasn't meeting her eyes. Behind the screen of his menu, his gaze floated somewhere over Dorothy's left shoulder. He seemed jumpy, Dorothy thought. She craned her neck, wondering what he was looking at. But she saw nothing unusual, just the typical crowd of lunchtime regulars and sunburned tourists. Maybe he was just as nervous about the date as she was.

Henry put down his menu, then picked it up again. He checked the time on his shiny gold watch. Dorothy stared at him, waiting for him to say something—anything. Her good feeling started to fade. Though he was even more handsome in person, Henry had seemed much more confident on the videotape. Now all of a sudden he seemed to be losing interest in their date.

As Dorothy racked her brain for something fascinating to say to keep the conversation going, it occurred to her that in-person dating was much more difficult than talking on the phone, even with someone like Henry. You had to worry about eye contact and if you had parsley in your teeth, for example. And it was much harder to hear each other over the clattering of plates and the conversations among other diners than it was on the phone.

*I'm pretty rusty at this dating game*, she thought when she realized none of this should be a surprise.

"So, what do you do for a living? Or are you retired?" Dorothy asked. In all of their previous conversations, they'd really only focused on their hobbies and interests.

At the same time, Henry opened his mouth and bluntly said, "How old did you say you were?"

Dorothy was stunned. *What kind of first-date question is that?*

A feeling of unease began to form somewhere behind her solar plexus, and her cheeks flamed with sudden anger. She drew herself up as tall as she could while sitting in a sticky leather booth.

"I am the exact same age as you said *you* were in your video," she said slowly. "Henry, do we have a problem?"

She tried to keep her anger in check. One of the reasons she'd zeroed in on Henry (besides his rugged good looks) was because they were the same age, so that it wouldn't be an issue. She'd seen him on video, but *he* hadn't seen *her*, she realized. Maybe she wasn't what he'd imagined.

*This whole date was a mistake*, she thought. Even though he knew her age, maybe he expected somebody who looked younger. Or maybe he was one of those men who said they wanted a mature woman but expected someone with the body of a twenty-year-old. She didn't need to be insulted over lunch. She could get that at home, without getting all dressed up.

Henry's mouth hung open like a mackerel's.

"Is that all you have to say?" Dorothy asked, her voice deepening with disappointment. Clearly, he didn't want an "educated and experienced" woman—he just wanted arm candy. She felt like a fool, and not a particularly youthful one.

Dorothy stood up, tossing her napkin onto the table. "I don't have time to get involved with self-centered, deluded, hypocritical men." Her voice was louder than she intended, and nearby tables stole glances their way.

Henry hurriedly got up from his seat, knocking over the

rest of his ice water. He put a gentle hand on Dorothy's arm, and she stiffened.

"Hey there, slow down. I'm sorry." He glanced around at the crowded restaurant and lowered his voice. "I've been under a lot of stress lately, and I was just trying to make conversation, and that slipped out. Can we start over? Please?"

Dorothy took in a long breath and thought about it. She'd been in bad relationships before, and Henry had hurt her feelings so quickly. But she'd also promised herself that she'd try—*really* try—to make an effort. Though her instinct was to give Henry a piece of her mind, she was determined to do things differently this time.

She offered him a wary smile. "Let's do that. I'd like a fresh start."

"Take two," Henry said. "I'd pull out your chair for you, but it's a booth. . . ." He mopped the spilled water with some paper napkins and gave Dorothy a sheepish smile. Maybe they could salvage this date, she thought. Anyone could have an off day—she herself had clearly overreacted to what was a perfectly normal question.

They placed their drink orders with a harried-looking waitress sporting bleach-blond hair and a name tag that said KIMBERLY, and Dorothy asked for an appetizer of pickles to share while they decided on their main courses. The restaurant grew even more crowded. A group of men in business suits squeezed by, seeming to linger by their table while they waited for another booth to clear.

Henry focused on the menu, bending his head down to pore over the specials. After a few minutes of chitchat about the sandwich offerings, Henry excused himself to go to the restroom.

"If the pickles come before I'm back, please dig in," he said.

"I'll try to save you a few. No promises, though," Dorothy quipped.

The waitress returned with their ice teas in sweating glasses with lemon wedges and a plate of pickles that she plunked in the center of the table. Dorothy waited, as it seemed rude to start without Henry, despite what he'd said. He'd be back any moment, anyway.

But the moment stretched into another, and another. Dorothy tasted her ice tea, which was perfectly tart and refreshing for a hot Miami day. When her drink reached the halfway mark in the glass, Dorothy felt a kernel of worry.

*Shouldn't Henry be back by now?*

Then again, who was she to judge how long someone took in the bathroom? She sipped her tea patiently.

When only ice and a squeezed-out lemon wedge were left in her glass, Dorothy realized with a sinking feeling that maybe Henry wasn't coming back. It hadn't been that long, but tables turned over quickly at Wolfie's, and she was starting to suspect that she'd been stood up mid-date. She couldn't very well go into the men's room to look, though.

She decided to give it a few more minutes, and if he wasn't back by then, she'd flag down the waitress, pay the bill, and leave. She felt keenly alone at this table set for two, with an untouched plate of pickles, surrounded by full tables of families and friends enjoying one another's company.

Defeated, Dorothy reached for her purse, preparing to leave. Just then the waitress appeared.

"You're all settled up, ma'am," she said kindly. "The gentleman paid the bill."

Dorothy tried to keep her face neutral, even though her chin wanted to tremble. Henry had clearly left their date on purpose. There wasn't a long line in the bathroom, or an emergency of some sort. This was even worse than being stood up. It was embarrassing, and Dorothy wanted to get out of there as quickly as possible. There was just one thing she needed to do.

"Thank you so much," she said to the waitress, who was already placing Dorothy's empty glass on a tray. "Could you wrap up the pickles?"

# THE SWEETS HEREAFTER

............. **5** .............

*T*he next day, Dorothy sat on the sofa in the living room, paging through the *Miami Herald*. She told the girls she was perusing the classifieds to see if anyone was selling a second-hand bookshelf for a reasonable price, as she needed another one in her bedroom. But really, she pored over the personals section, looking for anyone her age who *wasn't* Henry. After being abandoned at their lunch date, she'd licked her wounds but told herself that he just wasn't the man for her. Though she was done with video dating for good, that didn't mean she was done with the idea of finding someone to spend time with—or at least bring to Nettie's wedding. Preferably someone who wouldn't leave her right in the middle of the cake cutting.

Sophia played solitaire at the other end of the couch as Rose rattled dishes in the kitchen and Blanche flipped through the other sections of the morning paper from the rattan armchair. Sophia surreptitiously craned her neck every two minutes to peek over Dorothy's shoulder. "Make sure you find a strong, good-looking one."

"Excuse me?" Dorothy said, giving the diminutive snooper a death glare and tilting the newspaper away from her. Her mother always had to comment on everything Dorothy did—especially her love life.

"You know, to hold up the books! You don't want the shelf falling under the weight of *War and Peace*, or whatever it is you read for fun," Sophia said with a smirk.

Outside, a car horn honked to the tune of "Shave and a Haircut."

"Oh, that must be Jorgen!" Blanche said, jumping to her feet and fanning herself with the *Herald*'s coupon circular. "And me, not even ready to go."

Dorothy looked Blanche up and down, taking in her over-size coral blazer over a matching sundress with a flounced hem. "But you look lovely, Blanche."

"She's fully dressed, which is *over*dressed when a younger man is in her sights," Sophia said, grabbing her pocketbook from the coffee table.

"I just mean I haven't put on my perfume yet," Blanche said, rushing to her bedroom. "And I don't have anyone in my sights. Jorgen is easy on the eyes, that's all."

"He's not the only thing that's easy . . ." muttered Sophia before Dorothy silenced her with an eye roll. She really should talk to her mother about her outdated shaming of Blanche's healthy romantic appetite. After all, this was the 1980s, not the 1940s! Nowadays women should be able to act as freely as men did in the dating world without anyone criticizing them.

Rose emerged through the swinging kitchen door as steam billowed out, filling the air with a toasty scent of tuna and herbs. "I need two more minutes!" she shouted, waving her oven-mitted hands in the air.

Dorothy stood. "Don't worry, we'll get the centerpiece and everything else loaded into the car." She picked up a shopping bag stuffed with name tags and the vintage cow-shaped butter dish that Rose insisted on bringing to the venue, as well as tourist maps of Miami and a copy of *The History of St. Olaf: The Collected Works of Hans Christian Lukerhüven* that she intended to give to Jason's parents.

Blanche emerged from her room in a cloud of Poison by Dior, slung her purse over her shoulder, and picked up the modest floral arrangement comprised of coneflowers, black-eyed Susans, and other plants native to Minnesota and

Florida, meant to represent the union of two families from different regions. Blanche had helped Rose put the finishing touches on it that morning, and though it was certainly colorful, it was definitely not as picture-perfect as the centerpieces they'd tried to copy from *Ladies' Home Journal*.

Blanche, Dorothy, and Sophia filed out to Jorgen's roomy rented sedan, which idled at the curb. Jorgen popped out from the driver's seat and immediately took the centerpiece from Blanche and the heavy bag from Dorothy and placed them in the trunk, then opened the door to the back seat.

"You all look as beautiful as freshly milked cows in a pasture!" he said, beaming at them all but letting his admiring eyes linger on Blanche.

Blanche's coquettish smile disappeared as her jaw dropped.

"Why, I oughta," Sophia said, dropping her purse and drawing her white-gloved hands into fists, ready to spar. Dorothy laid a calming hand on her arm, hoping that none of the neighbors had seen. She'd already gotten a few phone calls from the time Sophia ran through the neighbor's sprinkler in her Playtex during a heat wave.

"I think that's a compliment where he comes from," Dorothy whispered. "He didn't mean to be rude. Remember, he's a farm boy. Think of him as a junior, male version of Rose."

Sophia slowly lowered her dukes, the slump of her shoulders hinting at her disappointment that she wasn't going to have a chance to use them. "Well, he shouldn't act like he was raised in a barn," she grumbled.

"He probably was, Ma," Dorothy said, gently leading Sophia to the car. They climbed in, and Jorgen took Blanche's hand.

"Oh, I'll ride up front with you," Blanche cooed, stepping into the passenger seat as Rose scurried out the door and down the walkway to the car with a casserole dish in her hands.

Jorgen settled Rose in the sedan on the other side of Sophia, then handed her the casserole dish. As they drove down Richmond Street, passing well-kept ranch houses and palm trees, the car filled with the aroma of tuna.

"Could you crack a window?" Sophia asked Dorothy.

"It smells just like home!" Jorgen chirped from the driver seat. "Is that smörgåstårta?"

"It's my famous tuna soufflé," Rose said with a note of pride in her voice. "The Bryants offered to handle the catering, but I just couldn't trust them to get the soufflé right, so I made it myself."

"Is that why you made the tuna salad sandwiches ahead of time, too?" Blanche said. She'd gone with Rose the day before to drop several trays of miniature crustless sandwiches off at the hotel along with the fleet of cheesecakes so they could be refrigerated overnight before the Tea. Rose had been a little nervous when they handed over the trays to the hotel staff, who had quickly ferried them into the hotel and out of sight. The two women had parted ways when Rose met up with Nettie and Jason. Blanche and Jorgen ran wedding errands on the other side of town. It had been far past Rose's bedtime when Jorgen had finally dropped Blanche off at home late that night.

"No, they could probably get my tuna salad right, if they followed the recipe," Rose said. "But Grandmother Lindstrom would arise from her watery grave and kill me if I ever shared her secret ingredient."

The girls shared a knowing look as they braced for a new St. Olaf story, but Rose had trailed off, quickly adding a few words to a list balanced on top of the casserole dish.

"I'm not even going to ask," Dorothy said. "But I'm sure it all will be delicious." She knew how important today was for Rose. This was the first official meeting of the families—the Bryant family on the groom's side, and the St. Olaf contingent from the bride's side. It was obvious that Rose wanted to make a great first impression from the care she took with every single detail, such as the hand calligraphy on the name tags, the fussing over her outfit and hairstyle, and making sure that there were plenty of St. Olaf touches in the food and decorations. Dorothy was glad that she and the others had pledged to help out in any way Rose needed, including keeping the conversation flowing between the two families. She had a feeling they'd need to.

"I'm just so nervous!" Rose said, pinching at the tinfoil edges of the casserole dish as the sedan rolled through the city, headed in the direction of Miami Beach. "What if something goes wrong?"

"You've planned every detail out to a T, and put a lot of

thought into it." Blanche turned toward the back seat to reassure Rose.

"Maybe the most thought you've put into anything!" Sophia said.

"It's going to be a lovely event," Dorothy added to smooth over Sophia's comment in case Rose took it the wrong way. "Everything will be just fine."

Jorgen drove down Collins Avenue, passing hotels and restaurants and the occasional palm tree. He pulled the sedan up a semicircular drive to the Cabana Sun Hotel, a cream-colored building accented with borders of teal and coral, an art deco wedding cake bathed in brilliant Miami sunshine. He parked under the portico awning, then helped each woman exit the car. Laden with bags and the casserole dish, he followed the three women through the revolving doors to the hotel lobby, a stylish space with marble black-and-white tiled floors, soaring columns, and artful arrangements of pink and white blooms. Every surface was polished to a glossy sheen, except for the teal settees in tufted velvet surrounding a small fountain of carved sea turtles and dolphins.

"This is a lot fancier than I expected," Sophia said, gawking up at the ceiling, which was painted with a scene of cherubs frolicking among fluffy clouds and palm fronds. Just then, a woman in a yellow sundress crossed the lobby ahead of them, holding a poofy white dog wearing a matching yellow ribbon around its neck. "It's like the love child of the Sistine Chapel and the Copacabana."

"I'm surprised they allow dogs in here," Dorothy mused, taking it all in.

"Don't worry, Dorothy, I called ahead to get permission for you," Sophia said.

"Stuff it, Ma," Dorothy said, clenching her fists inside her blazer pockets. "Why do you always need to be so mean? Did you put your adult diapers on backwards today?"

After getting her own verbal punch in, Dorothy decided she wouldn't let her mother ruin her mood. Yes, she was still dateless for Nettie's wedding, but there were a few days left to find someone new to bring. They were here to support Rose, and that's what she'd focus on.

As the girls and Jorgen made their way to the check-in counter, a thirtysomething woman with strong brows and sky-high cheekbones stepped from behind the desk, her white business suit cinched at the waist with a wide gold leather belt. Her permed ash-blond hair fell in perfect spirals to her padded shoulders, and Dorothy noticed the tasteful French manicure on her long oval nails as she extended her hand to Rose.

"You must be the midwestern in-laws," the woman purred, shaking Rose's hand while simultaneously casting an appreciative glance at Jorgen.

"Are you Jason's sister?" Rose asked.

"Yes, Jason's my brother. I'm Patricia, the general manager

of the Cabana Sun Hotel. I cover Housekeeping, Food and Beverage, you name it."

"Oh yes, we spoke on the phone!" Rose said warmly, wrapping Patricia in a slightly awkward hug. "So glad to meet you in person, and thank you for welcoming us to your beautiful hotel."

"It's no trouble at all." Patricia smiled, gently disentangling herself from Rose's arms. "As I said on the phone, we're planning to host the whole wedding here."

Just as Rose was about to reply, Jorgen stepped forward.

"I'm Jorgen!" He beamed. "You look just like Brooke Shields!"

Patricia stifled a laugh. "Nice to meet you, Jorgen. Jason told me you're the best man."

"I don't know about best," he said, blushing. "But I'm pretty good."

Rose gestured to her friends and introduced them one by one.

Blanche leaned over to whisper in Dorothy's ear. "I can smell a fake tan and surgical enhancements from a mile away."

Dorothy nodded in agreement. Patricia's measurements seemed very close to those of another leggy blond's—Barbie's.

"But a true gentleman prefers something real to grab on to." Blanche sniffed as she straightened her posture to show off her own unique assets.

"Let's hope at least some of them do," Dorothy whispered back. Even though Blanche always seemed so confident and in touch with her own sensuality, Dorothy could hear the note of insecurity in her voice. Dating after a certain age—or at *any* age—wasn't easy on anyone.

Patricia led the group through the hotel, pointing left and right. "Here's the concierge desk; over there are the elevators; the pool is that way, along with the bar. And we have a cigar clubroom with a humidor. That was my husband Chip's idea, and it's been a huge hit. Only the best for our guests."

Patricia led the girls and Jorgen to a corridor off to the side of the lobby. "The kitchens are back here," she said. "I'll have some of the staff help you set up on the patio by the pool, since we have perfect weather today."

"That would be lovely," Rose said, hurrying to keep up with Patricia's long-legged stride. "And are the mother and father of the groom here yet?"

"My parents will be down any minute. We had some international VIPs check in this morning, and as owners of the hotel, they wanted to personally welcome them to the Presidential Suite."

"Oooh, VIPS!" Blanche piped up from behind them. "Who are they? Do tell."

"Most of our guests expect complete privacy," Patricia said in an officious tone. "And I'm the soul of discretion." Then she cracked a wicked smile. "But I *can* tell you that we recently had Gloria Estefan's cousin stay with us for a week, and Philip Michael Thomas and Don Johnson have been known to frequent our cigar room."

"I love *Miami Vice*!" Rose said with a starstruck grin.

"We're planning to expand next year," Patricia said, her spike heels clacking on the marble flooring. "*If* we can get that run-down building next door. Then we can build an indoor pool and double our room count. Chip wants to add a nightclub."

International VIPs and television actors were a far cry from the small-town, farm-centric world of St. Olaf, Dorothy thought as Patricia directed them down a long corridor. She hoped for Rose's sake that the two families would find some common ground this week.

The group pushed through two wide swinging doors to a room that was partially under construction, with raw plywood cabinets and stainless-steel fixtures.

"Sorry for the mess—we're mid-renovation," Patricia said, gesturing to the fresh sheetrock and a few visible wires hanging from the ceiling. "Our previous kitchen could only handle a basic room-service menu, so this expansion and overhaul is long overdue."

The Bryants must be doing very well for themselves, Dorothy thought, with all this renovation work and their plans for expansion.

Rose looked worriedly around the half-finished kitchen. "Are my sandwiches still here? And the cheesecake?"

"Yes, they're in the industrial freezer toward the back. You can use this to get set up." Patricia pointed to a wide butcher-block table, upon which Jorgen deposited the heavy armloads he'd been carrying. "We'll serve everything on the patio. Those tables should already be set up, and I'll flag down José and Fred to bring out any servingware you need."

"Oh, thank you," Rose said. "But before you run off—here! I have name tags!"

Rose passed her a sticker with the name PATRICIA written out in slightly uneven calligraphy. Patricia held it carefully by one edge, as if Rose had handed her a loose sardine.

"I'm not sure I should put this on," Patricia said. "My blouse is silk."

Rose's face fell, and Patricia quickly recovered, tucking the name tag into the pocket of her blazer. "But it's a nice thought. I'll make sure to introduce myself to everyone from the St. Oliver branch of the family."

"St. Olaf!" Rose corrected.

"Of course," Patricia said. "And my apologies. I just have so much on my mind with managing the hotel, Chip's ideas to expand the business, and now Jason's wedding, it's amazing I remember anything."

"I know just how you feel," Sophia chimed in.

"Ma, that's because you're older than George Burns—when he played *God*!" Dorothy said. If her mother could dish it out, she should be able to take a few digs herself.

"I'm going to flag down José and Fred for you. If you need any other help setting up, the front desk can page me," Patricia said, sweeping out of the kitchen in a swirl of Jovan Musk and Aqua Net.

Blanche fanned her nose dramatically with her hand. "Well, she's certainly a lot to handle."

"A tall glass of cream," Jorgen murmured. "They don't wear heels that high in St. Olaf."

"I asked them to put everything in the fridge, not the freezer," Rose said worriedly. "But I suppose beggars can't be choosers. They've been very generous to offer us the use of their elegant facilities."

"That's the right attitude," Dorothy said. "Do you have any idea how much it would cost to rent a venue like this?"

"I can guess," Sophia said. "Probably enough to buy her an even bigger set of—" She gestured to her chest.

"Ma, please—we have more important things at hand. We have to get the food defrosted and set up the decorations before the wedding guests arrive," Dorothy said.

"That's right!" Rose said. "If we take everything out now, it should be ready in time." She headed to the other end of the kitchen where two large stainless-steel doors sat side by side, one with a wooden chair wedged against the handle.

"That's odd." Rose frowned. "Jorgen, could you move that for me?"

Jorgen tugged the chair to the side and Rose pulled open the freezer door. An array of cheesecakes gleamed on chest-high racks next to neat trays of sandwiches.

As she stepped forward to pull out the first tray, her foot hit something icy and hard. Then Rose looked down and screamed.

# THE WAY THE CHEESECAKE CRUMBLES

········· **6** ·········

*R*ose finally stopped screaming and covered her mouth with her hand. Blanche rushed to her side and threw an arm around her friend.

"What is it, honey? Are your cheesecakes all right?" Blanche asked breathlessly.

Rose pointed into the freezer. "The cheesecakes are fine . . . but *he's* not!"

Dorothy and Sophia stepped in close behind Rose and peered around her shoulders to see a man slumped face down in a cheesecake on the floor of the freezer. His features were hidden in the cream-colored mess that crumbled away from his head. Rose's eyes roamed in terror over his frozen body, and she screamed again when she spotted a knife clutched in the man's blue-tinged hand.

Now it was Dorothy and Sophia's turn to scream. Jorgen looked from one older woman to the next, then saw what they were screaming at and joined in himself. A surprisingly high-pitched series of notes emanated from his broad chest, echoing around the industrial kitchen.

When they all finally stopped screaming, they looked at each other in disbelief for several moments.

"Do you think we can revive him?" Rose said, her chest heaving as she tried to catch her breath. "Maybe help him . . . defrost?"

"He's not a pot roast," Sophia pointed out.

"I don't think it works like that, sweetie," Blanche added sadly. "I think he's a goner."

"This is terrible, just terrible!" Rose wailed. "That poor man." She devolved into sobs, and Dorothy, Blanche, and Sophia wrapped her in a hug. Jorgen didn't know quite what to do, so he patted each woman reassuringly on the back while he stole worried glances at the dead man.

When Rose calmed down, she looked at the other three women as tear tracks cut through the powder on her cheeks. Sophia opened her purse and handed her an embroidered handkerchief.

"What are we going to do?" Rose said, dabbing at her eyes.

"Don't worry," Sophia said. "I'll give my cousin Danny a call—he knows a few guys who can make a situation like this disapp—"

"Sophia!" Blanche scolded. "You know that's not what Rose meant."

"If we don't get rid of him, people are going to start asking questions." Sophia shook her finger in Rose's direction. "And one of those questions is going to be: What exactly did you put in that cheesecake?"

Rose gasped, stumbling back against Jorgen, who helped her back to her feet. "I didn't put anything in them!" she said, her face contorted with worry. "Just some extra vanilla!"

"Please, Ma, don't tease her. This is a very serious situation." Dorothy carefully led Rose away from the open freezer door. As she did, she craned her neck to look again at the dead man.

The man had thick salt-and-pepper hair and was dressed in a long-sleeve shirt with the words *Nassau Cup* on the back, madras shorts, and tennis shoes. His one visible ear was rimmed in ice crystals. He clutched a sharp knife in one hand, and the edge of a shiny gold watch face peeked out from his shirtsleeve.

"That poor man," Rose repeated. "Freezing has got to be one of the worst ways to die. Worse than being a victim of Gunilla Olfstatter, St. Olaf's Angel of Death, or falling into a butter silo, or being thrown into St. Olaf's most active volcano, or . . ."

"We get the picture," Blanche said gently. "But this isn't really the time for St. Olaf stories."

"We need to get help. I'll call 911," Dorothy said, turning to find a telephone.

Just then, two men in magenta bellhop uniforms burst through the swinging kitchen doors. "We heard screaming," said the mustachioed one bearing the name tag FRED on his uniform.

"Is everyone all right?" said the other, whose name tag read JOSÉ.

Rose ran toward the two men, wringing her hands. "We . . . we . . ."

"We do need your assistance, gentlemen," Blanche said, stepping forward. "We seem to have run into a bit of a problem."

"At your service," Fred said, adjusting his bellhop cap.

"The problem is right there!" Sophia said bluntly, pointing toward the open freezer.

The two men leaned forward and looked inside, their eyes bugging out in surprise when they saw the dead man. They stared at each other for a moment with knitted brows, then turned back to the ladies and Jorgen.

"We're sorry for the inconvenience," Fred said, almost automatically.

"This is . . . unexpected," José added. "We've never . . ."

"It's not some *inconvenience*," Rose said. "That man is dead!"

"We understand your concern," José said. "Perhaps you'd

like to speak to our manager so that we can rectify the situation immediately."

"I'm not sure you can," Dorothy said. "It's far too late for an ambulance."

"We need to call the police," Rose urged. "Where's the nearest phone?"

Fred and José looked at each other again. José bit his lip, hesitating.

"Let us alert Miss Patricia first," Fred said quickly.

"She will know the, uh, proper protocol for this unfortunate event," José added, crossing and uncrossing his arms. He gave another wide-eyed look to Fred, who practically ran out of the kitchen to find Patricia.

José closed the door behind him, then dragged two CAUTION! WET FLOOR! signs from the corner to block off their section of the kitchen. "We don't need anyone wandering through here by accident," he explained, sneaking darting glances at the dead man.

"Should we close the freezer door?" Rose said. "Maybe that will prevent him from . . . melting."

"Good idea," José said, and pushed the door closed, nudging the dead man's foot inside with his shoe.

The kitchen door swung open with a bang, making everyone jump. Patricia barreled through the room, trailed by Fred, her brow furrowed. Without saying a word to the ladies or Jorgen, she marched straight to José and whispered emphatically in his ear.

José nodded vigorously and whispered back a few words of his own, pointing in the direction of the freezer.

Patricia opened the stainless-steel door a few inches to peek inside, then quickly shut it again. She leaned against the freezer, her face pale beneath her expertly applied streaks of blush.

She closed her eyes, breathing loudly through her nose as if to calm her nerves.

"I'm the general manager, and I will manage this," she muttered under her breath. "I can handle it." Then she snapped her brilliant blue eyes open.

"Well, this is a first," she said with a forced smile. With brusque sweeping motions she began to shoo the ladies and Jorgen toward the other end of the kitchen. "I'll take care of this situation. You all can go right out to the patio, and José will bring out everything you need. Let's keep this just among us until I've had a chance to get it sorted, all right?"

"What do you mean?" said Dorothy. "Aren't you going to call the police?"

"I'm going to handle this properly," Patricia said smoothly. "This is an unfortunate accident, but I don't want Jason and Nettie to know about it just yet. I wouldn't want to upset them right before their wedding."

"Maybe you're right," Rose said, to everyone's surprise. "They have enough to worry about and I want them to enjoy today if possible—despite this terrible tragedy."

"We're just going to *carry on* with a tea party?" Sophia

asked, incredulous. "When I croak, could you at least take a few minutes to mourn before you pour the Earl Grey?"

"Shhh," Blanche said. "This man's death has nothing to do with us or this wedding. I agree that we shouldn't let it ruin things for Nettie."

Rose looked from one face to another, all marked with traces of shock at finding the dead man. But everyone nodded in agreement. Maybe the police would let them serve the remaining cheesecakes and sandwiches. Maybe they could all paste happy smiles on their faces and hide what they'd just witnessed, for Nettie's sake. She felt terrible for the man, but she had to wipe the tears from her eyes and make this wedding a success.

There was no use crying over smashed cheesecake.

# OUT OF THE FREEZER, INTO THE FRYING PAN

········· **7** ·········

*W*ith shaking hands, Rose placed the homemade center-piece in the middle of a large table crowded with sandwiches, plates, napkins, and her tuna soufflé, which had sunk a little as the day had grown more humid. She couldn't blame the soufflé. It had already been a long day, and it wasn't even noon yet.

The Welcome Tuna Teatime *had* to go off without a hitch, Rose thought. The event had been one of the first compromises that she'd made with the Bryants over the phone. They'd been delighted to host the event here, and if all went well, it would be easier for both families to convince Nettie and Jorgen to hold the ceremony and reception at the hotel. Mr. and Mrs. Bryant seemed more open than she'd expected to Rose supplying all the food, but perhaps that was due to their kitchen being renovated, she thought. She hadn't exactly told them yet about all the things they'd need to bring in for the wedding itself, including the live donkey for Jason to ride down the aisle.

One thing at a time, she reminded herself. For now, she'd have to put on a brave face. Not the face of a woman who'd just discovered a dead man.

She surveyed the patio area where they'd set up for the Teatime. An aqua swimming pool shimmered off to one side, and tables and chairs were set up to accommodate a group of around twenty people. There would be more, of course, at the wedding itself. The final guest list was still very much in question, as Nettie and Jason wanted the wedding limited to thirty people and the Bryants would likely want many more, now that the wedding was on their home turf.

In addition to contributing the space today, the Bryants had supplied white and silver balloons that José and Fred anchored to the wrought-iron patio furniture, working mechanically, as if they hadn't encountered a dead body just moments ago. As if nothing bad had ever happened in the world. The balloons tossed in the breeze as soft Cuban jazz music emanated from speakers hidden among the lush coral honeysuckle and hibiscus plants that lined the patio.

Rose straightened up, easing an ache in her back. She'd worked hard to prepare everything for this party, and even though she wanted to enjoy it, she couldn't shake the sadness of finding that poor man, and another, more unsettled feeling. What had happened to him? If it was truly an accident, as Patricia had said . . . then why had he been clutching that knife?

Just then Rose heard familiar sparkling laughter and turned to see Nettie and Jason stepping onto the patio. Jason looked handsome in a light linen suit that set off the tan he'd acquired after just one day back in Miami, and Nettie glowed in a yellow seersucker sundress, her hair pulled up in a banana clip. They walked arm in arm toward Rose, followed by the maid of honor, Bess, and a trail of St. Olafians who must have arrived last night or early this morning.

Rose was soon enveloped by a small crowd of people she hadn't seen in a very long time. Her sister Holly, her aunt Katrina, and some town elders, including her cousin Gustave Lindstrom, the current mayor of St. Olaf. A handful of relatives from Nettie's father's side of the family, a mostly blond, freckled bunch that spoke more Norwegian than English.

The women were all dressed in sensible cotton dresses in pale prints and sturdy flat shoes, and the men mostly wore plain slacks, button-down shirts, and thick-soled shoes that wouldn't be out of place on a farm or fishing boat. Several St. Olafians had worn wool cardigans and pullovers and were quickly removing them as dazzling sunlight heated the pool-side patio.

Springtime in Miami was very different from springtime in St. Olaf, where snow often still covered the ground and the trees were bare and the sky was gray, Rose thought with a touch of nostalgia. Every year she couldn't wait for spring, when she and Charlie would look for crocuses peeking their little purple heads above the crust of snow. Here, bougainvillea and hibiscus were in full bloom, and between the fronds of waving palm tree leaves, the sky was a sapphire blue.

"Rose Nylund," Aunt Katrina said in a lilting Scandinavian accent, wrapping her in a hug. "The last time I saw you was on Everybody Hide the Corn Day, some years ago!"

Rose hugged her back. "I've missed you, and everyone from St. Olaf."

Katrina drew back to get a good look at Rose. "You look so different," she said. "A real Miami lady."

"I do?" Rose said, looking down at herself. She was the same old Rose. Maybe her tutenbobels had shrunk a bit, she admitted, as she didn't consume quite as much heavy cream these days, and since Blanche would only allow skim milk in their kitchen, a bluish monstrosity that still unsettled Rose whenever she tried to pour a bowl of cereal. But that couldn't be it, she thought. Was it her outfit? She was dressed nicely, but not as flashy as say, Blanche or Patricia, but not as simply as everyone else from her hometown.

She was somewhere in the middle, she supposed, though

her hairstyle was a little longer than Aunt Katrina's, who still sported a severe wash-and-go style, or the braids that the younger St. Olaf women wore pinned around their heads like milkmaids. Rose realized she had a little more jewelry on and bright pink nail polish. In St. Olaf, she'd never painted her nails, since it would chip the moment she picked up a butter churn or deboned a walleye pike. Maybe she *was* a little more Miami than when she'd first left St. Olaf, she grudgingly admitted to herself.

But she could still milk a cow in under four minutes, win a round of Gügenspritzer, and chug eggnog with the best of them.

Couldn't she?

"Of course I'm the same old Rose," she insisted. "You'll see I'm still a St. Olaf girl through and through."

"I sure hope you are," her cousin Gustave said, giving her a kiss on the cheek. "The town elders and I are expecting this wedding to be a true expression of our St. Olaf traditions. This change of setting is most unusual."

"You don't need to worry about that," Rose said. "Everything will be just as if we were in our beloved village—I've been reviewing the town bylaws to make sure we have every single tradition covered."

Gustave cocked his head, listening skeptically.

"Do you have enough herring?" Katrina asked, her tone dubious.

Gustave nodded in harsh agreement. "A wedding without herring would be like St. Sigmund's Day—"

"Without the headless boy," Katrina finished, shaking a finger at Rose.

"Of course I have that under control," said Rose, mentally tallying the amount of herring she'd requested from the fishmonger and wondering if she should double it. "You can get any kind of fish here! And I'm personally overseeing each detail to make sure it's authentic," she continued, trying to put Cousin Gustave and Aunt Katrina at ease. "After all, as Nettie is a direct descendant of Heinrich von Anderdonnen, I wouldn't have it any other way."

"See that you do," Gustave said gravely. "If Nettie ever wants to settle in St. Olaf again she—and her future husband—will have to have completed every one of our wedding traditions to be citizens in good standing—and receive her portion of the Anderdonnen trust in the future."

Rose gasped. She knew that a real St. Olaf wedding would help Jason be accepted into the rest of her family and the community, but she hadn't realized that Nettie's future inheritance also hinged on it.

"But why does it matter who she marries, and how? Shouldn't she just get the trust automatically?" Rose asked, frowning. She loved St. Olaf, but sometimes their byzantine rules and regulations didn't exactly make sense. And sometimes they weren't fair. Especially Section 9, Article 1, of the

Me and My Pet Look-alike Contest rules, she thought with chagrin.

"Her parents earmarked their share for Nettie when they left St. Olaf for Pittsburgh," Gustave said. "For her to receive it once she gets married or reaches age thirty. But there were certain conditions attached."

Rose fumed, accidentally squeezing one of her mini tuna sandwiches into a pancake of mush in her hand. How dare Nettie's parents put conditions on their daughter after practically abandoning her for a troupe of—admittedly very talented—poodles?

"I have to tell you," Katrina said sternly, "it's been a huge mark against her that she got engaged to an outsider. A Miami boy, no less! From what I've seen just from the taxi ride from the airport, this city is full of the opposite values of St. Olaf."

"Hey, what do you mean by that?" Sophia chimed in as she wandered by, sweeping a cold glare over Katrina. "You don't know anything about Miami! It's a beautiful place, and you need to open up your small-minded, clodhopping eyes and give it a chance!"

Dumbfounded, Katrina opened her mouth but found no words to respond with.

Blanche quickly jumped in, trying to smooth over the tense moment. "What I think Sophia is trying to say is that Miami has a rich culture, in terms of the food, the music, the nightlife—"

"Exactly!" Gustave said. "It seems to be all about nightlife and dancing and nothing to do with family and community! Plus, there's all sorts of criminal activity, drug cartels, and smuggling. Haven't you seen the television show *Miami Vice*?"

"Oh no, it's nothing like that," Rose said. "It's more like . . . Miami *Nice*!"

She beamed, proud of herself for coming up with the perfect phrase to describe her life in her adopted city.

Just then Dorothy joined the group, having heard conversation getting animated. Rose realized introductions might be the perfect way to change the subject—and break the tension.

"Ladies," she said, "I want you to meet my cousin Gustave!"

As Gustave stepped forward with a hesitant smile, Blanche looked him over, taking in his white hair, short beard, and unruly eyebrows. He wore suspenders over a plaid work shirt and gave off a slight scent of hay and cigars.

Blanche leaned close to Rose's ear and whispered, "Is that the one who died?"

Rose looked at her friend, a little taken aback, since Gustave was clearly alive and well.

"You told me a story that back in St. Olaf there was a Gustave who was accidentally buried alive! And another one who—"

Rose let out a nervous laugh. "Oh, that was Gustav! As you can see, *Gustave* is alive and well," Rose explained, carefully enunciating both names with no discernable difference in intonation or pronunciation.

"Ah, I remember," Dorothy said. "Rose has mentioned her uncle Gustaf a few times."

"Oh no, that was his brother. This is *Gustave!*" Rose said.

Sophia threw up her hands, and Dorothy shared an incredulous look with her mother.

"Family tends to get confusing in St. Olaf," Rose admitted. "But one thing I know for sure is that we always stand by each other, right, Gustave?"

Gustave grunted. "In St. Olaf we do."

He shifted uncomfortably in his heavy work shoes, glancing around the glamorous hotel patio, gesturing at the tropical flowers and unfamiliar faces. "Why couldn't Nettie marry a nice local boy like Einar Nilsson? Or someone like Jorgen?" he asked.

"Young Einar throws hay very well," Katrina said approvingly. "And he plays the piano."

Nettie's voice rang out from behind Rose: "Because I don't *love* Einar and Jorgen!" Rose cringed, wondering how much Nettie had heard. "I love Jason."

"You tell 'em, honey," Blanche said, patting Nettie on the shoulder. "None of these gray-hairs know anything about true romance."

"And Jason loves St. Olaf, even though none of you are very welcoming when we visit," Nettie said, her voice trembling. "*He's* the one who wants to live there after we get married. *I'd* rather never go back." Spots of pink arose on Nettie's cheeks.

"Oh, sweetie," said Rose, mustering as much lighthearted

positivity she could, despite all the family tension and the specter of a nearby corpse giving her indigestion. "Let's all just take a breath and enjoy the party. It looked like everyone was meeting and mingling so nicely!"

She grabbed Nettie by the shoulders and pointed her toward the rest of the party while she surveyed the scene. Jason's parents were talking with Dorothy and their son-in-law Chip, and Patricia was busy pouring tea for a few of the St. Olaf elders. Rose led Nettie through the crowd, mentally checking everyone off the guest list. There were the Corzons, a well-to-do Cuban American family who owned a string of restaurants in Little Havana, the Petrosini clan, related to the Bryants by marriage, including a grandmotherly matriarch with a little boy about three years old clinging to her hand, and Mr. and Mrs. Walsh, a middle-aged couple who were friends of the Bryants. Everyone was well-dressed, down to the little blond toddler in a pint-size suit with a dolphin stitched on the chest.

Rose refilled Nettie's tea and left her chatting with Mr. Corzon and bustled around the guests, making sure everyone was helping themselves to plenty of cheesecake and sandwiches. She felt Jason at her side as he cut another slice of the St. Olaf's Kiss cake, stuffing his face with bites of creamy vanilla cheesecake with lingonberry sauce. Rose was glad he liked it so much, as she'd poured lots of love into that cake specifically, and its ingredients represented Nettie and Rose's hometown. Jason certainly didn't need to know what it had been sharing a freezer with, she thought with a shiver.

A fresh wash of sadness poured through Rose as she thought back to the grisly events of that morning. It must have been some sort of freak accident—like the time Lars von Dingelheim tripped over his own shoelace and fell into a well. No one heard his cries for help, since everyone was busy in town at the Founders' Day Pageant, a notoriously loud affair involving accordions, cottage cheese, and some of the best performances west of Broadway.

*That's life for you*, Rose thought. Tragedy and celebration, all mashed up next to each other like tuna salad and white bread. You needed both to make a sandwich. Thinking back on her joyful marriage to Charlie, and the devastating pain of being widowed, she figured that the sad times and the happy times were all part of the big picture. You couldn't get through life without a hefty serving of both.

Rose looked over and saw Sophia sitting poolside with the Petrosini grandmother, tying the shoes of the little boy in the dolphin suit. The Walshes chatted animatedly with Jorgen, and Mr. and Mrs. Corzon were deep in conversation with Cousin Gustave. She didn't see the Bryants or Chip at the moment, but Rose figured they must have stepped away from the party to handle the freezer situation. Despite the earlier unpleasantness from the town elders, everyone was getting along and going back for seconds and even thirds on cheesecake, she noticed. She'd done it! The Miami contingent was happily mingling with the St. Olafians, and despite the tension with Sophia and Aunt Katrina, no one had been pushed into the swimming pool yet.

Jason threw his arm around Nettie, and she leaned on his shoulder with a happy smile that lit up her eyes. Rose let out a relaxed sigh. The very first wedding event was clearly a hit. Even with minimal prep time and the delicate task of managing everyone's feelings, she'd pulled off a rather wonderful party.

Rose smiled to herself, just as a line of uniformed police officers burst onto the patio.

# MIAMI 5-OH NO

## 8

*D*orothy clocked the police as soon as they muscled their way into the party. All conversation stopped abruptly, leaving only the harsh sound of boots over tile. She and Sophia put down their half-eaten slices of cheesecake and hurried over to Rose. Without a doubt, she'd need their help managing this situation.

Across the table, Patricia excused herself from the conversation she'd been having with Jorgen and Bess and power walked across the patio to intercept the police. Mr. and Mrs. Bryant were hot on her heels.

It was clear from Dorothy's point of view that Patricia was trying to draw the police out of sight, away from the patio. But it was too late. Everyone was gawking at the newcomers and looking nervously from one face to another.

"What did you do this time?" Mrs. Walsh asked Mr. Walsh.

"Nothing, I swear!" Mr. Walsh said, his face growing a tad ruddy. He took a long sip of his gin and tonic, then ordered another.

"Maybe it's something to do with one of the guests," Mrs. Corzon said in a rich Cuban accent.

"Probably something routine—perhaps they're checking a gas leak in the area," Mr. Corzon said, patting her arm. "Most likely nothing to worry about."

Dorothy caught up with Rose by the tuna table just as Nettie jogged over, her brow knit in confusion. "What's going on?" the young woman asked.

"Not anything to concern yourself with, dear," said Rose. "Nothing we need worry about today."

"You don't want to tell her the truth?" Sophia whispered. "Better she hears it from you."

"Shhh, Ma," Dorothy said, exasperated. They were trying to keep everything going well—or at least looking that way—for Rose's sake. They had to help her spin this. "We're not going into detail about the . . . *expired cheesecake*, remember?"

"Detail about what?" Nettie said as Jason showed up at her side. "This is my wedding. Are you all keeping something from me?"

"Hey, babe," Jason said. "Are you okay?" He wrapped his strong arms around her.

"I'm trying to figure out why there are a bunch of police at our wedding tea," Nettie said. "Can you go over there and figure out what they're saying?"

By now, Patricia had moved the officers into an area partially shaded by a lattice wall, but Dorothy could see them and the Bryants talking heatedly.

The St. Olaf contingent shifted in their sensible shoes, pulling on their sweaters as if in preparation for a quick getaway.

"Is this a bust?" Aunt Katrina said. "A *shakedown*, a *sting*?"

"I knew this city was full of danger," Gustave said, shaking his head. "The TV news says there is criminal activity in every nook and krugel in these big cities. No one is safe."

"Should we go back to St. Olaf?" Katrina said. She wrung her hands.

"Don't be silly," Sophia snapped. "You're overreacting. You're more likely to get run over by a cow in that one-horse town than get into any trouble here."

"And you wouldn't want to miss the wedding," Blanche added hurriedly. "Whatever that's about, it has nothing to do with this joyous occasion, the merging of two wonderful families."

"That's right," Rose added, clearly grateful for Blanche's help in trying to calm the families and keep the wedding party together. "I'm sure it's nothing to worry about." She offered a fresh slice of cheesecake to Katrina with the biggest smile she could muster, but Dorothy could see the strain behind it.

Just as the words left Rose's mouth, a tall policewoman with a golden-brown complexion and a serious expression stalked over to the group, circling the four of them. Dorothy felt anxiety twist in her stomach, which she tried to stifle. Just because the police had shown up didn't mean *they* were in trouble.

"Dorothy Zbornak and associates?" the officer said in a stern voice, pointing to each woman in turn, then whirling to locate Jorgen. "I'm Detective Silva."

"We need you all to come with us," a second, portly policeman with gray hair said. He placed his hands on his hips, which only served to highlight the firearm at his waist.

The four friends stared at each other, biting their lips. *So much for carrying on as if nothing bad happened this morning,* Dorothy thought. *So much for not making a scene.*

"Right now!" the policewoman said, making Rose jump slightly at Dorothy's side.

"Let me just grab my things," Sophia said, bending to get the purse she'd placed on a chair. The she tugged on Dorothy's arm and whispered, "Never tell the police anything more than you have to, *capisce?*"

"Nothing to worry about!" Rose warbled to those nearby as she stepped forward to follow the officers, Patricia and Mr. and Mrs. Bryant hot on their heels. But Dorothy could tell from her tone—Rose was definitely worried.

"Probably just a parking ticket," Blanche tossed over her shoulder at the other party guests, attempting a casual air.

As the policewoman led them back to the interior of the

hotel, Dorothy noticed that the rest of the wedding party had gotten over their initial surprise. Everyone was whispering to each other and sending suspicious glances everywhere. So much for the party, Dorothy thought. Poor Nettie. Poor Rose.

"Oh dear," Rose said. "This party is ruined!"

"Let's simply speak with them and then calmly return," Dorothy said, trying to sound more levelheaded than she felt. "I'm sure they just want to talk to us about finding the body. They're just doing their jobs."

"I know, but can't they do their jobs more discreetly?" Patricia said. "I *told* them I'd bring you over, one by one. I really didn't want them to make a scene. They must have marched right through the lobby," she complained. "I hope our other hotel guests didn't see them."

"I don't think the police care too much about appearances," Blanche said, trying to keep up with the others in her high heels as they filed inside the hotel.

"But appearances affect *business*," Patricia said. "I can't have guests thinking this is some kind of low-rent criminal enclave. We have an esteemed clientele, and we've cultivated a reputation for excellence. If word gets out, people will stop coming to the hotel and we'll lose money. We're already in the hole with renovations as it is!"

"I'm sure you'll make them see reason," Mrs. Bryant huffed. "That this is some fluke event."

"We'll keep this as quiet as we can," Mr. Bryant added. "I know you won't let us down."

Patricia nodded at her parents, a determined glint in her eye.

"This would never have happened if we weren't doing this renovation, having workers coming in and out at all hours," Mrs. Bryant said, in a tone that conveyed that it was somehow Patricia's fault. Dorothy recognized it loud and clear from decades of her own mother's passive-aggressive tendencies. Speaking of which, where *was* her mother? Sophia had moved to get her purse but somehow had slipped away in the time it took them all to walk from the pool patio to the hotel hallway.

"Well, I couldn't have known that would happen, Mother," Patricia said tightly. "Oh, why did he have to die in *our* kitchen?"

"It's crummy luck, that's what it is," Mr. Bryant said. "The important thing is for the police to know that none of us knew him or had anything to do with him. He was here completely at random, and he has nothing to do with the hotel.

"If people start asking questions about it, tell them that there was a medical emergency with a staff member," Mr. Bryant continued, gripping Patricia's forearm so tightly that it wrinkled the fabric of her blazer. "Set up a free cocktail hour, throw in some canapés. Anyone who saw anything will forget all about it."

"Okay," Patricia said. "I'll find Chip and get him started right on that."

Mrs. Bryant looked at Patricia, an icy expression on her face. "Are you being willfully dense? Your father asked *you* to take care of it. Any idiot can see that this is too important to delegate."

"Yes, Mother," Patricia said, her head drooping under the harsh words.

Dorothy was starting to see why Jason had wanted to move away from his family, if this was how they talked to each other in times of stress. He was so sweet with Nettie, probably trying to be the opposite of how he'd been brought up.

The police escorted the group through a frosted-glass door at the other side of the lobby. They entered a spacious room with low amber lighting. After her eyes had a chance to adjust, Dorothy took in the mirrored walls, leather club chairs, mahogany tables, gold accents, and a gleaming glass humidor in the center of the room.

*This must be the cigar room*, she thought.

"Officers," Patricia said, changing her tone from chastised daughter to smooth hotel impresario. "Can I offer you a cigar while you work, or to take home?"

The gray-haired policeman looked eagerly at the humidor and rubbed his hands together. Detective Silva shot him a glare.

"No, thank you," she said. "Officer Pierno and I will decline. And I'm sure these are all sourced appropriately?"

"Of course they are." Patricia smiled. "Nothing but the best American cigars for our guests. Everything here is aboveboard."

"Including the dead body?" Officer Pierno said flatly.

Another look from Detective Silva, and he stepped down, clasping his hands behind his back.

"Well, I'll leave you to it," Patricia said. "I'll be right outside if you need anything." She closed the door and Detective Silva glanced around the room.

"Please, take a load off," she said.

Dorothy lowered herself into a black tufted leather chair, feeling herself sink into it as the others sat as well. Jorgen looked from woman to woman and picked at a loose thread on his sleeve. Rose sat on the edge of her chair, not allowing herself to lean back.

"I feel like I've been called to the principal's office," Blanche whispered.

Detective Silva stalked in a circle around the chairs, leaning forward with piercing intensity. "I'm told you all discovered the body?"

Officer Pierno flipped open a small notebook, his pencil poised for their answers.

"Yes, I saw him first," Rose began. "Then I screamed, and everyone ran over."

"You all saw the deceased?" Detective Silva said.

Everyone nodded. Dorothy remembered the shock of seeing the body, the thin icy layer over the man's skin. Jorgen made a small whimpering sound.

"Did anyone touch the body?"

Dorothy shook her head.

"Well . . . I *kicked* him," Rose said, her voice full of sincere guilt. "I mean accidentally. I wasn't mad at him or anything."

Detective Silva looked over at her. "Would you like to clarify your statement, Miss . . . ?"

"Rose Marie Nylund, maiden name Lindstrom, born Karklavoner-Martin, resident of 6151 Rich—"

The officer held up a hand to calm the spinning Rose. "Please. Just what happened with the body."

Rose stammered for a moment, searching for her words. "My foot hit his leg when I stepped into the freezer."

Officer Pierno wrote something in his notebook.

Detective Silva continued. "Did any of you notice anything suspicious?"

"Other than a dead man and a ruined cheesecake?" Rose said. "Isn't that enough?"

"Shhh, Rose," Dorothy said. They needed to get this over with as quickly and painlessly as possible so they could help her salvage what was left of the tea party.

"Well, there *was* a chair leaning against the handle when we walked in. I asked Jorgen to move it so I could open the freezer," Rose noted, recounting the chain of events.

Detective Silva pinned her big brown eyes on Jorgen. He gulped audibly and shifted in his seat.

"Can you elaborate, sir?"

"Ja," Jorgen said. He looked to Blanche for reassurance.

"Go on, honey," she said. "Just tell them what happened."

"I . . . I moved the chair," he said. "It was stuck a little bit—under the handle."

"Take his prints," the detective said. "Pierno, continue questioning him and report back to me." Jorgen allowed the officer to lead him out of the cigar room, his face as white as a cloud.

*"I didn't do it!"* he said urgently, looking to Blanche. "Tell them I didn't do it!"

"We know, sweetie," Blanche said in a calming tone. "Just do what they say and we'll clear this all up."

"We're simply eliminating him from the suspect pool, should we be able to pull prints from the chair," Silva said. "If he's innocent, he has nothing to worry about."

Of course they had nothing to worry about, Dorothy thought. None of them were responsible for that man's death, or even had any idea what had happened. It was preposterous to even think that they would.

Over the next thirty minutes, the police questioned the ladies on the appearance of the corpse, the condition they'd found him in, the time of day, and each of their initial reactions. The detective repeated her questions, making notes in her own notebook, and checking and double-checking the answers. Rose was questioned heavily about the cheesecake ingredients and who had taken the cheesecakes and placed them in the freezers. Rose repeated the recipes for the traditional cheesecake and the St. Olaf's Kiss version so many times that she was starting to mix up her tablespoons and teaspoons.

"We'll be testing the cake that the deceased was found on," Detective Silva said. "And any others as well."

"Oh, but you can't," Rose cried. "We've already served the others. . . ."

The policewoman raised an eyebrow.

"Oh dear."

"I'm sure it's fine, honey," Dorothy said. "We know there was nothing bad in those cakes. You made them yourself." She turned to the officer. "Anyway, can you tell the cause of death yet? I'm assuming it's something to do with the freezer."

"Wait a minute—you removed evidence from the crime scene?" Detective Silva's jaw dropped.

"I didn't mean to!" Rose insisted. "And surely it's not a crime scene—it was just an accident, right?"

"This is a very serious matter. We're exploring all angles," Detective Silva replied. "And we're not obligated to share those details with you at this time."

Dorothy started to feel hot, and she removed her blazer for some relief. She noticed that Blanche was fanning herself with her hand and wondered how much longer this interrogation would last.

"And *none* of you had ever seen this man before?" the detective said in a tired voice. She looked at her watch, seeming ready to move on in the investigation. Dorothy was relieved that the questioning was almost over and shifted in her seat, ready to get up and stretch her legs.

Just then Officer Pierno reentered the room. He whispered into Detective Silva's ear. Her brow furrowed, and she shot a piercing glance at each of the women in turn.

"Which one of you is Dorothy Zbornak again?" she said.

Dorothy felt a cold fear spread across her insides. "I am," she said.

Silva leaned forward, only a few inches from Dorothy's nose. "Why don't we speak privately?"

Dorothy fought the urge to gulp. Why would *she* be singled out?

Rose and Blanche stared wide-eyed at their friend as Pierno led them out of the room. Silva pulled Dorothy over to two chairs on the far side of the cigar bar, next to a painting of a woman and man dancing a passionate salsa.

Silva crossed her legs and fixed Dorothy with a level gaze. "How did you know the victim?" she said.

"I *didn't*," Dorothy said. "We just found him, like I've told you."

*Over and over again*, she muttered to herself.

"Are you sure about that?" Silva said. "Nothing about him is familiar to you?"

Dorothy shook her head. For a second, the shiny face of the man's watch swam in her mind's eye. That had seemed slightly familiar, but lots of men in Miami wore flashy watches.

"I have nothing to do with this," Dorothy insisted.

"Then why," Silva said, leaning back in her chair with a smug smile, "was your name written on a slip of paper found in his pocket?"

Dorothy's mouth hung open. "What? What are you talking about?"

"Dorothy Zbornak: Z-B-O-R-N-A-K. That's how you spell it, right? How many Dorothy Zbornaks do you think there are in the area?"

Dorothy looked down at her lap, then up to the other woman, then down at her lap again. She was flustered, confused, and downright incredulous. Why *would* the dead man have her name in his pocket?

"Look, I want to help you," Dorothy said. "But I honestly have no idea. Did the note say anything else?"

The policewoman ran her gaze up and down Dorothy's face, seemingly taking in every pore, expression line, and minuscule muscle movement. She paused as if considering whether to divulge anything. After a few seconds of silence that felt like an hour, she spoke. "It said . . . Well, see for yourself." She pulled out a scrap of paper that looked like it had been torn from a day planner. It read:

*Dorothy Zbornak,*
*12:30, Wolfie's.*
*WEDDING NEXT WEEK.*

Dorothy clapped a hand to her chest, feeling her heart pound. It was suddenly incredibly difficult to take a breath. The dead man had salt-and-pepper hair and a watch she'd seen somewhere before. Not to mention there had been something familiar about his build, though he'd been face down in the freezer.

It is her—she knew that man. It was Henry, who she'd been very recently on a date with.

The man who'd walked out on her at Wolfie's. The man she'd almost brought as her date to this very event. In a T-shirt and shorts, he was dressed very differently than he had been on their date. And with him facedown in a cheesecake, she hadn't immediately recognized him.

After a few moments of stunned silence, Dorothy told the officer everything she could remember about Henry Pattinson.

Silva pressed Dorothy for details, which Dorothy helpfully provided. She told them all about Lucky Chances Dating Service. She told them that she'd invited him to be her date for the wedding, which explained what was written on the note in his pocket.

She said that once she got home, she would give the police his phone number from her address book. No, she didn't have the number memorized. No, they weren't close. Like she'd said, they'd only gone on one date. No, they hadn't made plans to see each other again. No, she wasn't his girlfriend. No, she had no idea what happened, or what his home address was.

Even as she was trying to be factual and helpful, Dorothy did not mention how her date with Henry had ended, remembering what her mother had said. She didn't need to go overboard on giving them extraneous details that they didn't ask for. Those simply weren't relevant. The topic hadn't come up—Detective Silva hadn't asked, and Dorothy had answered every single one of their questions as honestly and completely as she could.

But then the other officer rejoined them and whispered in Silva's ear.

The questions got harder.

"Why do you think Henry Pattinson was here at the

Cabana Sun Hotel?" Silva asked, tapping her pencil against her teeth. She looked at Dorothy as if she were trying to peer inside her head.

"Well, I have no idea," Dorothy answered truthfully. "I was incredibly surprised to see him in that freezer. I was incredibly surprised to see anyone in a freezer, to be perfectly honest."

"Maybe we should look at all of the wedding guests," Pierno suggested. "That note—and Dorothy—seem to be the reason he was here."

"Who else from the wedding party knew him?" Silva said.

"I don't know. I assume just me."

"Were you meeting him here at this hotel? A lovers' rendezvous, perhaps?"

"No, no, no," Dorothy said, trying to keep her cool. She knew the police were just doing their jobs, but they were barking up the wrong tree. "I told you, we'd only been on one date. That was it. We hadn't planned to see each other again, and we certainly weren't meeting up for any *rendezvous*, as you call it."

"C'mon, Silva," Officer Pierno said. "She's what, sixty?"

"It's *Detective* Silva," the woman said calmly. "And they could have been having an evening of mature passion. An elderly encounter, as it were."

Officer Pierno's eyes widened so much they looked like they'd bounce from their sockets. "That happens?" he said, looking at Dorothy with a new appreciation in his eyes.

"You should see what they get up to in nursing homes,"

Detective Silva said, all seriousness. "It's not out of the question."

Dorothy thought back to the time that Sophia had complained about Harry Hornswagle, the Caligula of Shady Pines, who threw special "parties" in the activity room after the day nurses had gone home. She'd figured it was just another one of her mother's exaggerations. Now she wasn't so sure.

Officer Pierno was still staring at Dorothy. "I'm sorry, ma'am—miss—madam—I didn't know ladies your age got up to such things."

"Oh, please," Dorothy said, placing her hands on the leather armrests and pushing herself up to leave. "This is ridiculous. I'm being given the third degree *and* being insulted along the way."

"I'm sorry," Silva said. "It wasn't my intention to offend you. I'm just trying to paint a full picture here."

"Well, I've cooperated, as has everyone else here. Now we've got a family event to attempt to repair. Am I free to go now?" Dorothy stood, folding her arms. They didn't need to boss her around any more than they already had.

The detective nodded and handed Dorothy her card. "Call me if you think of anything else that might help us. And yes, you're free to go."

"Wonderful," Dorothy said flatly and stalked out of the cigar room to the hotel lobby, where Sophia and Blanche waited right outside the door.

"Oh, and Ms. Zbornak?" the policewoman said. "You're the only lead we have so far. Don't leave town. Got it?"

# A MATTER OF TRUST

........... 9 ...........

*R*ose sat next to Nettie on matching chaise longues by the hotel pool. All the guests had dispersed, leaving partially eaten cheesecakes and crumpled napkins in their wake. The St. Olafians had hurried back to their hotel rooms, no doubt double-locking their doors behind them.

Jason rubbed Nettie's shoulders as she sniffled into a tissue. Rose had just finished telling Nettie the truth about that morning and why the police had come.

"It's a bad sign!" Nettie sobbed. "We should have eloped like we planned."

"I don't want to have any more wedding events here," said Jason. "We're just not comfortable with it."

"But it's not the hotel's fault. Or your family's, Jason," Rose said, handing Nettie a fresh tissue. "It's nobody's fault! It's just a horrible coincidence."

"It's *somebody's* fault," Nettie said. "Someone killed that man."

"Oh, hush," Rose tutted. "You don't know that. It was most likely an accident."

"Jorgen said the door was wedged shut with a chair," Nettie said. "You think that man did that to himself?"

Jason grimaced. "It's very odd. Weird things have happened at the hotel over the years, but nothing so sinister."

Rose was about to explain that the wooden chair didn't mean that man had actually been murdered but then realized that was very likely exactly what it meant. Even if an unusual chain of events occurred, for a man in good health to get stuck inside a freezer that long . . . which meant that someone must have pushed him in there—or at least made sure he couldn't get out. And she certainly wouldn't mention the knife in his hand to Nettie. It hadn't looked like the kind you'd use to cut a slice of cake.

Rose shivered, leaning toward Nettie and putting a motherly hand on her arm. "In any case, it's not an omen about the wedding. And this doesn't mean that you should elope. We're going to have a real wedding without any more hitches."

"Why should we?" Nettie said. "Isn't it up to us—you know, the people who are getting married?"

"Yes, of course," Rose said. "But don't you want to get your portion of the trust?"

"What?" Nettie said. "What are you talking about, Aunt Rose?"

"Cousin Gustave was just telling me that if you get married in the St. Olaf tradition, you'll be able to receive your share of the family trust, passed down from Heinrich von Anderdonnen."

Nettie shook her head blankly. "What trust? My parents don't communicate with me, except for the occasional postcard about their stupid poodles."

Rose sighed and brushed Nettie's hair from her face. She wasn't completely surprised that Nettie's parents had left her without much information about her past or much thought for her future. It had been Rose and the community of St. Olaf who had raised her from a young age, and she'd grown up to be a sweet, compassionate woman despite her selfish parents.

"I'm sorry, sweetheart. I should have told you about it when you were younger, but I confess I haven't given it much thought since I married my dear Charlie so many years ago. It's not a lot of money, but we were able to buy our first cow with our portion of the trust. I just assumed you knew."

Nettie shook her head. "There's a lot I wish they told me," she said sadly. "So how does this trust work?"

"I'll dig up a copy of Heinrich's will—I'm sure I have it somewhere," Rose said. "And the terms may be listed in the original town bylaws. But from what I understand, your parents relinquished their share when they left St. Olaf to ensure their portion would be passed along to you, on top of your own share, to help set you up in life. Even with a double share it's a modest amount, but it's never wise to look a gift trout in the mouth."

"That's very nice," Jason said. "Nettie, isn't that good news?"

Nettie nodded. "At least they did *one* thing for me. But why do we have to get married a certain way to get the money?" she asked bluntly. "It's very odd, and it's not fair."

"I think our ancestor Heinrich wanted to keep St. Olaf going for generations to come, so that's why he wanted to keep its traditions alive and encourage families to stay there."

"I don't care about keeping its traditions alive," Nettie said. "I just want to get married without everyone telling me what to do—and without any dead bodies!"

"Is it because Nettie is marrying me that she can't just get the trust now?" Jason asked, looking glum. "I don't want to be the reason she's not getting her inheritance."

"She can get it when she turns thirty, and sooner if she gets marries in the St. Olaf tradition. I have to look into the details, but there are various conditions for every circumstance," Rose said. She vaguely remembered her unmarried sister Holly getting the money on her thirtieth birthday, but she'd had to paint a mural in the town square and plant a dozen oak trees on St. Olaf property first, then walk backward from the courthouse to the post office with a baby sturgeon on her head, which came naturally to Holly. Birds had always loved perching on her head. It wasn't fair.

Jason nodded. "Sounds like my family. They'll give you the moon, as long as you do every single thing they want, whether *you* want to or not."

"I don't care about the money," Nettie said, putting her head in her hands. "I just want to start my life with Jason."

"She's right, Aunt Rose," Jason said, squeezing onto the chaise longue next to Nettie. "At the end of the day, we don't care about the trust. Whether it's modest or—whatever the opposite of modest is."

Rose sighed, impressed with the principles and amount of love between these two young people. But she also wanted to bounce a beach ball off their heads. After being widowed and having to share a home and living expenses with three other women on a fixed income, she knew how important it was to have money in the bank. You never knew what was coming in life, and it was better to be prepared.

She also didn't mention the other thought working its way through her mind, one that she was less proud of. She wanted to pull this wedding off in grand style and show Gustave and

Katrina and the rest of her relatives that they should never have underestimated her.

She wanted to prove that she knew their traditions inside and out—even better than they did. If she could pull this wedding off perfectly, it would make up for the Butter Queen upset, losing the chicken singing competition, and all the other injustices she'd faced growing up. They'd all see that Rose was a true St. Olaf girl, whether on the fjords of Minnesota or the beaches of Miami.

"Why don't we all take a break from this trust business? When you're ready, we can discuss these details. How about we focus on something fun, like trying on your wedding dress? Would you like that, dear?"

Nettie wiped the tears from her cheeks. "That would be kind of nice," she admitted.

"And, Jason, you and the boys can help secure the rest of the items we'll need for the wedding."

"I don't know, Aunt Rose," he said. "Like Nettie said, we're not sure we want to go through with all of this."

Rose took a moment to choose her words. She stood up from her chaise and leaned close to Jason. She didn't want to be bossy like the Bryants, but an entire Viking ship's worth of St. Olafians had traveled to Miami to celebrate this couple, and things were too far along to stop now. "You listen to me, young man. If you're going to call me Aunt Rose, you need to pay some respect. I will honor whatever you and Nettie decide. But in the meantime, I'm going to need a goat horn, fifteen tubs of grass-fed butter, twelve yards of ribbon, at least sixteen white towels, loofahs, and shower caps, suits for you and the groomsmen to wear to the wedding, and a tin whistle. I'll also need extra tubes of concentrated herring paste, a few willow branches, and twenty ounces of canned or jarred lingonberries. I don't think you'll be able to find fresh ones around here. After you gather all those supplies, *then* you can decide if you want a real St. Olaf wedding. But I think once you see the whole dazzling vision, you'll make the right choice."

Jason's eyes widened at the long list of demands. "I'm pretty sure I can get the towels from the hotel." Jason gulped. "That's easy."

"That's the spirit," Rose said, slapping him gently on the knee. "I knew you were a resourceful young man. You know, if you can handle each and every wedding tradition, that will go a long way in helping you feel fully welcomed in St. Olaf. No one would be able to even *try* to look down on you anymore, despite the hay incident."

Jason hung his head. "The wind was against me that day . . . I'd practiced and everything."

"Of course you had," Rose agreed. "But there won't be another chance to prove yourself until next year's throwing of the hay. Do you really want to live as an outcast until then?"

"No," Jason said. "St. Olaf is the one place I truly feel at home. Where people don't care if you drive a Porsche or wear designer clothes. Where Nettie and I can be ourselves and start a family."

Rose felt a little thrill at the idea of a gaggle of little children running around, tumbling over hay bales and giggling under the watchful eyes of Nettie and Jason.

"Then you know what you need to do," said Rose. "And I have my own work cut out for me. I'm going to speak to your parents, Jason, and see if we can't work out some more compromises for the bridal shower and the wedding itself. And then I have to speak to the St. Olaf contingent and make sure they haven't hopped on the first toboggan home."

"Thank you, Aunt Rose," Nettie said. "You're doing a lot for us."

Rose allowed herself a moment to lean against the back of Nettie's chair. They'd only had one wedding event so far, and she was exhausted. This certainly was a lot on her shoulders. But the thought of Nettie's happiness gave Rose another boost of energy. She kissed her young cousin on the head and patted Jason's shoulder.

As she headed toward the elevator bank to look for the Bryants, she peered out the window overlooking the patio, where Fred and José were busy cleaning up the half-eaten plates of food and unpoured pitchers of lemonade. The party had come to a screeching halt once the police arrived, and no one had had much of an appetite once word begin circulating that a dead man had been found not far from the very cheesecake they'd been savoring.

When the elevator dinged and opened, Rose stepped inside, wondering what she might have done differently.

*Chin up, my little dumpling*, her Charlie would have told her. He always said that when she was dealing with something difficult. And so that's just what Rose would do. She'd pull her chin up and try again. There were more wedding events to plan, and perhaps if each one went swimmingly, everyone would forget about the one that happened to have a dead body.

She'd throw her all into making the rest of this wedding week so joyous, so celebratory, and so full of all the right foods and songs and games and traditions that no one would have time to feel anything other than happy.

Rose's meeting with the Bryants that afternoon had been anything but happy. They'd spoken harshly to her, criticizing her decision to serve the cheesecakes after the incident and demanding full control of the wedding and menu going forward. Defeated, Rose took a taxi back to Richmond Street, armed with printouts of the Bryants' guest list, their preferred menu, and the schedule of events. She wanted to go straight back to her bedroom, too tired to even say hello to her roommates, who sat in the living room in their pajamas and robes, unwinding from the day. She thought she might be able to sneak by as Sophia regaled Dorothy and Blanche with the story of how she disappeared before the police could interrogate her, too.

"Like I said, talking to the authorities is never a good idea, whether it's the OVRA in the old country or Miami's finest." Sophia shook a tiny fist to emphasize her point. "I hid behind a dirty towel bin at the edge of the patio and slipped a few bills to the pool boy to let me hop in. He wheeled me out the back entrance. . . ."

As Sophia spoke, Rose noticed Dorothy listening to the recounting with a serious look in her eye. She stood and pulled Rose to one side of the living room and shared everything she'd gleaned from her conversation with Detective Silva, including the identity of the victim and the note found in his pocket.

Rose listened, aghast. Her face went from ghostly white to an angry pinkish red.

"Oh, Dorothy, I *told* you to be careful who you were meeting!" she said. "And now look what's happened!"

Dorothy jerked backward at Rose's words. "But he's the *victim*, Rose, not a criminal. And it doesn't make sense that he'd be in the hotel kitchen several days before the wedding. Surely it doesn't have anything to do with our date."

"That may be true," Rose said. "But it doesn't look good. He had your name in his pocket! And the fact that the wedding party's now dragged into all this . . . I wish you'd never gone on that stupid date!"

Dorothy nodded in resignation. "I do, too, Rose. I'm really sorry."

"You just can't be so trusting of strangers!" Rose snapped, whirling on her heel and disappearing into her bedroom. She normally saw the bright side of everything, but today had just been too much for her.

Rose flopped onto her bed and kicked her shoes off. She couldn't believe that this horrible tragedy was directly tied to them—to Dorothy! She groaned into her pillow. What would Charlie say about all of this? He'd say to focus on what she could control, and not on what she couldn't.

She'd focus on the wedding planning. She'd create an event so special that no one would remember this week's rocky start. She pulled her face out of the pillow and sat up.

Rose spread out the Bryants' guest list, comparing it with her original handwritten one. Right now, the combined guest list looked to be about 90 percent Bryant invitees and 10 percent from St. Olaf. There were many invitees who would not have been at the smaller St. Olaf wedding that would have taken place had the Storslagen Hotel not burned down. That wasn't so bad, she thought, considering that they were on the Bryants' home turf, but they'd added nearly a hundred new names!

The Bryants' list included a column detailing each guest's relationship to the groom, such as cousin, aunt, godfather, etc. But as Rose read further, she realized that many of the names didn't have any family connection noted, reminding Rose of what Jason had said. That this wedding was a chance for the Bryants to show off in front of their business associates and rivals—a way to showcase the hotel to get more business. This wasn't them giving their son a big wedding out of the goodness of their hearts. Plus, Rose noticed, there was a lot of media on the page—the *Miami Herald*, the *Standard*, anchors from the local TV stations, gossip reporters, and more. Rose eyed the paper sprawled over her bedspread and searched for guests that actually belonged at the wedding. She ticked off the people she'd already heard of: the Corzons, the Petrosinis, and the Walshes. A bunch of friends from Chip's fraternity days and the croquet club. Then she put a line through everyone who didn't have a strong connection to the bride or groom. That narrowed down the list significantly.

Rose was jolted from her work by the ringing of her bedside phone.

Gustave's stern lilt emanated from the other end of the receiver, so loud that Rose held it an inch from her head. "Did you see what was on the TV news? A national herring shortage! I hope you have enough for the wedding banquet."

Rose hung her head as she took in the devastating seafood news. She'd placed her order with the fishmonger already but hadn't picked up any herring yet. It was too early.

But now the guest list had tripled in size. Her mouth went dry. If she couldn't get enough herring for everyone, then it wouldn't be a real wedding. Not by St. Olaf standards, anyway. She needed it for the herring balls, the ceremonial candied herring, the smoked herring-leek casserole, and of course, the herring-juice chasers that would follow shots of Aquavit during the Spin the Groom Dance. And that was just for starters. She hadn't even begun thinking about the herring quiche for the Happy Hangover Breakfast or the herring cream popsicles for the children. Rose pressed a hand over the phone handset and scrunched her face up in distress.

In as clear a voice as she could muster, Rose said, "I've got it all under control, Gustave. You don't need to worry."

"But I'm *very* worried," Gustave intoned gravely. "Considering how today went. We didn't even get to do the traditional In-Law Square Dance."

Rose clenched the hand that wasn't holding the phone. She couldn't believe her cousin's nerve. He must be pulling her leg, she thought. "You know just as well as I do that it's the In-Law Triangle Dance," she said. "And we'll make time for it another day. The bylaws don't specify that the dance has to be at the first meeting of the families. It just has to happen at some point during the festivities."

Rose heard Gustave chuckle on the other end of the line.

"Well done, Rose," Gustave said, sounding slightly relieved. "I thought I'd get that one past you. You must have done your homework."

"I certainly have," Rose said. "And I would greatly appreciate it if you all would believe in me to organize this. I have a great deal of respect for St. Olaf and its traditions, but I'm not feeling like you have the same respect for me!"

"Rose, you have to understand that it's hard. You left us behind years ago, to live so far away. Miami is like another world—everything is different! The weather, the food, the languages you hear walking down the street. Your life is so removed from ours, it's hard for us to imagine that you're still the same Rose who played Gowakanoggin as a child and delivered fresh potato juice on the Velcome Vagon."

"Well, this is my chance to prove myself," Rose said. "And I think I'm doing a darn good job." She erupted into tears, trying to stifle them with the lacy corner of her pink bedspread.

"If it's too much for you, maybe you should give up," Gustave said softly. "Let Nettie elope with her outsider. It's all the same to me."

Rose paused in her sniffling to think a moment. "But don't you *want* them to have a real St. Olaf wedding? To fully be a part of the community you keep going on and on about?"

Something wasn't adding up. No one in the family would want the lovebirds to elope instead of having a big family wedding . . . right?

"Well," Gustave said. "It wouldn't be the end of the world. People have flown the coop before. St. Olaf endures yet. In fact, we just redid the town rec hall, and added central heating."

Rose frowned, remembering how many times as children they'd played Catch the Elf-Cat on frigid winter nights, their fingers almost blue.

"You really don't care if we finish this wedding, St. Olaf style?"

"It's not up to me, Rose. It will be a miracle if it happens."

Rose stretched her tired shoulders and thought. All this pressure to have the perfect St. Olaf wedding wasn't coming from the town elders. It was coming from herself. Unless . . .

"Gustave," she said slowly, "it sounds to me almost as if you don't want Nettie to get married and complete all the St. Olaf wedding traditions. Is there a reason for that?"

Gustave let out a dismissive snort. "That's nonsense. Of course we want Nettie to get married. Even if it's to an outsider."

Rose narrowed her eyes. "Are you sure you don't want to just keep that Anderdonnen money in the town's coffers, hanging around and bearing interest so you can spend it on more town improvements?"

Gustave chuckled in that slightly condescending way he'd done since they were both children. "You're being irrational, Cousin. You don't sound like yourself. I suggest you drink some hot milk with cinnamon and get a good night's sleep."

Rose hung up the phone with a clatter and threw herself face down on her pillow. She didn't know what to think, but Gustave was right—she certainly wasn't feeling like herself. She wept into her frilly pillowcase until she finally fell asleep.

# SHOWERED WITH LOVE

## ·············10············

*T*he next morning at noon, Jorgen drove Dorothy, Rose, Blanche, and Sophia to Corazón Del Mar, the Corzons' beachside restaurant that they'd generously offered as a venue for the bridal shower. The restaurant was a wide building near the South Pointe Park Pier, with outdoor tables shaded by oversize umbrellas and a uniformed waitstaff serving a well-dressed crowd.

Nettie stood outside the restaurant, twisting her hands and shifting from foot to foot in her pale green jumpsuit.

"I'm famished," Dorothy said, looking forward to the sit-down lunch with the female members of both sides of the family. She'd recently read some rave reviews for the restaurant's Cuban cuisine in the *Miami Herald*, and just remembering them had her stomach growling.

"We're not eating right away," Rose said. "We have the shower before the shower, remember?"

"Right," Dorothy said, casting a dubious glance at the baskets that Jorgen began unloading from the trunk.

Gloria Corzon flung open the restaurant doors, resplendent in a silver-and-blue caftan that matched the azure ocean behind them. She gave a wide smile to Jorgen as he hefted the baskets of supplies, admiring his strong back and bulging biceps when he lifted a series of wood panels from the trunk.

"What do you need all that for?" said Blanche.

"I painted them in the driveway last night when I couldn't sleep," Rose said. "When you put them together, it will show a pastoral scene from our hometown. I included the town church, the Tree of Giggles, and other landmarks for people to pose in front of for photos. It'll look just like we're in St. Olaf!"

Blanche shared a pointed look with Dorothy. It was clear that they both wondered if Rose was going overboard for this wedding. Probably to compensate for the disastrous Welcome Tuna Teatime, Dorothy thought, which was understandable.

"I'll bring you a glass of water," Gloria purred as a

sweat-spangled Jorgen carried the heavy panels inside the restaurant.

Blanche eyed Gloria with a cool expression as she expertly took in the other woman's stunning outfit, complete with four-inch peep-toe heels. Blanche stood a little straighter in her three-inch slingbacks. She tilted her head to show off her best angles, letting her dangly earrings catch the sunlight.

Dorothy was amused that they both had the hots for Jorgen, and she had to admit she could see why. He was nearly six feet tall, handsome, and helpful. What more could a woman ask for? And both women actually had a chance with him, Dorothy thought. In their late fifties, they both exuded similar levels of confidence, charisma, and simmering sensuality. And Jorgen lapped it all up like a kitten with a saucer full of milk, completely oblivious to the daggers the two women shot at each other when they weren't busy making eyes at him.

Soon the St. Olaf contingent and other members of the groom's family arrived in taxis. Rose led the group from the front steps of the restaurant to a spot a dozen yards down the beach, an area with public changing rooms and showers enclosed by a wall of pink-painted cinder blocks.

"Normally we'd set up the shower with hoses and shower curtains right in the town square," Rose gushed, leading Nettie and Mrs. Bryant over to the cinder-block structure, across which she had draped in colorful streamers. "The St. Olaf boys would always try to hang out of their windows or climb up on their roofs to get a peek at the ladies." She wagged one finger. "But we were always too careful."

Rose led the line of women inside the open-air space with a line of changing stalls on one side, and a line of showerheads on the other, partially hidden by shower curtains.

Aunt Katrina looked disapprovingly at the plain white shower curtains flapping in the brisk sea breeze. "In St. Olaf, we always used *yellow* shower curtains. This isn't exactly how it's done back home. The proper way."

Rose tugged Aunt Katrina into one of the changing stalls and shoved a towel in her arms. "That's just because Mean Old Lady Hickenlooper's shower curtains were covered in mildew. They were *supposed* to be white, like these."

Aunt Katrina sniffed as Rose quickly handed out towels, loofahs, and shower caps to everyone in the group as they clustered into the stalls. Gloria and Mrs. Bryant skeptically unwrapped the plastic bonnets, turning them over in their manicured hands and looking up at Rose with confusion.

"Is this really necessary?" Mrs. Bryant asked. She'd clearly been to the beauty shop that morning, and her short white-gold strands had been blow-dried and sprayed into a hard-looking shell. Meanwhile, Gloria was valiantly struggling to fit her glossy brown waves with a few hints of silver into the shower cap.

"You can't have a bridal shower without a shower!" Rose chided. "Everybody knows that."

Mrs. Bryant pressed her lips together in an expression that

one would give to a one-legged dog, or perhaps to a child who hadn't made it to the bathroom on time. She leaned over to Rose, her voice gentle. "But of course you know, it's meant to shower the bride with gifts she'll need as a future wife. . . ."

"Of course," Rose said. "But in St. Olaf, the shower has a double meaning. It's a ritual cleansing before making the big commitment to a life together. You shampoo away your single life to prepare for your married one. Then you exfoliate with the loofah, so that you don't have any rough patches in your marriage."

"Rough patches." Sophia laughed, poking Mrs. Bryant in the arm. "Get it?"

Mrs. Bryant and Gloria nodded politely but snuck wide-eyed glances to each other. Rose knew that St. Olaf traditions could sound silly—occasionally crazy—to many people. Sometimes they didn't make sense even to her, and she'd grown up with them. But she herself had stood under the bridal shower decades ago, surrounded by her sisters and the other women of the town. It had been a wonderful celebration of female bonding and personal hygiene. She'd seen every type of female body that day—all ages and shapes and sizes, women who had had surgeries and scars and stretch marks, and it made her feel more connected to the women in her community. She wanted Nettie to share in that feeling.

"Do we really have to . . . get fully nude?" Mrs. Bryant asked. "I'm wearing a girdle," she confessed, "and it'll be murder to unhook everything."

"And I've got a full face of Lancôme on," Mrs. Corzon said, pointing to her elegant lapis lazuli eye shadow. "I wasn't planning on quite such a . . . production."

"As long as you're wrapped in a towel and have your shower cap on, it's okay if you stay in your clothes underneath," Rose assured them. "You can stand on the outer edges of the shower, and you just need to get a little bit wet for the ceremony to be complete."

Grateful and very relieved, Mrs. Bryant and Gloria proceeded to wrap the towels around the outside of their outfits.

"Some people wear bathing suits. It's really more about the symbolism of the shower," Rose said as the St. Olaf women quickly stripped down and stepped toward the showers with towels hung over their arms, fully unselfconscious.

Nudity was part of their culture, originating from running naked through the snow and jumping into natural hot springs on the winter solstice. It was one of their top ten health practices and was credited as one of the main reasons that St. Olafians tended to have long lives. That and the fact that after the hot tubs, they'd beat each other with reeds to stimulate blood flow.

Blanche wiggled out of her dress, keeping her lacy slip on, and Dorothy kept on her sensible satin camisole and half-slip. She wanted to support Rose, but ever since Rose had accidentally booked them into a nudist hotel a year or so ago, she'd felt that she'd already blessed Rose with her full quota of bodily exposure for the foreseeable future.

Sophia kept her skirt, blouse, and yellow cardigan on, opting instead to throw a fluffy robe over everything, including her compression stockings and orthopedic shoes.

"At my age, it'll take me so long to get out of this outfit, I might not live long enough to get back into it," she said, wrapping an extra shower cap over her ever-present wicker purse.

"Please stop, Ma," Dorothy said, placing another crinkly shower cap over her mother's fluffy white curls. After the shocking moment of finding Henry dead as a doornail, she'd had much less patience for her mother's constant joking about her demise. It just wasn't funny anymore, Dorothy thought sadly.

Blanche sashayed out of the changing area, the lacy peach straps of her lingerie visible above the straight line of the towel, which was wrapped so tight that it gave her cleavage an extra helpful boost.

"I think I left my loofah outside," she said. "I'll be back quicker than a June bug."

"I bet she's hoping that Jorgen will catch a glimpse of her like that," Sophia said. "That woman has no shame."

"Who cares if she has a harmless flirtation with that young man?" Dorothy said. "He certainly doesn't seem to mind."

"That's my point," Sophia said, waving a bar of soap at Dorothy. "At his age, his mind isn't even fully formed yet."

Just then, Blanche swept back in with a loofah in hand and a twinkle in her eye.

"What were you saying, Sophia?" Blanche asked.

"Oh, nothing," Sophia said. "Did you happen to run into your boy toy when you shimmied out there looking like a Dodge Polara with the top down?"

Blanche blushed. "I *did* see him for a moment before he drove off." A wide smile spread across her face. "Isn't he just darling?"

"He's decades younger than you!" Sophia scolded her.

"Technically, that may be true," Blanche said, her eyes still twinkling. "But he seems to have an appreciation for a woman with some experience. Someone to help him navigate the twisting byways of love and romance to a delightful destination."

Sophia rolled her eyes. "Well, I hope he checks under the hood first!"

Rose hushed the crowd, shooting a look at Sophia. Dorothy stifled a laugh and hitched her towel up under her armpits, trying to look like she was paying attention.

Once everyone had piled into the shower area, Rose led the group in a rousing sing-along, starting off with "Scrubenrinsedottir," an old St. Olaf folk song to the tune of Bobby Darin's "Splish Splash."

After many songs, much laughter, and the liberal use of Ivory soap, the shower finally ended. Rose wiped her face dry with the fluffy towel. She dabbed at her eyes, realizing she'd been crying a little bit with happiness. Nettie was giggling with her friend Bess and the Petrosini women, and everything had gone off without a hitch. Even Aunt Katrina was smiling as she changed back into her sensible cotton dress.

*One more tradition down*, Rose thought, mentally checking it off on her list.

She longed to grab her legal pad with all the traditions and really cross it off in ink. There were many more to go.

Back at the restaurant, everyone was fully dressed and being directed to their seats at a long table in a cheerful back room, the walls of which were lined with framed photos of celebrity patrons including Sidney Poitier and Debbie Harry. A Cuban jazz band played on the nearby deck, the music a pleasant undertone as they entered. Dorothy watched as Rose settled Nettie at a seat in the center of the table. Rose gave her cousin a motherly hug, then placed a hand-woven circular crown made of willow branches on her head.

Nettie reached up to push it back from her forehead.

"I remember when I first wore the Glugelfluger," Rose said. "I felt like such a princess, even though one of the twigs scratched my cornea and I had to wear an eye patch until my wedding day! Everyone called me Captain that week—I could never understand why."

"I'll be careful, then," said Nettie, pushing the crown back another inch.

After Dorothy got Sophia settled in her seat with a hot cup

of tea, she and Blanche helped Rose set up, placing trinkets, name tags, and place cards along the big table. There were homemade bingo cards that Rose had meticulously cut out of oaktag, listing common phrases overheard at a wedding. There were slips of paper on which people could write their best marital advice and an empty tin milking pail to collect them all.

*She's really thought of everything*, Dorothy mused as she stepped up to the Bucket of Love. She wondered what she should write down for Nettie. *Never go to bed angry? Say I love you at least once a day? Don't worry about the dead body?* It really was hard to narrow down. Her own wedding had been such a hasty affair, and her marriage so rocky that she really didn't know what advice to give.

Meanwhile, Sophia was scribbling away, filling several pieces of paper with her tiny all-caps handwriting. Her mother was certainly opinionated, Dorothy thought, but she wondered how she could write so much. Curious, she glanced over Sophia's shoulder and saw detailed instructions on how to get marinara stains off a duvet cover, the best roast chicken recipe to help couples make up after an argument, and the phone number for a divorce attorney she'd seen on an ad at a bus stop, just in case.

Blanche was also busy giving advice, filling a notecard with loopy cursive. Dorothy craned her neck to see what she was writing, but Blanche held the paper to her chest.

"This is meant for a *young bride*," Blanche said. "I wouldn't recommend you try this technique yourself."

The rest of the party filed in and took their seats. Rose made sure Mrs. Bryant got a seat right next to Nettie, and craned her neck, looking for someone.

"Where's Patricia?" Rose asked, realizing she hadn't seen her yet today.

"Ah," Mrs. Bryant said. "I have to express her regrets. She had to take Chip to the doctor as he's had a croquet injury flair up. Then she'll be handling some important business at the hotel today, and we're both so sorry she couldn't make it to the shower. But she sent her contribution with me." She pointed to a large Neiman Marcus gift bag overflowing with tissue paper.

Dorothy noticed that Rose seemed to take this news in stride. She herself wondered if the "important business" had anything to do with the investigation into Henry's death.

But soon the first course was brought to the table, and Rose directed the group in various party games meant to stimulate conversations between individuals. Everyone was having a good time, though talk of the Welcome Tuna Teatime kept cropping up in conversation. Whispered questions about the sudden appearance of the police were exchanged between the St. Olafians and Miamians throughout the meal, and Dorothy did her best to change the subject when those questions reached her.

When it was time for gifts, each ribbon that Nettie removed was taken by Rose, twirled into a flower shape, and pinned to the Glugelfluger on her head. Soon she had a colorful riot of blooms towering half a foot around her face. Sophia muttered that it looked like Frida Kahlo had asked the Cat in the Hat to dress the poor girl, which did elicit a little chuckle from Dorothy. Nettie giggled each time the beribboned hat slipped over her eyes and she had to adjust it.

Everything was going swimmingly, and Dorothy could see the pride in Rose's face. The St. Olaf traditions harmonized beautifully with the beachside ambiance of the restaurant, and the waitstaff delivered dish after dish of mouthwatering Cuban delicacies, to everyone's delight.

*Rose is really pulling it off, despite the horrors of yesterday*, Dorothy thought, feeling proud of her dear friend.

As she leaned forward to take a sip of her mojito, a sudden hush fell over the previously boisterous crowd at her end of the table. Nearby had appeared Detective Silva, or, rather, her head, which poked through the door to their private room. Dorothy momentarily froze, hoping that the other end of the table hadn't seen her yet. Though the detective was dressed in plain clothes, a sharp khaki pantsuit, and mango-colored pumps, Dorothy immediately recognized the imposing woman from the last time they'd seen her, in full uniform, flashing her badge poolside at the Cabana Sun Hotel—and taking Dorothy and the others away for questioning.

"Detective," Dorothy said, quickly rising from her seat and

trying to head off the policewoman before she fully entered the room, where Rose and Nettie might see her. She would try to deal with this discreetly, away from the shower.

"Just who I was looking for," Detective Silva said, taking in Dorothy with a stern expression. Silva put her hands on her hips, which opened her blazer just enough to reveal an ivory silk blouse, as well as a firearm neatly tucked into a holster at her side. "You're a hard woman to get in touch with."

"I've been busy," Dorothy said, gesturing to the party in full swing. Well, Dorothy thought, the party was more accurately in half swing, since half the guests were paying attention to Nettie and the gifts she was opening at one end of the table, and the closer half were stealing glances at Dorothy and the detective over their maduros. "Detective, can't you see we're in the midst of a big celebration? I'm not exactly sitting at home waiting by the phone."

"Fair enough," said Silva, crossing her arms and making her sidepiece disappear from view. "But you need to come down to the station."

Dorothy leaned back in surprise just as her mother marched over with a frown to their end of the table, giving the detective a glare that could sear a veal parmigiana from a mile away. So much for moving this conversation to a more private space.

"*What's going on here?*" Sophia demanded. "Why are you bothering my daughter? You know she had nothing to do with that man's unfortunate demise."

"I know nothing of the sort," Detective Silva said coolly. Though she did keep an eye on the tiny fist that Sophia shook in her face.

While Detective Silva spoke with Dorothy, Rose tried to distract her cousin from what was happening near the entrance to the room. She rotated the handle of a metal eggbeater that had just been unwrapped, making the tines whir right in front of Nettie's face.

"Be careful, Rose, don't take her nose off!" Blanche said.

"Isn't this wonderful?" Rose said. "They didn't have these when I got married. I had to beat and fluff everything by hand!"

Blanche erupted into giggles, then covered her mouth. Then kept giggling. Nettie blushed and looked down at her plate of ropa vieja.

"What?" Rose asked. "What's so funny?"

"Nothing, sweetie," Blanche said. "You were saying?"

"I bet you can't wait to use all these new inventions! They make life in the kitchen so much easier," Rose said, her eyes darting around Nettie, trying to see what was happening at the other end of the table.

"Jason does all the cooking," Nettie said. "I'm sure he'll be thrilled with all of this stuff."

She started to turn her head to see what Rose was looking

at, but Rose quickly dangled a colorful Tupperware lid in front of her, successfully blocking her view.

"A modern man," Blanche cooed. "You certainly found yourself a real gem."

"I sure did," Nettie said. "His dad always wanted him to take up golf like him or croquet like Chip, but Jason loves cooking."

"He's a real sweetheart, isn't he," said Rose, thinking about the high-stress, fast-paced hotel atmosphere the rest of the Bryants inhabited. It made sense that Jason would prefer the simpler things in life, like cooking, and the slower St. Olaf lifestyle.

Suddenly raised voices broke through the conversation and the sound of the live Cuban jazz band playing out on the deck.

Rose—and now Nettie—saw Detective Silva speaking emphatically to Dorothy as she pulled her toward the back deck, in full view of the entire wedding party.

When Silva slapped a pair of shiny silver handcuffs on Dorothy's wrists, Dorothy shifted from one foot to the other, her face alternating between expressions of fury and mortification.

# COPPING AN ATTITUDE

## 11

*A*t the police station lobby, Dorothy crossed her arms and tried to get comfortable on a battered wooden bench as Detective Silva spoke to a young Asian officer manning the front desk. Dorothy wished she'd brought her mother along, or another one of the girls, for moral support, but she didn't want to disturb the bridal shower any more than she already had. It wasn't her first time at the precinct, and as an educated woman, she knew her rights.

She hadn't dreamed that they would arrest her, even

if the police's "invitation" to come down to the station immediately hadn't felt like a request. Still, when the cuffs came out she was shocked at how serious it had gotten, and so quickly. As a model citizen, Dorothy had no problems cooperating with the authorities. But she knew how often a misunderstanding could get blown out of proportion. She'd seen some of her own students get in trouble with the law, simply because of their accent or the color of their skin. The system wasn't perfect, and though Dorothy was a law-abiding woman, she knew she'd have to be a strong advocate for herself.

"Should I be getting a lawyer?" she asked Officer Pierno.

"Well, are you guilty? Of course, it's your right." Then, looking her up and down, he added, "The guilty ones always lawyer up."

She wondered why she was getting this treatment when back at the Cabana Sun Hotel they'd been interrogated with more respect and less suspicion.

Finally, Detective Silva motioned for Dorothy to follow her through a dented metal door, and she found herself inside an interrogation room.

The fluorescent lighting was a flickering, sickly green, and Dorothy found herself going from a hard wooden bench to a hard folding chair. She surveyed the peeling beige paint and a mirror on one wall, which she imagined was one-way glass. The reflection in the mirror showed an older, scared-looking woman with nervous eyes. Dorothy quickly tried to rearrange her features into an innocent, blank expression. There was no reason for her to look scared. She certainly didn't want to look guilty. She'd simply do her best to clear this all up.

Detective Silva entered the room and took off her blazer. "Ms. Zbornak," she said. "We ran all the prints from the hotel's freezer and kitchen area. Yours, along with your friends, are the only ones that showed up outside of the hotel staff. So there are no other suspects."

Dorothy gulped just as a sharp knock landed on the door. A man in a crisp gray suit that matched his gray buzz cut marched inside.

"This is Special Agent Crum, FBI."

Dorothy raised her eyebrows. Why was the FBI getting involved? Her stomach started to plummet. Maybe she was in more trouble than she'd thought.

"You've been read your rights?" Special Agent Crum said, looking down his aquiline nose at Dorothy. The scent of cigarettes and Drakkar Noir rolled off him like a cloud, and she tried not to recoil.

Dorothy nodded. "Yes, and I want to know what all this is about." She tried to sound stern and powerful. The way she'd talk in classrooms to unruly students, to let them know who was in charge. Though, at this moment, she felt like she was anything but in charge.

Agent Crum sat on the edge of the table, looming menacingly over Dorothy. But she didn't shrink away and kept her head held high.

"This is about your boyfriend," he said in a slightly con-descending tone.

"I already told Detective Silva, that man is not—was not—my boyfriend," Dorothy said. She didn't want to come off as too aggressive and risk angering the cops. It was a delicate balance, one she hoped she could get right.

Agent Crum clapped as if he'd caught her in a lie. "So you know who I'm talking about."

*Well, there* was *only one murder victim* . . . Dorothy wanted to say. But instead she went with "I'm assuming you're talking about Henry, the man who was found dead. I told you all, I'd been on one date with him. That doesn't mean anything."

Crum scrunched up his mouth as if considering her words. "Okay, say I believe you. But the fact of the matter is, you've been keeping vital information from this investigation." He buttoned his suit jacket as he stood up.

"I don't know what you mean," Dorothy insisted. "I've told you everything. I even called you to give you his phone number and the information from Lucky Chances Dating Service."

Agent Crum looked to Detective Silva, who nodded.

"So you did," he said. "But during that time, and in your statement taken at the Cabana Sun Hotel, you failed to mention the public screaming match you had with him the day before he died."

Dorothy's stomach fell several stories to the precinct's subbasement, and she gripped the cold metal edge of her seat. Somehow they'd found out how her date had ended, and now they thought she was a guilty liar at best . . . and perhaps a murderer at worst.

"It was hardly a screaming match," she said, trying to keep her voice calm and even. "We'd had a miscommunication, I thought he'd said something rude, and I firmly gave him a piece of my mind, that's all."

"And you didn't think to mention that yesterday when you were being questioned?" Silva chimed in from the back of the room. "You *conveniently* left that detail out."

"I honestly didn't think it was important," Dorothy said, opening her hands and shrugging. "It was a simple misunderstanding. And we weren't *yelling*. I stood up to leave, we exchanged words, and then I sat back down again and we worked it out."

"Witnesses say he stormed off," Agent Crum said.

"That's also not true," Dorothy said.

*Who the heck are these witnesses?* she wondered. She'd seen hungry families, sunburned tourists, and that group of businessmen having lunch. Had any of them wildly misinterpreted what they'd seen? It wasn't impossible, she supposed. It's not like she'd paid a lot of attention to *them* either.

"Is it?" Detective Silva said. "The waitress reported that he paid the bill and left you at the table."

Dorothy's head dropped slightly, the embarrassment of the day flooding back through her memory. "That part is true. But it wasn't like that. He ended up standing me up, in a sense. He excused himself to go to the bathroom, and never came back. I assume that I wasn't what he was looking for in a romantic partner and he bailed. Simple as that." It hurt her pride to admit it out loud, but that's what must have happened, she thought.

"Are you sure that was the end of it?" Agent Crum asked. "He didn't come back to your place later? Or previously?"

"No," Dorothy said. "I never heard from him again! Nor did I want to."

"Did he ever ask to borrow money from you, or did you write him a check?"

Dorothy looked from Agent Crum to Detective Silva, confused.

"And did you still have all your jewelry at the end of the date? Was anything missing from your purse?"

Dorothy subconsciously touched her earrings as she remembered what she'd worn that day. "No, everything was in order. . . . Nothing missing from my purse. What are you getting at?"

"We've had several reports of a man close to Henry's description taking ladies out on dates, or having short-term relationships with them. When these relationships ended, he'd leave, along with the contents of their jewelry boxes. Sometimes savings bonds, if they kept those in their nightstands, or anything else valuable that was easily accessible."

Dorothy's mouth hung open. Henry had been so nice—until

he wasn't. Polished and cultured and interesting. But as she listened to Special Agent Crum, she had to wonder—had it all been an act?

"You're lucky you didn't bring him home with you," Detective Silva said. "He couldn't have stolen from you, or the other women in your household."

Dorothy frowned. If they had hit it off, and he'd earned her trust, maybe they would have gotten to that point. . . . And if they'd taken that step and then she'd found out about all this, that would have been terrible and exactly what Rose had warned against. Even airheaded Rose had more street smarts than she did, apparently. Four older women on a budget could not afford such a costly mistake. Their rent, utilities, and medications weren't cheap.

"Are you sure it was *Henry*?" Dorothy asked. "I have to say, except for unceremoniously abandoning me at the restaurant, he seemed like really a good guy."

"They never are," Silva said.

Clearly she had some dating baggage of her own.

"We're looking into it and gathering accounts," Crum said. "But you can see, anyone he dated or screwed over is definitely on our short list."

"Some of the women he dated claimed that he had a mustache, making him look even more like Tom Selleck," Silva said. "Sometimes he wore an earring. And he went by a number of names. Henry must have been his newest alias."

"When I met him, and in his dating video, he didn't have

a mustache, or an earring," Dorothy said, recalling how hand-some he'd looked in his button-down shirt and aviator frames. She couldn't believe the same man was this thieving lothario Silva and Crum were talking about. It boggled the mind. But then again, she had been so desperate for a date, maybe she wasn't able to see the warning signs.

"Did any of these other women mention if he wore glasses?" she said. "He wore light-gold aviators. But when we found him in the freezer, he was face down, so I'm not sure if he was wearing them there."

"Interesting," Agent Crum said. "Do we have a photo?"

Detective Silva flipped through a manila folder and slid a glossy photo across the table.

It was Henry, the familiar, handsome planes of his face clearly visible despite the pale smears of cheesecake that ran from his chin up to his hairline, covering his ear. She felt a pang in her heart seeing the once-vibrant man as a motionless corpse. Even though it was just a photograph, Dorothy felt she was finding the body all over again, and she clutched the edge of the metal table. But something was missing here, she noticed.

She tapped at the picture. "No glasses," she said. "What do you think happened to them?"

Agent Crum grunted. "Check into that," he told Detective Silva.

The detective made a note in her notebook and chewed the end of her pencil thoughtfully.

"I supposed he could have been wearing nonprescription glasses on our date," Dorothy said. "If he was a con man like you say, he might have all kinds of disguises. But I got the feeling he needed them." She remembered how he'd leaned over the menu to read it. But then another thought occurred to her. What if he'd been doing that to hide his face from someone he'd seen at Wolfie's? Another woman he'd dated, perhaps. Someone he might have stolen from.

Dorothy looked closer at the crime-scene photograph on the table. It looked like there was a mole on Henry's cheekbone, which she hadn't remembered seeing on their date. It was hard to tell, though, through the smears of cheesecake.

"In the spirit of being as forthcoming as possible," Dorothy said, "I should tell you that Henry *did* act a little strange at our meeting. Jumpy, maybe. I thought it was just first-date nerves like I had. But he seemed to be looking over my shoulder a lot, and at one point he seemed to be hiding his face behind the menu. I don't know if that's useful, but I thought I'd mention it. Also, I don't remember the mole."

"Well, well, well. All of a sudden you're full of helpful details," Agent Crum said. "Interesting." He made eye contact with Detective Silva, who scribbled menacingly in her notebook.

"How can you still be treating me like a suspect?" Dorothy blurted out. "I've told you everything I know. I'm trying to be helpful!"

"We'll need to check all of your statements," Silva said. "So far, we only have your word that he didn't come home with you another time or take anything from you."

"Many of these women who were scammed are quite angry about it," Crum added ominously. "As you might imagine."

"Of course," Dorothy nodded. "No one wants to be stolen from. Or made a fool of."

"*Exactly*," Special Agent Crum said. "*You* understand. Someone in your position might even want to get back at him. Someone might be so angry that they just might kill him."

He stared deep into Dorothy's eyes, so close to her face that she could see each and every pore on his skin. She pulled back an inch but kept her eye contact stable. She'd had plenty of practice with men who had tried to intimidate her.

"Well, *I* didn't kill him," she said, straightening her shoulders and keeping her head up. Her height lent her gravitas, she knew, even when she was sitting down. "I wouldn't hurt a fly. Even if Henry had stolen from me, which he didn't. I would think that might lead you to rule me out."

"We'll see about that," Crum said, flicking his eyes up and down Dorothy's frame. "You're officially a person of interest. Though, at this point, you're free to go."

Dorothy felt a wave of relief roll through her body. She wasn't out of the woods yet, but at least she could get out of this god-awful interrogation room. She grabbed her purse and pushed out of the room into the police station lobby, where she immediately saw her mother, Sophia, standing there waiting for her, a shower cap still on her purse.

# A ROSE AMONG THORNS

## ········12·········

*B*ack in the comfort of her living room, Rose sank onto the rattan couch and kicked off her shoes. With a groan, she reached down to massage one foot and then the other. Then she reclined and pulled a throw pillow over her face.

This wedding had gotten off to a terrible start. Not one but two events ruined by a dead body and the ensuing investigation. Trying to hide the truth from Nettie had only made things worse, and now Rose wondered if there'd even be a wedding at all.

"Sweetheart, you did the best you could," Blanche said, kicking off her own shoes and pulling the pillow from Rose's face. "This isn't your fault."

"Blanche, I know *that*." Rose sniffled. "I didn't kill him!"

Her friend sat on the couch by Rose's feet and patted her leg affectionately. "Oh, honey, you're running hotter than a Louisiana July. Nobody blames you."

"They shouldn't blame me, but they do," Rose said. "How could I know that something like this would happen right before the Welcome Tuna Teatime?"

Blanche gently smacked Rose's nyloned feet with the other throw pillow. "You couldn't," she said. "It's just plain bad luck."

"And is it just bad luck that he had Dorothy's name in his pocket?" Rose pushed herself up to a seated position, pulling her knees into her chest. When Blanche looked at her quizzically, she added, "I'm not saying that Dorothy knew that this guy was a con artist. I'm just saying her association with him is the reason that this wedding is a disaster!"

"Surely Dorothy couldn't have known that he was so dastardly, or that he was about to get murdered," Blanche said reasonably, pursing her lips and giving Rose a stern look. "If she did, she probably wouldn't have made a date with him."

"That's not funny," Rose said. "I'm in a serious pickle—and not one of those delicious fried ones. I *told* Dorothy to be careful with that VHS dating service. I warned her about the dangers of dating strange men. And now look what's happened!"

"Rose, this could have happened to anyone. It was pure

chance that Dorothy happened to cross paths with this unfortunate man. It's just a terrible coincidence."

"I don't know," Rose said, shaking her head. "I don't think people should go out with total strangers. Even if you have seen them on a videotape or talked to them on the phone first. It's better—and safer—to stick with someone you know. Or somebody someone you know has vouched for."

"So you're against blind dates now? Everyone should just date within their own little circle?" Blanche said, raising her eyebrows. "You're starting to sound like some of the more conservative elders of St. Olaf."

Rose lightly flung the throw pillow at Blanche.

"I am not!" she said. "I'm not as slow, boring, and provincial as—"

Just then, a loud knock echoed from the front door as it opened to reveal an older man with a shock of white hair.

"—Cousin Gustave!" Rose said, quickly bringing her feet off the couch and smoothing her hair back into place. "What are you doing here?"

"I've come to speak with you," he said cryptically. "In private." He darted a glance at Blanche, who watched him through narrowed eyes.

"Blanche and I have no secrets," Rose said. "She can stay."

Gustave looked at Blanche for a moment, then shrugged. He seated himself in the rattan armchair to Rose's right, placing a sheaf of papers on the coffee table.

"I was very concerned to hear about the bridal shower

today," he began. He unbuttoned the top button of his plaid shirt, far too hot for the Miami weather. "Katrina told me everything. And then she notified the other town elders via telegram."

"Did she tell you how wonderful the shower ceremony was? How delightfully everyone sang?" Rose said, ticking off items on her fingers. "Did she mention how the conversation flowed at the restaurant, how delicious the food tasted, how beautiful Nettie looked and how much she laughed, or how every step of the ceremony went off without a hitch?"

Gustave grimaced and loosened his collar. "She . . . ah . . . she felt the event was overshadowed by the intrusion of this police person, and the fact that your roommate, or whoever she is, was taken away in handcuffs!"

"But that was just maybe five or ten minutes out of an entire afternoon!" Rose said. "At the very end of all the festivities!"

"That may be so, but in light of all this criminal activity, the elders have added a few more conditions to the trust." Gustave exhaled slowly, then dove into a torrent of Norwegian, pausing only to wipe his perspiring brow with a handkerchief.

Blanche looked from Gustave to Rose, clearly not understanding a single word, but fully comprehending the meaning. With each guttural consonant, tiny flecks of spittle flew from Gustave's mouth. He gestured to the stack of paper on the coffee table, then shuffled through the pages, pointing out line after line marked in bright yellow highlighter.

Rose looked down at her hands, then back up at the

ceiling, trying to prevent tears from rolling down her face.

When he was finally done speak-yelling, Rose leveled her gaze to Gustave's piercing baby blues. "Cousin, if you're finished venting your klager, perhaps you'd like to shut your stoyhull and listen to me." She stood up from the couch and straightened her shoulders. "Things may have gone a little haywire, but that has nothing to do with this wedding. Every single wedding tradition thus far has happened fully in accordance with St. Olaf's bylaws. These additions that you've brought to my attention will be included seamlessly into the wedding program we already have underway. As will all the new guests the groom's family is insisting on. Now if you'll excuse me, I have work to do." Rose pointed toward the door, trembling slightly. "Perhaps it's best if you leave now."

Gustave stood, his knees audibly cracking. He looked down his freckled nose at Rose, his eyes wide as if in shock at how she'd spoken to him. Rose looked back up at him, rather in shock herself.

She stood firm, even if inside she was shaking. She'd never spoken to her cousin that way. Or any of the town elders. She never dreamed she'd ever stand up to them, for any reason. But that was just what she'd done.

As soon as the door shut behind Gustave, Rose collapsed onto the sofa again. She clapped a hand to her forehead, still in shock. She'd always hated being yelled at, criticized, underestimated, and confronted, and in the last twenty minutes, she'd had to endure all four at once. It made her feel just like the time she was chastised for accidentally breaking the family's china gravy boat on the dining room floor, when she was playing pirates with her sister Holly and they needed another vessel for their dolls. Or like the time she'd spilled ink all over her teacher's desk in St. Olaf's one-room schoolhouse. Or the time—it was with Cousin Gustave, actually—that they'd snuck out to catch fireflies and accidentally left the pasture gate open, causing their cow Petunia to escape. Come to think of it, Cousin Gustave had blamed that on her, when he was the last one through the gate, and the eldest. He should have taken responsibility for that, Rose thought. He loved to tell other people what to do, but never apologized for any mistakes himself.

"Oh, honey . . ." Blanche began.

Before Rose could even reply, there was another loud knock at the door.

"We need a 'Do Not Disturb' sign for our front door," Rose grumbled.

"Or at least one that points out we do have a doorbell," Blanche added.

Rose started to get up again. She had half a mind to tinker with the doorknob so no one else could walk over that threshold again. She'd had enough for one day. For several days, she thought.

But Blanche waved her gently back into place and went to the door instead. "Give your feet a rest, honey."

"This better be the evening paper," Rose said. "Or a singing telegram."

When Blanche opened the door, there stood Mr. and Mrs. Bryant, both dressed to the nines. Mrs. Bryant had changed out of the Diane von Furstenberg wrap dress she'd worn to the shower into a tailored St. John knit in crisp white and navy. Mr. Bryant wore a dark suit with an immaculate white button-down and shining gold cuff links.

"Blanche, Rose," Mrs. Bryant said, "may we come in?"

Blanche angled herself to look over at Rose, who was lost in thought for a moment. What if she said no? Or what if they just shut the door in their faces and went right to bed? The thought was preposterous. She'd never do something like that. She was just too polite. She hadn't been raised that way.

"Of course," Rose said, groaning inwardly. "I was just about to retire for the night." That was as direct as her midwestern upbringing would allow, hoping they'd get the hint to keep this visit short.

The Bryants stepped into the living room and glanced around, taking in the pink walls, framed art, and potted plants. Mr. Bryant paid extra attention to the satin nightgown and robe clinging to Blanche's curves.

"Please, don't let us keep you from . . . whatever you get up to at night," Mrs. Bryant said, giving a disdainful look in Blanche's direction.

"I'd love to stay and chat, but I'd rather eat glass," Blanche said frostily. "Rose, remember that one shouldn't let uninvited visitors keep one up late."

Rose sent Blanche a pleading glance as Blanche disappeared

behind her bedroom door. She really could have used more of Blanche's moral support right then. Heck, she wished Dorothy and Sophia were here, too, to provide backup, but then again, Dorothy was the reason they were in this mess to begin with.

"Please sit down," Rose turned to say, but the Bryants had already seated themselves on the sofa. Rose sat in one of the armchairs, feeling like she was about to face a firing squad.

"Thank you for seeing us like this," Mr. Bryant said. "We felt this was a conversation that needed to happen face-to-face."

Rose gulped. She couldn't take getting yelled at anymore. She tried to keep a pleasant smile on her face, but she felt at any moment that she would shatter into tears.

"All of this . . . police activity is really distracting from the wedding, don't you think?" Mrs. Bryant began.

*That's an understatement*, Rose thought.

"And it's bringing the wrong kind of attention to the hotel. We just can't have this kind of thing continue. I hope you understand."

Rose nodded. Of course no one wanted more of this kind of thing.

"Great," Mr. Bryant said. "Glad we've come to an agreement."

"I'm sorry . . ." Rose said, looking from Mr. Bryant to Mrs. Bryant. "What do you mean?"

"*We'll* handle the rest of the arrangements from here on out," Mrs. Bryant said. "We'll take care of the rehearsal dinner, the ceremony, and the reception. Overall, I'd say there's really no need for your participation any longer, or that of your . . . roommates."

Rose frowned. This didn't sound good.

"But we have lots of St. Olaf traditions we need to incorporate into those three events, and we have other pre-wedding ceremonies that need to occur." Rose twisted her wedding ring, trying to tamp down the mix of anger and anxiety that was bubbling up inside her.

Mr. Bryant cleared his throat. "I hate to speak plainly, but you and your friends have caused disaster after disaster. And frankly, our business and our family are suffering because of it. So you see, there really isn't further discussion to be had."

Though Mr. Bryant's jowls were turning slightly red, his expression remained cool and composed. He was good at getting his way and seemed like he was used to it. Rose remembered him saying he'd built his hotel business from nothing but a ten-dollar inheritance from his uncle Bull when he was a boy in the Great Depression.

Rose opened her mouth to protest and fight harder for her hometown's traditions. But she was so exhausted from standing up to Cousin Gustave that she didn't know if she could. Maybe it would be better this way, she thought morosely. Nettie and Jason could have a nice wedding. Maybe they didn't need the Anderdonnen trust. And maybe Rose didn't really need to prove herself to everyone by making this a true St. Olaf wedding. The challenges were just too great.

It would be sad, of course, and somewhat embarrassing to

have to explain everything to her relatives. To waste all that herring, and to have to return the goat horn, the donkey, and the other essentials she, Jorgen, and Jason had been working so hard to procure.

"Fine," Rose said quietly. "I'll tell Nettie."

She thought she'd feel relief at this decision, but regret and a sense of failure washed over Rose. She hadn't felt this way since the Butter Queen crown had been stolen right out from under her. She felt worse. Because this time, she wasn't just disappointing herself. She'd be disappointing everyone she grew up with and loved.

Maybe Nettie and Jason didn't care about the St. Olaf traditions, but they also didn't want a wedding completely controlled by the Bryants.

*I've failed everyone*, she thought. *I should never have thought that simple old Rose Nyland could pull this off.*

"Wonderful," Mrs. Bryant said. "We'll see you on Saturday, at the ceremony. We've pulled a few strings and gotten our priest from Our Lady of Sorrows to officiate the ceremony in our ballroom. You may attend with a plus-one."

Rose gasped. "What do you mean? What about all the other guests, from Nettie's side of the family? And what about the rehearsal dinner?"

"Those events will just be for *immediate* family." Mrs. Bryant sniffed. "I'm sure you understand."

"You're telling me that you are *disinviting* everyone else from the wedding?"

Rose couldn't believe the gall of the Bryants. Cutting out Rose—and everyone else—from the rest of the wedding festivities—and, except for her and her paltry plus-one, of the wedding itself!

"This is ridiculous!" she said, clenching the rattan arms of her chair. "This is unnecessary, barbaric, rude . . . and . . . and just plain cruel!"

"I'm sorry you feel that way," Mr. Bryant said, "but we can't introduce any more criminal activity or suspicious characters in this wedding. Take it or leave it." He tossed a white wedding invitation on heavy cardstock onto the coffee table.

"It's going to be a *lovely* affair," Mrs. Bryant said coldly.

"You can't be serious," Rose said. Her mouth set in a hard line, and Rose felt the heat of anger swelling up inside her. "You can't cut out Nettie's family from this wedding!"

"We're only inviting you as a courtesy," Mrs. Bryant said. "Or should we rescind the invitation?" She picked the heavy envelope up from the table as she and her husband stood up and walked to the front door.

"We'll let ourselves out," Mr. Bryant said. "I'm sorry it had to be this way. It's most unpleasant for all of us."

Rose followed the Bryants to the door as they opened it and stepped over the threshold, bathed in the yellow porch light. Before the couple stepped into the humid Miami night, Rose snatched the invitation from Mrs. Bryant's hand and held it to her chest.

*Thank goodness that's over*, Rose thought as she walked to

her kitchen. The Bryants' visit was the camel that broke the scarecrow's back, and she was now feeling like the scarecrow! Rose longed to let sleep bring her a reprieve from this unbearable wedding stress, but she had too much work to do.

Just then, the phone rang.

Rose's heart sped up. Only bad things came from phone calls so late at night. She reached out to the receiver with a trembling hand, praying that no one was hurt, or worse.

Nettie's voice streamed through the handset, words tumbling over each other with Jason's calming tones in the background.

"My wedding dress has been stolen!" Nettie cried. "It was hanging right here in the closet, and now it's gone!"

Rose's eyes went wide. "Perhaps it's hanging in another closet?" She knew she was grasping at straws, but what other possibility could there be?

"There's only one closet in this hotel room, Aunt Rose," Nettie said. "And it's nowhere to be seen!"

"All right, we'll find it," Rose said, in as calm a voice as she could muster. "Maybe someone took it to be steamed. It's got to be somewhere. I'll come over first thing in the morning and help you find it."

"Thank you," Nettie sniffled. "Jason's already going to ask the staff if they know anything about it. But I can't help but wonder if this wedding is cursed!"

# THE GAME'S AFOOT
## 13

*T*he next morning Dorothy carved a groggy path to the kitchen to brew some coffee. Her head was pounding after a long night at the police station, getting peppered with question after question under unforgiving (and unflattering, based on the sallow reflection staring back at her in the mirrored glass) fluorescent lighting.

As she flicked on the kitchen light, she nearly stumbled over Rose, who was slumped at the kitchen table, fast asleep. Still fully dressed, Rose clutched a large envelope in her hand, and her head rested on a pile of papers next to a cold cup of tea.

Dorothy reached for the cup of tea to take it to the sink. As she did, she saw some of the typewritten text next to Rose's face.

THE ANDERDONNEN TRUST: CONDITIONS, she was able to make out, before the ink dissolved in a small spot of Rose's drool.

*Definitely not some light reading*, Dorothy thought as she wondered what Rose had been poring over all night. Usually her wedding-related checklists and paperwork involved lists of ingredients, old recipes, Norwegian limericks, and the names of family members, with any pets and farm animals added in parentheses.

Dorothy filled the teakettle with water, then put it on the stove. As she poured fresh grounds into the coffeemaker, Blanche entered the kitchen in a violet satin robe, followed by Sophia in a blue terrycloth robe and fuzzy slippers.

"What's with Rose?" Sophia asked. "Did you bump her off, too?"

"Very funny, Ma," Dorothy said. "It looks like the poor thing had a long night."

"You did, too, pumpkin," Sophia said, then turned to Blanche. "The police kept her for questioning until after ten o'clock!"

"Oh, that's terrible," Blanche cooed. "But did you meet any handsome officers? They always look so important in their crisp blue uniforms."

"I didn't notice," Dorothy said flatly. "They were so busy giving me the third degree, I didn't have time to notice how adorable they might be. And remember, the lead detective is a woman."

Blanche raised her eyebrows and sat down. "Well, how did she look in her uniform?"

"I don't happen to swing that way," Dorothy said. "But even if I did, there's nothing friendly about the treatment I got. They were acting like I was a . . . a *suspect*, or some sort of criminal!" Dorothy slammed her hand down for emphasis, accidentally waking up Rose.

"Who's a criminal?" Rose said, rubbing the sleep from her eyes and looking around wildly. Her gaze landed on Dorothy, and her confused expression hardened into a frown. "Oh, it's you," she said, in an uncharacteristically chilly tone. She gathered up her papers, placing the envelope on top, and pushed her chair out to leave the table.

"I'm sorry I woke you," Dorothy said. "I'm making you some fresh tea, if that helps. It's Earl Grey, your favorite."

"No thanks. I'm not thirsty," Rose said. She stood up from the table, clutching her papers to her chest. Dorothy noticed the dark circles under Rose's eyes and the faint transfer of typewritten lines across her cheek.

"Didn't you go to bed last night?" Blanche said. "Is everything all right?"

"No, everything is not all right," Rose groused. "I was up all night going around and around in my head."

"Well, that couldn't have taken long," Sophia said. "Unless you got stuck in all that cotton you keep between your ears."

Dorothy placed a quieting hand on her mother's arm. Something told her that Rose wasn't in the right frame of mind for, well, anything Sophia.

"I'm stuck between a log and a hard place," Rose said. "And I just can't figure any way around it."

"A rock," Sophia said.

"Yes, exactly," Rose said. "I'm stuck between a rock and a log and there's no way out. It's worse than the time I icinged myself inside a life-size gingerbread house at the Nilssons' holiday smorgasbord. I was stuck in there for hours!"

"How'd you get out of that?" Blanche asked.

"I had to eat my way through," Rose said. "It was harrowing. And delicious. But I ruined my chances of winning the gingerbread house competition, since mine had bite marks all over it. I've never been able to enjoy that particular cookie since."

"But, Rose, that proved you can find your way out of any challenging situation," Dorothy pointed out.

"I can't *eat* my way through this one," Rose said. "I've looked at it from every angle and tried every single thing I can think of."

"How many is that, two?" Sophia said.

Rose bristled at Sophia and shook the sheaf of papers at her. "It's a whole lot more than two. Basically, thanks to Dorothy, none of us, and no one from St. Olaf, is welcome at the wedding anymore. We won't have any St. Olaf traditions,

Nettie won't get her inheritance for years, if at all, I won't get to show everyone that I'm not as simple and useless as they thought I was," Rose wailed. "And it's all Dorothy's fault!"

"You wait just a minute," Dorothy said, rising from her seat. She'd had quite enough of this at the station. Now even sweet-natured Rose was turning on her.

"Everyone thinks you had something to do with the murder at the Cabana Sun Hotel," Rose said, glaring at Dorothy. "And that's why all of this is happening."

"This is preposterous," Dorothy said, raising her voice slightly. She didn't want to yell at one of her best friends, but she was sick and tired of being accused by everybody.

"My goodness," Blanche said, fanning herself with the Bryants' wedding invitation.

"You all make me sick," Sophia said. Everyone stopped to stare at her. "All we have to do is clear Dorothy's name. Then everyone will know she had nothing to do with the dead body. If she's not the murderer, we can make a case for the wedding to go on as planned." She scooped a teaspoon of sugar into her coffee. "Simple!"

Dorothy blinked. Her mother wasn't wrong. Dorothy had been starting to worry that she should hire a lawyer—or a fleet of them—based on the way she'd been treated at the police station and all the admonitions not to leave town.

She also had to admit to a niggling feeling in the back of her head: she wanted to know what had really happened with Henry. She'd had such a connection with him, then an odd first date, and then there was his sudden death. But the police's theory about him being a con man didn't jibe with the man she'd gotten to know by phone. The person she'd traded salmon recipes with. The one who'd mentioned having dinner on his boat. They'd discussed their favorite bookshops in Miami and Coral Gables, and bonded over the challenges of being empty nesters and finding themselves on the dating scene again.

She just couldn't imagine that he was a liar. Could he really have been a grifter, someone who took advantage of others? Even with his odd behavior at Wolfie's, it just didn't add up. But maybe she was being as naive as her dear friend Rose. Certainly other women must have also felt a romantic connection with him, based on what the police had said about the number of people he'd successfully conned. He was probably very good at adapting to any woman's tastes and desires—at playing the part of Wonderful Guy. And the fact that he had rugged good looks and a full head of hair? Dorothy shook her head ruefully. She and the other women never stood a chance.

There was obviously so much she hadn't known about him—or even thought to question. Her curiosity was piqued—but more than that, she also wanted to know for *herself*. She clearly needed to recalibrate her instincts about people. Getting answers about Henry might just help her do that—a side benefit to clearing her name.

"What do you all think?" Dorothy said, looking from one

woman to the other, hoping they'd say yes. She didn't think she could do this alone—she needed her friends.

Blanche shifted in her seat, then looked down at her frosty coral manicure. Rose took a slurp of the tea Dorothy had made for her, conveniently avoiding her eyes.

"Come on, you two!" Sophia said, lifting her hands in disbelief. "You know if it was one of you in trouble, Dorothy would do everything in her power to help you."

Blanche looked up from her nails with a tortured expression. "It's not that I don't want to help you, Dorothy, I do," she insisted. "But I'm no Jessica Fletcher. I have no idea how to solve a murder."

"We all have our different talents," Dorothy said. "Can't you think of any that would be helpful in our own investigation?"

Blanche tapped a finger against the side of her face. "I see. Like maybe if we're spying on someone, Jorgen could lift me up to peek in a window with his big strong hands around my waist. Maybe a stakeout on a secluded beach at sunset, huddled together for warmth as the sun dips below the horizon. Or, if there's trouble, he could fight off some bad guys and catch me in his arms when I faint at the sight of blood. . . ."

Having clearly been mentally transported to a soft-focus daydream, Blanche stared into space for a moment. "I think I'll be able to help," she said at last with a slow smile.

Sophia peered at Rose over the rim of her glasses. "And what about you? How can you help my poor, wrongfully accused daughter? The one who's treated you like family all these years and would never blame you for going on the worst of the worst bad dates?"

Dorothy turned to Rose, locking eyes with her. Rose's were bloodshot from being up all night worrying. Dorothy's probably looked the same after being at the station so long.

"What do you say, Rose? Will you help me?" Dorothy asked.

Rose sank back in her seat and nodded. "I don't like any of this," she said. "This whole wedding—it's made me turn against you and even some members of my family. And I'm so exhausted already. I *want* to believe we can fix everything, but . . ." Rose dropped her head and dissolved into sobs. Dorothy patted Rose's heaving shoulder.

"I don't see why we can't do it all, if we work together," Dorothy said.

A plan started to form in her head. Whenever she engaged her intellect, instead of giving in to feelings of anger and helplessness, she started to feel calm and clear-headed. "Most likely the real suspect is someone in the Miami area. Based on what the police said, it was probably a crime of passion—or revenge—on Henry for his dirty dealings with women. It could be a jealous ex-lover, an angry husband, or a concerned family member." The possibilities laid themselves out in Dorothy's mind as if she were drawing a diagram on a chalkboard. As a teacher, she always encouraged her students to look at the information they had, ask questions, and follow the answers to a logical conclusion. She simply would have to apply that method to herself if she were going to get out of this troubling situation.

"And we already know—and have access to—the scene of the crime!" Blanche said, getting excited. "We could start there."

"That's the ticket!" Dorothy said. "The killer had to be at the Cabana Sun Hotel at some point to trap Henry in that freezer. There might still be clues at the scene, and at such a bustling hotel, someone must have seen him—or her—before or after the murder was committed."

"Okay, but what do we *do*?" Rose said. "I'm ready to help! But—and this may come as a shock to you all—I'm afraid I'm also not the best detective. Back in St. Olaf, somebody stole a cherry pie that I'd baked and left on the windowsill to cool, and I never found the culprit. I put up signs, offered a reward, and grilled everyone in town in case they'd noticed anyone sneaking around my house. But even the neighbor boy with that sticky red face didn't see who did it."

Dorothy and Sophia exchanged smiles, and Sophia started to laugh, which she hid with a cough.

"None of us are trained police officers, it's true," Dorothy said. "So we'll have to work with what we have. Rose, you're the closest to the Bryant family. You have the perfect reason to get to know Nettie's future in-laws, and any possible ties they might have to Henry or to what happened. Especially that Patricia—she manages the hotel, and she seems to know the most about the goings-on there. She also manages the staff, who may have seen someone hanging around the kitchens that night."

Rose nodded solemnly. "Maybe I can do that . . ." she said. "I already have a lot of questions for them. And to be honest, a few things that the Bryants said last night gave me pause. They're so laser-focused on their business, and there are clearly tensions in that family. Normally I don't like to pry, but this is a good reason to."

Then Rose's face fell and she bit her lip. "But I'm not very confrontational. I don't think I'll be able to get them to spill their guts like the boys on *Miami Vice* do."

"But that's the beauty of our investigation," Dorothy said. "You don't have to be confrontational like the police. You'll be subtle. You'll find out things over the course of getting to know them, just like any prospective family member. Anything that seems odd or doesn't add up—make a note of it and we'll discuss it together. Your approach will be more delicate, nuanced, and sophisticated than what they do on *Miami Vice*."

"Sophisticated?" Sophia said. "Ha!"

Dorothy shot a silencing look at her mother. She was finally getting everyone on board—and needed everyone to stay that way.

"As a matter of fact, Ma," Dorothy said, "Rose is the perfect undercover detective. She's so sweet and sincere that no one will suspect she has ulterior motives."

"Ah, I get it," Sophia said, winking at Dorothy. She leaned over and whispered close to Dorothy's ear. "You want her to play the role she was born to play: dumb."

Dorothy cleared her throat loudly to cover up her mother's crack. "What my mother is trying to say is that, Rose, you can just be yourself. That's the best thing to be."

Rose smiled. "People always underestimate me. They think I don't have anything going on beyond what they see. A simple girl from St. Olaf, blessed with a knack for milking and churning, just a farm-raised, corn-fed beauty with an undeniable talent for tap-dancing, chicken-calling, and cow-brushing, with dancer's legs and perfect pitch and—"

"We get the point," Sophia said. "We all know you're very special. Now can you use that wining personality of yours to help my daughter avoid the slammer?"

"Yes, sir!" said Rose, her spirits clearly lifted.

Dorothy hugged Rose. "Then let's get started. Since there are four of us, we can divide and conquer different aspects of the case."

Sophia rubbed her hands together. "*There's* my genius daughter. Your father said educating a girl was like trying to teach a duck the tarantella, but you proved him wrong!"

Rose grinned and pulled out a notebook and pen from beneath the papers she'd been reading overnight. "I'm going to start on my list of questions for the Bryants," she said. "I could go to the hotel this morning and offer to help them with their version of the wedding plans. I'll get in good with Mrs. Bryant, under the guise of just wanting to be included."

"Good thinking, Rose," said Blanche. "But what if they give you the brush-off? You already said they like to steamroll people, and they clearly weren't very happy with you last night."

Rose scrunched up her face in thought. "I suppose then I'd try to get close to Patricia, or her husband, Chip, and see if they need my help with anything. And I could always stick close to Nettie. After all, no matter what type of wedding she has, there's still so much to do—which can be a reason for all of us to spend some time together."

"Very smart," said Dorothy. By dividing this case up into manageable sections, they just might be able to solve it together. "Now, Blanche, while you help Rose with the wedding, I want you to talk to everyone you may meet along the way. Find out if any similar crimes have occurred in the city, or if anyone has an aunt or a grandmother or a friend who got taken in by a charming con man who looks like Tom Selleck. And of course, pump Jorgen for information on anyone else in the wedding party."

"That I can do," Blanche said. "I'll make plenty of notes and report back. You've never seen someone who can pump information out of a man as well as I can."

Sophia snickered.

"And what about you two?" Blanche asked Dorothy and Sophia.

Dorothy thought it over. Should she pore over old news-paper crime reports on microfilm at the library? Should she call Lucky Chances, or locate their offices, to try to get more intel on Henry—or the man who called himself Henry? Maybe she should go back to Wolfie's and try to re-create their first (and last) date minute by minute. Her head began to spin with all the options spiraling out before her. Even with everyone's help, solving a murder was a daunting task.

Sophia watched Dorothy's face as if she could read the churning thoughts in her head.

"Don't overthink it, pussycat. I've figured out our next move. We're going to do a stakeout," she declared. "We're going to watch that hotel like the FBI watched Lucky Luciano. No one will go in or out without us making a note of it—including a full description. If there are any suspicious characters lurking around, we'll find them."

Dorothy looked dubiously at her mother. The idea of them parked in an unmarked van, wearing fedoras and tossing back corn chips and lukewarm coffee all night like television detec-tives seemed like a stretch. Her mother would need plenty of bathroom breaks, for starters. And even if she gave Sophia a phone book so that she could see over the dashboard, her mother's eyes weren't the sharpest. Dorothy wasn't sure if Sophia's hips—or lower back—would allow for that much sitting. Or if Dorothy's would, for that matter.

"I'm not sure lurking in the car with a set of binoculars is the best idea," she said.

Sophia sighed with annoyance. "I'm not talking about *outside* the hotel," Sophia said. "I'm talking about inside! We'll set up right in that fancy lobby of theirs."

"So more like a stake-*in* . . ." Blanche drawled.

Rose frowned. "But that won't work at all. Dorothy is the whole reason this wedding is in limbo—and the Bryants don't want her anywhere near their precious hotel."

A sparkle lit up Sophia's eyes. "That's why we're going to use disguises! Blanche, get your makeup kit. We're going to need all the spackle and paint you slap on for a Friday-night date."

# MISTRESSES OF DISGUISE

·············14·············

*T*he four women piled into Dorothy's car. Blanche once again took the front seat, muttering under her breath about Jorgen not answering the phone when she'd called his hotel room that morning.

"I'm sure he was just in the shower," Rose said. "You can try him again from the hotel lobby."

Soon the quiet residential streets turned to high-rises with glittering balconies as they reached the heart of Miami. They drove over a small bridge, and on one side the ocean glittered a brilliant aquamarine, cheering Dorothy a bit. Everything seemed a little more possible when the sun was shining, she thought. Thank goodness they were in Miami, where excellent weather was the norm. Dorothy tried to hang on to that sunny feeling as they approached their destination. Even though she was in a storm of her own, she could try to prevent it from becoming a hurricane.

Dorothy dropped Rose and Blanche off at the hotel, then drove off with Sophia still in the back seat.

Dorothy circled a few blocks, tapping her fingers against the steering wheel as she waited for throngs of tourists in sunglasses, visors, sundresses, and guayaberas to amble through the crosswalks. She didn't want to shell out for some of the more exorbitant parking lots, but if she didn't find a spot soon, she'd have to. Miami was truly booming as a vacation destination, despite the efforts of the local news to make it sound like there were drug busts and organized crime happening on every corner. That just wasn't the Miami she knew. But this sun-soaked paradise was attracting so many tourists to its beaches and nightclubs that now no one could get a decent parking spot.

After finally finding one on a quiet side street several blocks from Collins Avenue, Dorothy flagged down a taxi and helped her mother into the back seat. This was all part of their act, to look like tourists loitering at the hotel—rather than themselves.

To that end, Dorothy pulled on a broad straw-brimmed hat that covered her hair and hid most of her face, especially when she angled it correctly and dipped her head down. She wore a pair of Blanche's sunglasses in a vibrant teal color that she never would have chosen herself. Blanche had also done her makeup, overlining Dorothy's lips with an exaggerated cupid's bow and filling it all in with a bright tube of Million Dollar Red lipstick. Being a tall woman made it more difficult to fade into the background, but the idea was to at least look different from the Dorothy Zbornak everyone had met at the Welcome Tuna Teatime and at the bridal shower.

*And I look different, all right*, Dorothy thought. *Like a clown on holiday. Or a lady of the evening caught in the harsh morning light.* Instead of her usual blousy tops, long vests, and flowing trousers, Dorothy had squeezed her long legs into a pair of blue jeans that belonged to her daughter and had been left behind on a recent visit. She'd been amazed that they fit, even though she'd had to take a deep breath and suck in her stomach to get the button fastened, Blanche pulling on one side and Rose on the other. At least they hadn't needed to use pliers to yank up the zipper. She'd also borrowed a stretchy magenta top from Blanche that hugged her curves, topped off with a baggy jacket in white denim. The boxy cut and the generous shoulder pads helped Dorothy feel less exposed, as if the Jordache jacket were a type of armor as well as a disguise.

She'd drawn the line at borrowing shoes from any of her roommates. All their feet were tiny, and if she was going to wear uncomfortably tight pants, then, darn it, she was going to wear shoes that fit. She slid on a pair of white huaraches that she'd bought optimistically during her shopping spree at Aventura Mall, thinking they'd be perfect for a date on Henry's boat. She hadn't had the time to return them yet. After all, there was no chance of another date with Henry, and she couldn't imagine going on more dates—or doing anything fun—until she got herself out of this mess. She prayed that these disguises would work. They had to.

She looked over to her mother and let out a guffaw. They'd toyed with the idea of dressing Sophia up as Dorothy's daughter, since she was so much shorter. But even with makeup, there was no hiding the fact that Sophia was elderly. Not to mention the massive bifocals that she couldn't do without.

The four of them had done their best to disguise Sophia's short, white hairdo under a dark wig, with a drab cotton scarf tied under her chin. "I'll look like Strega Nona!" Sophia had bellowed before admitting that the scarf did help obscure her face.

They draped a camera around Sophia's neck to complete the picture of a tourist staying at the Cabana Sun Hotel, though its bulk almost overwhelmed her petite frame. Sophia needed her glasses to see, so there was nothing they could do about that, but Blanche did her best with contour, bronzing powder, blush, and lip liner to change the appearance of Sophia's features. In the bright sunlight coming through the taxi window, the results looked even more garish than Dorothy had realized.

"Stop looking at me!" Sophia said. "I know what you're thinking."

"I'm only thinking that you definitely don't look like your-self," Dorothy said. "Which today is a good thing."

"I've seen morticians do a better job," Sophia grumbled. "Take a picture. Go ahead and tack my photo up at the funeral home as a demonstration on what *not* to do!"

"Oh, Ma, it's not that bad," Dorothy said, crossing her fingers behind her back. "You look ten years younger. And maybe a little sunburned."

"I look like the victim of a plastic surgeon's personal vendetta, which doesn't exactly go with my backstory." Sophia gestured to her dark dress and cardigan and matching ortho-pedic shoes. "If anyone tries to talk to me, I'm going to play the part of an Italian widow."

"But you *are* an Italian widow," Dorothy said. "You'll need a better cover story."

"I already have one, pumpkin, inspired by my great-aunt Neeta. Picture it: Sicily, 1884. A woman on the run from a ring of corrupt priests trying to take over her convent. Did you know in those days, you could be excommunicated for disobedience? They did that to Aunt Neeta. But she took one donkey, a bottle of Communion wine, and the finger bone of St. Agatha and disappeared into the hills. In my version, it happened a few decades ago. She made it to Napoli and boarded a boat to Ellis Island. She had seventeen children, became widowed, and is now on spring break from her job as a notary public."

Dorothy shook her head, her mouth agape at each twist

and turn of Great-Aunt Neeta's backstory. "That's—that's very unique, Ma," she said. "How did you come up with all that?"

"It's all true, except the part where she becomes a notary public. I wasn't sure if she should be a part-time go-go dancer instead."

"I think the part about the seventeen children is what you need to worry about. How would she have had time to get her notary license?"

The taxi swung around a corner, and Dorothy could see the bright white facade of the Cabana Sun Hotel just half a block away.

"Look—I even brought the finger!" Sophia pulled out a small, dried-out bone from her purse, along with a few loose bobby pins and a roll of Certs. She winked. "Don't worry, it's really a chicken bone."

Dorothy rolled her eyes. "We're almost there. You ready, Ma?"

"Ready as I'll ever be," Sophia said, tucking the chicken bone back into her purse. "You better have your backstory ready. Tell it to me quick, so we can keep our details consistent."

"I don't think we need—" Dorothy began.

"You could be one of my seventeen children," Sophia mused. "Although . . . I would never let my daughter leave the house looking like that!"

"Well, that's too bad, because you already did—in real life," Dorothy said, self-consciously untucking her tight shirt from her tight jeans. "Maybe I can play the role of an independent woman taking her elderly mother on a nice vacation so that she can heal from a difficult bout of laryngitis. The mother has doctor's orders to rest her vocal cords—and can't speak a word!"

"Ha, ha," Sophia said. "Try again."

"Fine," Dorothy huffed. "I'm a woman on vacation with her elderly mother. We're here to see the sights and we're waiting around in the lobby for the rest of our family to go to the Seaquarium and eat cotton candy, okay?"

Sophia shook her head. "That's too generic. You need more detail."

Dorothy threw her hands up in exasperation. "My name is Tiffani. I'm here on vacation. I love the color hot pink, I watch *Days of Our Lives*, and my drink of choice is a fuzzy navel. How's *that*?" she snapped.

"Not buying it," said Sophia. "You've gotta work in a little kernel of truth, to make it believable."

Dorothy gritted her teeth as the taxi pulled right under the hotel portico.

"I'm a woman on vacation with her *difficult* mother. We're here to see the sights. I have a pet parakeet at home in Akron whom I miss terribly. I'm newly divorced and I'm wondering if I'll ever find love again."

"There it is," Sophia said, pointing a finger at Dorothy. "That kernel of truth."

Dorothy quickly paid the cab fare, avoiding her mother's

eyes while they exited the car. As they pushed through the hotel's revolving doors, Dorothy wondered if they'd made a mistake. The silly costumes, the elaborate backstories—would it be enough to conceal their identities long enough for them to find some leads? She took a deep breath. She hoped so.

Dorothy scanned the lobby, taking in the large family waiting at the check-in desk, an older man reading a newspaper on one of the velvet settees, and a few bellhops standing around, smoking at their station. A middle-aged couple had taken over another one of the settees to pore over a map of Miami. Both had ineptly applied their sunscreen, giving them a greasy white cast over their already pale skin.

*Tourists*, she thought. Just like she and her mother were supposed to be. Looking at these others, she reminded herself that they'd have to act like everything was all new to them. That they didn't know where they were going. Her mother acted that way a lot anyway, Dorothy thought wryly as she guided Sophia to a set of velvet armchairs in the near corner of the lobby.

"Try and look like you're on vacation," she muttered under her breath.

"How about I take your picture, *Tiffani?*" Sophia said, lifting the heavy Minolta that hung around her neck on a thick strap. They hadn't had time to buy new film, but it was good for their tourist act.

"No, just, you know . . ." Dorothy trailed off as the man across from them put down his newspaper and walked past, casting an eye over Sophia, then Dorothy, and raising his eyebrows as if he liked what he saw.

*I knew I looked like a lady of the evening*, Dorothy thought. She made a mental note to write down his description as soon as he was out of view.

"Say *formaggio*!" Sophia said, holding the camera up to her face. "This is what the tourists do."

Dorothy pretended to pose for the picture, then moved to grab the older man's discarded newspaper. Like the camera, it could be a helpful prop, and maybe she could study the crime pages while they waited for more people to observe.

In the meantime, she reached into her purse and pulled out *Lucky* by Jackie Collins, a paperback she'd snagged from Blanche's bedside, the exact thing that someone would read on vacation. But this copy had a slim notebook tucked inside. With a pencil nub, Dorothy noted down the date, the time, and a description of everyone in the lobby.

After several uneventful minutes, Sophia groaned and stretched, several popping noises emitting from the direction of her left hip. "I have to stand up," she said. "My joints are killing me."

"I knew this wasn't a good idea," Dorothy said. "Let me take you home."

"That's not what I'm saying. And don't give up so soon. I simply need to stretch my legs. I'm going to go for a walk and see what I can see in the other areas of the hotel. There could be people in the cigar room, or the patio, or the kitchens."

Dorothy thought of Henry in that very kitchen, pushed into the freezer by a cruel hand. An icy feeling gripped her from the inside. She didn't want her mom wandering around alone—especially not in that industrial kitchen.

"Then I'm going with you," she said. "You're not leaving my sight."

"Good," Sophia said, collecting her purse from where it had been hooked over the arm of the chair. "Nothing interesting is happening in this lobby anyway."

Dorothy tucked the book back into her purse. Just as she was about to stand up, a man and a woman hurried through the lobby. They weren't holding hands, but the intimate way they leaned their heads together and whispered as they walked suggested that they were an item.

The woman was resplendent in emerald silk shantung capris and a matching sleeveless top. Something the man said into her ear made her laugh, and she briefly placed a manicured hand on his arm. Dorothy snatched up the newspaper, lifting it up to cover her face. She peered over the top edge of the sports section to watch the couple. A photo of Dan Marino on the page facing her stared back as Dorothy gasped.

She recognized them. The woman was Gloria. And the smiling man on her arm wasn't Mr. Corzon. It was Jorgen.

Behind the protective screen of the newspaper, Dorothy and Sophia exchanged wide-eyed looks.

# RESTING SUSPICIOUS FACE
## 15

*R*ose and Blanche stood outside the firmly closed doors of Mr. and Mrs. Bryant's shared office on the second floor of the Cabana Sun Hotel. They'd been kicked out and Rose's feelings were still a bit bruised. It had been done politely, of course, as Mr. Bryant had gestured to a stack of computer printouts on his desk, stating that he and Mrs. Bryant were doing their weekly accounting review and would be tied up for hours; Mrs. Bryant had strongly suggested that Rose and Blanche enjoy some complimentary refreshments on the poolside patio instead of unnecessarily worrying themselves about wedding details that were already being taken care of.

Now Rose and Blanche found themselves in a white stucco hallway, far less luxurious than the lobby and the guestroom levels. This was a behind-the-scenes area, like the kitchens, more about the practical functioning of the hotel rather than the polished hospitality that faced the public. There was a long side table that held wire baskets of incoming and outgoing mail, as well as neat stacks of business cards and replenishments of paper clips, staples, rubber bands, and mimeograph paper. There was a case of Tab cola on the floor, probably waiting to be loaded into the Bryants' office mini fridge. Instead of the soft piano music that could be heard in the lobby, here the only sound was the roar of air-conditioning.

"What are we supposed to do now?" Blanche said, putting her hands on her hips.

Rose glanced around the hallway. They'd have to go to Plan B—whatever that was. She hadn't been exactly clear on Plan A in the first place. There wasn't anything they could find out about the Bryants with those office doors firmly shut behind them. Or was there? Rose wondered. Sometimes you could find things in unexpected places. Like the time she found a silver dollar in a pasture. Or like Lindstrom Surprise (her second-favorite dessert), which only *looked* like apple pie.

She peered down at the office supply table and the wire bins full of mail. "If I were a clue, where would I hide?" Rose mused. As an idea formed in her mind, she widened her eyes, trying to use her bulging baby blues to direct Blanche's attention to the pile of letters. She tilted her head down toward the table.

Blanche huffed. "Well, what are we waiting for? We could at least get a piña colada by the pool."

"Ahem!" Rose cleared her throat meaningfully, widening her eyes even more and then staring down at the mail bins.

Blanche cocked her head in concern as Rose continued dramatically clearing her throat. "Maybe we should get you a hot tea, sweetie. You sound a little scratchy."

"*Oh, for goodness' sake!*" Rose said in a stage whisper. "*Take a look at their mail!* Maybe there are some clues in there."

"Ah, I see," said Blanche, pursing her lips. "But isn't that . . . Oh, what's the word I'm looking for? A felony?"

Rose furrowed her brow as she thought. "It might be, but I think that's just for *opening* someone else's mail. Or stealing it."

Blanche narrowed her eyes. "I do believe you're right," she said. "And if our eyes just *happened* to fall upon something that was sitting out in plain view, that wouldn't be a crime, would it?"

"I don't think so," said Rose. "It certainly doesn't sound like a felony to me."

"Let me just put my purse down for a few minutes," Blanche said. "It's getting heavy and my shoulder hurts."

She gently placed her purse on the table, setting it down

with exaggerated care as she peered into one of the mail bins. "Oh, my poor arm," she said, rubbing her left shoulder with her right hand. She rotated her shoulder, causing the elbow of her other arm to knock one of the mail bins off the table. "Oops! Was that little old me? I'm so clumsy!" she said in a faux-concerned voice as she winked at Rose.

Rose gave Blanche a surprised open-mouthed smile as if she couldn't believe what her friend had just done. She carefully and slowly lowered herself to her knees on the gray industrial carpeting.

"It's all right, Blanche," she said in a stilted voice as if she were reciting the answer in a spelling bee. "Accidents happen! I'll just help clean this up."

Rose gathered the spilled envelopes in her hands and rifled through them. A batch of large cream envelopes had been loosely tied together with a ribbon, with a note saying *FOR COURIER*. As Rose peeked at the addresses, she noticed that several were names Rose vaguely remembered from one of the guest lists the Bryants had shared with her.

"They sure aren't wasting any time," she said through gritted teeth. She placed the invitations back into the bin and shuffled through a stack of business-size envelopes. It looked like correspondence—or maybe payments—to suppliers for the types of goods and services a bustling hotel would need: Lawrence's Laundry & Linens, Blue Marlin Liquor Distribution, Florida Power & Light, BellSouth, Five Star Carpet Cleaners, Corzon Catering & Dining, LCC, General

Sugar Co., Estrella Contracting & Plumbing, and more. Rose paused at an envelope addressed to the Miami Police Benevolent Society.

"That must be a donation," Rose mused. "Let's bring that up to Dorothy."

"This all seems pretty normal for the hotel business," Blanche said. "I'm not sure we've found anything that relates back to the murder."

Rose frowned. She felt that there might be clues *inside* those envelopes, but that was a line she wasn't ready to cross. At least, not yet. She placed the envelopes back in the bin and lifted it onto the table, next to the one filled with incoming mail. She pressed her index finger down on one end of that bin, flipping it over so the contents spread over the table.

"Ooops, now I've done it!" she giggled. "I guess I'm clumsy, too."

"Hurry up," Blanche said. "Let's not push our luck." She glanced up and down the empty hallway nervously.

Rose flicked through the incoming letters, tossing them back where they belonged after a quick skim of the return address.

"A few collection notices," she whispered, tapping at the typed words *FINAL NOTICE* with a pale pink fingernail. As a widow who always had to watch her pocketbook, envelopes like that sent a chill down Rose's spine.

"That's odd," said Blanche, peering over Rose's shoulder. "I thought they were doing very well for themselves."

"Me too," said Rose. "But Patricia mentioned something the other day that made me think maybe they're really stretching to make this expansion happen."

Blanche raised an eyebrow. "Well, it's not exactly the same thing as finding a murder suspect to swap out for Dorothy."

"No," Rose said. "But it's something that seems a little out of place. I'm not sure if it's a clue, but it is something that seems different from the picture the Bryants would want the rest of us to see. It reminds me of what Mr. Bryant said: that they can't afford to lose any business. I'm not sure if it means anything, but let's make a mental note of it."

"Oh, honey, I'm committing it to paper," Blanche said, pulling out a silver ballpoint pen and writing on the back of a receipt from Melina's Lingerie. "Though certain aspects of mine are as sharp—and as firm—as ever, I think it's best if we as a group don't fully rely on notes of the mental variety."

"Good point," Rose acknowledged. She scanned through the rest of the mail. Mostly flyers, junk mail, and typical business correspondence. "Nothing else here is jumping out at me. If there are any clues here, I'm not seeing them."

"Well then let's get out of here, before anyone sees us snooping!" Blanche motioned for Rose to follow her. They picked up their purses and hurried down the hall. As they went, Rose peered at the other closed doors. One was marked JANITOR'S CLOSET, one was marked LINENS, and a third TOILETRIES.

"Oooh!" Blanche said. "Maybe we can get some of those

teeny-tiny shampoos!" She tried the door, but it was locked.

"Come on," said Rose. "Let's try to find Patricia's office. Maybe she'll be a little more helpful than her parents."

"Where do you think they keep those chocolates they put on your pillow?" Blanche said, jogging to keep up with Rose. "Perhaps we could find some of those."

When they reached the elevator banks, Rose stopped, wondering if she should push the up or down button. "I didn't see an office for Patricia," she said. "And she's the manager. Where do you think it is?"

"We've always seen her running around the main floor. That's probably our best bet for finding her."

Rose nodded, and they took the elevator to the first floor. Patricia wasn't behind the front desk, so the two women circled the lobby, keeping an eye out for the statuesque woman. A man in a magenta blazer was checking in a family of four. Other than a few bellhops at their stations and a tourist couple applying ever more sunscreen, no one else was visible in the lobby.

"We'll have to go farther than just the lobby," Blanche said, waving Rose to follow her down a hallway behind the front desk. "Maybe she's in one of the other areas."

As Rose and Blanche rounded the corner, they bumped into two mysterious figures—literally. As their bodies collided, Rose tottered backward into Blanche, who caught her under the armpits, preventing her from falling to the floor. A drab little figure was similarly held under their arms by a sexy woman in tight, alluring clothing in a swirl of colors.

*A lady of the evening!* Rose thought. *How exciting!* She didn't know they came out during the day.

As Rose blinked, the stranger snapped into focus. The woman's full pout transformed into a frown.

"Oh, for Pete's sake," the lady of the evening said. Her voice was deep, sultry, and stern. And oddly familiar.

The lady lowered her sunglasses; Dorothy's eyes bored into Rose's.

"Oh my!" Rose gasped. "I didn't even—"

"How could you not recognize us—*you* dressed us!" Dorothy growled. "These jeans were *your* idea!"

"Well . . . the way you wear them . . . is very convincing," Rose said, untangling herself from Blanche's arms.

"Is everybody all right?" said Blanche. She picked up Sophia's purse, which had fallen to the floor in the collision. Rose dusted off Sophia's shoulders and straightened her kerchief.

"I thought I was a goner!" Sophia cried, pushing off their attempts at helping her. "I always feared the end would come in the back of some hotel, pressed between a couple of floozies!"

Blanche laughed so hard she snorted, and Dorothy groaned. "Oh, Ma, please. For everyone's sakes, wield your vivid imagination more carefully."

"Please keep your voices down!" Rose hissed as she smoothed her pale green button-down shirt. "We don't want to draw any attention to ourselves."

"You're right," Dorothy said, pushing her sunglasses back up her nose and trying to hide her face with the tourist map. Rose's eyes darted around the hallway. In the skintight jeans and dramatic makeup, the woman before her was hardly recognizable as her friend, but she didn't want to take any chances.

"Have you all found out anything? Seen any suspicious characters returning to the scene of the crime?" Blanche whispered.

"Oh, us?" Sophia said. Her tone was suspiciously casual, and she looked down at her orthopedic shoes. "Maybe we should wait and compare notes at the end of the day."

Dorothy grimaced, then turned to Blanche. "We did see something suspicious, but you aren't going to be happy about it."

Rose and Blanche leaned forward. *Maybe they've seen the perp!* Rose thought. Maybe, just maybe, they could pinpoint the killer, get Dorothy off the hook, and triumphantly place Nettie's wedding back onto the cowpath. Blanche stared at Dorothy expectantly.

Dorothy sighed. "We saw Jorgen walking through the lobby with Mrs. Corzon."

Blanche tilted her head and frowned. "Okay, but he's staying here! That doesn't mean that delectable young man is the"—her voice dropped an octave—"*murderer.*"

"I'm not saying he's the murderer," Dorothy said. "But he

looked very cozy with Mrs. Corzon, if you get my drift. It's somewhat suspicious."

"Very cozy," Sophia added. "Like two cannelloni under a blanket of mozzarella."

Blanche's eyes narrowed, and Rose noticed spots of pink appearing on Blanche's cheeks.

*"That woman,"* Blanche practically spat. "She's been trying to get her claws into him, when I clearly found him first! Maybe that's why he didn't answer the phone this morning—she could have been . . . seducing him over room-service eggs Benedict!" Blanche pressed a hand to her chest, as if the idea were too terrible to bear.

Rose thought that sounded rather unsanitary, but she didn't have time to ask questions. She looked from one woman to the next, exasperation flooding her veins—even the varicose ones. The romantic entanglements of Nettie and Jason's best man were not at the top of her priorities right now.

"Blanche, I know you're not happy to hear that, but honestly, we have bigger Tørrfisk to fry! Well, first, you have to salt them, then dip them into a batter of cream, flour, and butter . . . but you know what I mean! Could we *please* focus on catching the killer? We need to find Patricia, and you two need to skedaddle." She looked pointedly at Dorothy and Sophia. It struck her that they did, in fact, look ridiculous, despite the fact that she'd helped them pick out their outfits. Instead of tourists, they looked more like a mismatched vaudeville duo, or perhaps a nun and the lost soul she was trying to save. Either way, she didn't want any of the Bryants recognizing them, or thinking that she'd invited ladies of the evening into their hotel—in broad daylight.

Seeing a familiar figure up ahead, Rose yanked Dorothy behind a colossal potted fern and motioned for Sophia and Blanche to join them just as Patricia appeared at the other end of the hallway. Chip trailed a few steps behind her. He stopped to catch his breath and leaned against the wall. Patricia paused and turned back toward him, jabbing a finger at something on her clipboard, her face stormy. Chip shifted his weight, resting one foot against the wall as she continued her tirade. Thanks to whatever Patricia was yelling about, neither of them noticed the four senior citizens hidden in the greenery.

Rose peered around the fern, watching as the pastel-clad couple disappeared around a corner and out of sight.

"That was close," Blanche said, batting a low-hanging frond away from her décolletage.

"I'll say," Sophia said, waving a hand in front of her nose. "Someone needs a spritz of Binaca! Either that or I'm having a stroke."

"You're fine, Ma," Dorothy said, pulling out her Jackie Collins novel/notebook. "But I'm not so sure about the Bobbsey Twins. I'm adding what we just saw to our case file."

"It did look suspicious, now that you mention it, *Tiffani,*"

Sophia said. "I thought we'd stumbled onto the set of *Who's Afraid of Virginia Woolf!*"

"But what if it was just a lovers' quarrel?" Blanche interjected. "Or something about the running of the hotel? Are we really going to suspect everyone we see?"

Rose bit her lip. She hated suspecting *anyone*, let alone the sister of the person her niece was about to marry. After all, she wanted to think the best of people. She believed that everyone had a good heart, and if they did something wrong, it was because they didn't know better or they were trying to help someone, like the time Dorothy and Blanche overstated Rose's accomplishments for the St. Olaf Woman of the Year Award. Or the time that Rose saw a young mother at the supermarket with a loose thread on her sweater and had secretly yanked on it, thinking she was just helping the girl look nicer but ending up accidentally causing the entire sweater to unravel into a pile of yarn right next to the cantaloupes.

But Patricia had looked different during that heated exchange, with her modelesque good looks distorted in anger. *Can anyone commit a crime of passion if they get angry enough?* Rose wondered. She drifted off into a mental daydream where Sophia was a soot-smudged pickpocket in Dickensian London, lifting watches and wallets from unsuspecting crowds and leading a band of ragtag seniors through smoggy alleyways. She imagined Blanche as a carjacker, enticing men to pull over to pick her up next to a supposedly broken-down Buick, then speeding away in their Corvettes and Porsches with a chiffon scarf blowing in the breeze. Her daydream shifted to Dorothy rappelling down a rocky cliff in a black tactical suit and sunglasses, lifting a shiny gun outfitted with a silencer. A heartless assassin who could kill with her sharp wit or the blade hidden in her boot. Finally, she saw herself, dressed in a flannel shirt, gleefully lighting match after match and dropping them onto a pile of kindling that caught fire against the side of the home of Lacy Lindstrom, the woman Rose strongly suspected had tampered with her churn before her ill-fated Butter Queen upset. The blaze crackled and grew, the orange glow casting devilish-looking shadows across Rose's face as she set fire to the wooden house.

Rose gulped and shook the images from her head, now eyeing each of her dear friends with a fearful expression. Anyone could be a criminal, she realized. Anyone.

Maybe she had been too trusting of humanity. She knew that some would say that Rose Nylund was naive. Actually, many had said it. Rose vowed then and there to treat everyone except her housemates as a potential suspect, no matter how innocent they seemed.

"I'm going to interrogate anyone who even looks the least bit suspicious, and nothing—absolutely *nothing*—can stop me!" Rose said, drawing herself up and straightening her shoulders. She whirled around to follow Patricia and walked straight into what felt like a side of beef.

She looked up to see Cousin Gustave glaring down at her. Behind him, the rest of the St. Olafians eyed Rose expectantly.

# THE BIG SCHLEP
## ·············16·············

*J*ust who I was looking for!" Gustave intoned in his lilting baritone. "The wedding week schedule indicates a tour of Miami, led by you. You're fifteen minutes late."

Rose's insides turned to ice. She'd completely forgotten about the tour, what with all the hubbub of Dorothy getting arrested, the Bryants taking over the wedding, and the excitement of the stakeout. She clapped a hand over her mouth, internally chastising herself. If she'd forgotten about this, what other wedding details might she be forgetting?

This was one more screwup in her list of wedding disasters.

The crowd behind Gustave murmured uneasily. Being late was seen as a moral failing in the Midwest, and punctuality was so important to the town that it was actually written into the bylaws. If a business said it was open at nine a.m., it had better be open at nine a.m. Otherwise the townspeople were legally allowed to throw rotten eggs at said business or proprietor. It was a rule that hadn't been enforced often during Rose's upbringing in St. Olaf, but the sulfurous smell of the eggs tended to hang around the occasional offender for days. To her that scent was synonymous with shame.

Blanche swept to Rose's rescue. "Actually, she's early for Miami time. It's considered rude here *not* to be fifteen minutes behind schedule."

Rose turned to her in surprise.

"Just go with it, honey," Blanche muttered out of the side of her mouth.

"It's my mistake," Rose said. "I should have told you about the customs here."

Gustave harrumphed. "Well, we are here. Where is the charter bus?"

"Oh, the charter bus!" Rose said brightly, stalling for time. She remembered scheduling it days ago, but she'd never called to confirm. Or had she? If only she had been focused on the wedding planning instead of playing detective! Either way, she'd lost track of time, and now had a busload of relatives to wrangle. "I'll just locate the . . . uh, itinerary." Rose rummaged in her purse. But she only had her wallet, a tube of lipstick, some tissues, a few sticks of Juicy Fruit, a wooden yo-yo, and a Swiss Army knife that Charlie had given her when they'd been on a family road trip and she'd needed to trim a hangnail.

She rummaged some more, buying time. She hadn't had a chance yet to speak with Nettie and Jason about the new wedding upheavals—let alone her plans to fix everything. That conversation needed to happen in private. It would be delicate, and possibly unpleasant—at least until she was able to get Nettie and Jason to understand that all would be back on track as soon as could be. Now the entire bride's side of the wedding was standing in the Cabana Sun lobby staring at her, waiting for her to take them on a tour of Miami's sights and culture.

"The tour I have planned is actually going to be led by me and . . . Sophia. She has a wonderful knowledge of the city, having lived here for many years. She's a pillar of the community and can show us all the culturally significant locations."

Sophia winked. "Eh, I know a few things. Like where the bodies are, and also where to get a good nectarine." She pulled off her kerchief and stuffed it into her wicker purse. "Come on, and *bienvenidos a Miami*, as they say."

Rose let out a grateful sigh that Sophia was able to switch gears and play along so quickly. Sophia may not have been the fastest on her feet, but she could sure think on them.

Gustave looked at Blanche, a rare smile of appreciation stretching the stern lines of his face. "And will your other friends be joining us? The lovely belle of the South, and the ah, murderess?"

As Blanche preened, twisting her hips from side to side as she absorbed the compliment, Dorothy glowered beneath the brim of her hat and a pound of makeup.

"Well, Dorothy's not a murderess, or a criminal of any sort. But she can't make it anyway," Rose said, seeing Dorothy slowly edge backward toward the abundant fern. "She's sick, actually. With . . ."

Rose paused. All she could think of were ailments that had afflicted her family's farm animals over the years: worms, mites, and bumblefoot. *Can people get hoof-and-mouth?*

As Dorothy disappeared behind the fern, Blanche stepped forward. "Oh, she just has a touch of a summer flu. I'm just on my way back to take care of her. I'm the nurturing sort, you see."

"I see," said Gustave, seemingly entranced by Blanche's fluttering hands, the silky belted orange jacket that floated around her hips, and the aquamarine necklace that twinkled just above her solar plexus.

*"Andiamo!"* Sophia bellowed, shocking him out of his state. Motioning for the rest of the group to follow her out of the lobby, she led them all out at a pace as slow as their hometown.

Blanche leaned close to Rose and whispered, "Now what do we do? Our plan has wilted like an unwatered camellia, and now our teams are split up."

While Rose listened, she pasted a broad midwestern smile on her face as she nodded and waved to her array of cousins. "We'll just have to improvise. Let's do what we can, and I'll do my best to catch up to you before you can say Heidi Flugendugelgurgenplotz."

Though Rose put on a pleasant expression, her stomach twisted in knots as she faced her latest mess. How in the world would she be able to pull off a tour of Miami with a bus full of people who didn't yet realize they'd been disinvited from the wedding *and* catch a killer? She simply couldn't do it. She wasn't at all capable.

Maybe Gustave had been right all along. She wasn't up for the job.

"I just can't do this!" Rose whimpered, trying to control herself. "I can't do it all."

"Oh, honey, you don't have to," said Blanche, putting an arm around her. "I'm here to help you. And so is Dorothy."

"It's *Tiffani*," Dorothy said, as she emerged from the leafy fern's embrace and huddled close to Rose, keeping much of her face hidden beneath her hat. "You're not alone, Rose. You have us. So *use* us."

Rose let out a little laugh, taking in the sincerity of Dorothy's expression under the layers of makeup, which had gotten smudged in their collision.

"You certainly are," Rose said, gesturing to Dorothy's outfit, when a loud beep, presumably from the bus, echoed from beyond the lobby doors and made her jump. "But how can I make progress on the investigation, or the wedding, if I'm tied up for hours on this bus?"

"That is a predicament," Blanche acknowledged.

"It'll be like a self-contained family reunion on wheels—without a smorgasbord! And what if someone uses the bathroom on the bus?" Rose shivered at the thought.

"Let's try to look at this as an opportunity," Dorothy said, pointing toward the outside. "*That* out there is a busload of suspects."

Rose let out a half whimper, half snort. "But those are my relatives! People from St. Olaf are kind and honest. They couldn't have had anything to do with the murder."

"Perhaps," said Blanche. "But didn't you just say that you were going to investigate everyone, no matter how innocent they seemed? *And* that you'd let nothing stop you?"

Rose's own words echoed in her head. So did the visions she'd had of herself cheerfully committing (justified) arson, and *she* was from St. Olaf. Anyone could be a criminal, she reminded herself.

Anyone.

"You're right," she said. "And maybe I can keep an eye out for a wedding venue as we traverse the city. The Bryants want to hold it at the hotel, and we cannot have it at the scene of a crime!"

"That's the spirit!" Blanche said, squeezing Rose's arm.

"It's settled, then," Dorothy said. "You two do the tour and Blanche and I will continue to investigate here."

Her friends were coming through for her, yet again. Rose hugged them both. "Thank you," she said. "Now I've got a bus to catch!"

"Don't let Ma take you on a detour to Shady Pines—those good people can't handle it!" Dorothy yelled after her friend.

Rose raced through the revolving doors to find an idling charter bus under the portico with the phrase YOUR ONLY AFFORDABLE OPTION! painted in peeling blue paint along the side.

Sophia sat in the front seat just behind the driver with a lavalier microphone pinned to her dress. Jason and Nettie sat in the row opposite, both rosy-cheeked and glowing. They must have had a really good breakfast complete with Florida orange juice, Rose thought.

Nettie wore a red-and-white striped sundress that coordinated nicely with Jason's navy polo shirt and white shorts. They didn't look like tourists from St. Olaf, but they didn't quite look like Miami locals either. A bit of both, Rose decided.

Rose grabbed onto the back of Nettie's seat as the bus lurched away from the hotel.

"And we're off!" Sophia said a bit too loudly into the microphone, causing it to screech. "This is the famous Collins Avenue, in the neighborhood of North Beach. Here you'll find many art deco buildings, hotels, restaurants, and the place where I once lost a button. Keep an eye out for a small mother-of-pearl. Also keep an eye out for a short guy named Mickey with one eye. He owes me fifty cents."

A few of the St. Olafians snapped photos of the hotels with festive awnings, terraces full of people dining al fresco, and the glamorous sports cars carrying equally glamorous people.

"Cher did a press conference right there," Sophia said, pointing out the Boulevard Hotel, a white building outlined in red. "Pretty nice restrooms there. When you're my age, you want to know where the best ones are." A few of the older bus riders murmured in agreement.

Rose settled herself behind Jason and Nettie, leaning forward into the space between their seatbacks. The two of them were looking at each other, and not at any of the sights visible through the bus windows.

Rose cleared her throat. "I hate to interrupt you two lovebirds, but I have some wedding details to discuss with you."

"That's wonderful," Nettie said, turning to Rose. "We've been talking about it, and we've decided that we're totally on board with all of the St. Olaf stuff. We want to fully honor all of the traditions!"

Rose raised her eyebrows. "You do? What made you change your mind?" Inside, her heart sank. If only she could give that to them. Clearly the Bryants hadn't said anything to them yet about their draconian change of plans.

"I've always loved St. Olaf, and all its traditions," Jason

chimed in. "But we've given more thought to the trust. Nettie and I have been talking about starting a family, and with that help, we could move out of our little apartment and get a starter home." He blushed a little bit, then looked out the window as two men roller-skated by on the sidewalk holding hands.

"And I want to get my master's in teaching," Nettie said. "So we could really use the money. And since Jason loves St. Olaf so much, we might as well. It's not that I hate the traditions. Some of them are kind of fun. There just are *a lot* of them!" she said with a giggle.

"That's true," Rose said, thinking of the long list plus the additions Gustave had given her. She had to admit, the ceremonies, outfits, foods, and songs were extensive and often elaborate. They didn't seem that way back in St. Olaf, when you had an entire village participating and helping to prepare everything. It was a whole other kettle of ham when you had to do it all yourself in a completely different location.

She struggled to keep her expression upbeat. This was exactly what she wanted them to want, but now that it was all in jeopardy it seemed cruel to tell them that it might not happen after all. But she *had* to tell them—it was the right thing to do. Plus, sooner or later they'd hear about the new plans from the Bryants.

"I have to tell you something, but I'd like you to keep it between us for now," Rose said. She couldn't bear to tell her other relatives that they were disinvited from the wedding—even if it was just temporary. She'd need to gather her talking points, courage, and about a liter of Aquavit before she could begin to broach that topic with Gustave.

"We're passing through Midtown on our way to Little Havana." Sophia's voice crackled over the bus speakers. "Also, the bus driver asks that all passengers refrain from eating seafood products for the duration of the ride."

Rose's third cousin Cheryl, twice removed and once replaced, lowered a plastic baggie of dried fish back into her purse. One of Nettie's relations on her father's side recapped a jar of smoked whitefish and tucked it back into his sweater pocket.

"As you know, there has been some tension regarding the wedding and . . . certain unfortunate events," Rose began, twisting her wedding ring around on her finger.

"You mean the expired cheesecake?" Jason asked.

Nettie stiffened. Jason rubbed her arm. "Sorry, I mean the deceased gentleman whose demise is absolutely not an omen about our wedding or future happiness?"

"I've been trying not to think about it," Nettie said quietly. "You know I'm not superstitious, Aunt Rose, but it didn't seem like a good sign, you know?"

Rose smoothed the back of Nettie's hair. She fought the urge to part it and twist it into two braids, just like she'd done when her cousin was little. Sometimes, Nettie would ask for a French braid. Those had always been too hard for Rose, turning out lopsided and lumpy, with wisps of the girl's hair coming loose before Rose could even tie a bow at the bottom. So Rose had invented the St. Olaf braid, which was much easier: three regular braids, braided together. She wondered if Nettie remembered asking for that braid on her first day of kindergarten, saying that only her aunt Rose knew how to do it right. Once, she hadn't had any ribbon to add, so she'd used a shoelace, which had made Nettie giggle.

"It's not a bad omen," Rose said. "In St. Olaf lore, there are only good omens mentioned when it comes to weddings." Rose tapped her fingers on the back of the bus seat. "Let's see—there's the obvious one, that if it rains on your wedding day, that's good luck."

"Isn't it ironic, then, that we're getting married in Miami, where the sun is constantly shining?" Nettie said. "Are there any other good omens?"

"Well, sure." Rose racked her brain. "If a bird flies over the head of the bride, that's good luck. Usually it's a common loon or a great blue heron, but seagulls work too."

"There are lots of seagulls here," Jason pointed out. "And those noisy green parrots—I bet those are extra lucky."

Nettie smiled. Jason always knew what to say to cheer her up. Rose liked that about him.

"And of course, if you get kicked by a mule, or even a donkey, and survive, that's *very* good luck. . . . That only applies to the groom, though," Rose said thoughtfully. She smiled suddenly. "Oh, we do have a donkey reserved from a petting zoo to carry Jason down the aisle, so there's still a chance!"

Jason gulped.

Rose continued. "If a baby cries at the ceremony, you'll have good fortune, and if a goat breaks loose from its pen, that means your life together will be an adventure, and of course we'll arrange for the uninflated balloon drop."

"Why uninflated?" Jason asked.

"It's because back in St. Olaf, the choir boys once used balloons to make some very rude noises, so they made a new rule that only uninflated balloons are allowed at weddings," Nettie said, grinning. "I like to think there's at least one St. Olaf tradition I know better than you." She patted Jason lovingly on the leg.

"I'm sure we'll have more good omens," Rose said. "And I'm working hard to make sure that everything we need for each tradition is in place. However, we've temporarily hit a small snag." She paused, waiting for her niece's face to fall, but Nettie only looked at her expectantly.

"What's the problem?" Jason asked. "Is it my parents? Are they insisting on lace napkins or something? They're such bulldogs when it comes to what they want. I had to move ten states away just to break free of their iron fists."

"Well, yes," Rose began. "I hate to say it, because you have a lovely family, Jason." She crossed her fingers behind her back. She didn't want to hurt the young man's feelings, even if he agreed with her about their behavior. "It seems that because of the attention on Dorothy related to the, um, unexpected contents of the hotel freezer, the Bryants are under the impression that they will be taking over the wedding planning."

"What!" Nettie cried. "Why would they be under that impression?"

Jason put his head in his hands and groaned. "I knew they'd do this! If you're in a fifty-mile radius of their domain, they will try to control everything!"

"They, uh . . . they informed me of this," Rose said. "They basically gave me an ultimatum."

Nettie threw her head back and let out a ragged noise that was 50 percent groan, 25 five percent sigh, and 25 percent shriek. It was a sound Rose hadn't heard since her own daughters were teenagers. It was a sound that made her want to jump out of the bus window for fear of hearing it again. The audible frustration of teenage girls, with a healthy dose of disappointment in their mothers (or aunt, in this case) felt like being dipped in boiling molasses, and Rose couldn't stand it.

"Now listen here. I have a plan to fix this. It's already underway. You will have a wonderful St. Olaf wedding if it kills me!"

"Don't say that!" Jason said. "We can't have anyone else die this week, okay?"

Rose didn't tell them how harsh Mr. and Mrs. Bryant had been or how coldly they'd disinvited the entirety of St. Olaf. She wanted to protect the couple from that as much as she could, even though she wished she could share exactly what a difficult undertaking this all was for her.

"The thing is," Rose said, "I think it's best if we keep this between us for now. Cousin Gustave and our other relatives don't need to know about this. As far as they're concerned, the St. Olaf wedding will continue as planned. Do you understand me?"

Rose stared at Jason, who nodded obediently.

She looked at Nettie, waiting for her to do so as well.

"So you want me to lie?" Nettie said. "That's, like, the opposite of what you've always taught me."

Feelings of guilt and trepidation square-danced in Rose's chest. She was doing the right thing—she knew it. She just had to convince Nettie.

"You don't have to *lie*," she said. "Just don't bring it up. Carry on as usual. Once I finish handling this, it will have always been the truth. Can you do that, for me?"

Rose tamped down her worry and tried to project a confident demeanor.

Nettie looked up at her. "I'll do it for you, Aunt Rose."

Suddenly the bus lurched to a halt. "We're stopping at Haulover Beach for photos," Sophia announced. "You can all take turns posing like Farrah Fawcett or acting out that famous scene with Burt Lancaster and Deborah Kerr."

# LEAVE NO PICKLE UNTURNED
## ·············17···········

*B*ack at the Cabana Sun Hotel, Dorothy and Blanche stared at each other, wondering what to do next.

"Ma and I had been about to explore the back rooms," Dorothy said. "Maybe we should continue with that plan?"

Blanche looked dubiously at Dorothy. "Your disguise is good, but if Patricia or anyone else sees you with me, they might guess that it's you."

"Or they might just think we're a couple of working girls," Dorothy said dryly. "I haven't felt like this since, well, *the* other *time we went to a hotel and people thought we were working girls.*"

"Oh, hush," Blanche said. "I can't help it if I exude sensuality, like a magnolia blossom offering her delicate scent to the languid breeze. Besides, I'm dressed much more respectably than you."

"It was *you all* who dressed me—" Dorothy stopped herself and took a breath. "Well, I'm not sure what I'm exuding, but I'm sweating. Is this top polyester? And we need to find some answers. Because I cannot go to jail!"

"Right," said Blanche. "I think we should nix the hotel and try somewhere else."

"Hmmm." Dorothy thought. Where else could they investigate? Though the murder had taken place in the hotel, surely the perpetrator didn't spend all their time there. But where would they have come from, or gone to?

Dorothy wondered how all those detectives in her beloved novels did it. Even though Dorothy knew she was bright, she wasn't Sherlock Holmes. She didn't know if a smudge on someone's shoe meant that they had been fishing at the Newport Pier or that a broken palm frond meant that a man in a purple hat had crossed NE 125th Street three days ago. Come to think of it, how could Sherlock even have known that, *really*?

One thing that detectives did—at least on those TV shows that Rose loved—was to retrace the steps of their victim. But Dorothy didn't know what Henry had been up to in the few days between when she saw him alive and not alive.

She felt more like the bumbling Columbo and less like the my-bumbling-had-a-purpose-all-along Columbo. Thinking of Columbo made her think of all those scenes where dreamy Peter Falk was eating chili. Which made her a bit peckish.

Which made her realize that she *did* know one place Henry had been just a few days before his death.

"I've got an idea," she said. "Follow me."

"Do you want to go home and change first?" Blanche asked as she hustled to keep up with Dorothy's long-legged stride.

"No time!" Dorothy called, already out the revolving doors and pulling the hot hat and wig combo from her head. The fresh air felt cool on her scalp, and she took a deep breath—or as deep as the waistband of her daughter's jeans would allow.

Wolfie's was bustling—even busier than the last time Dorothy had been there. She pushed past the line of people waiting to be seated, Blanche bobbing and weaving in her wake.

Dorothy swiveled her head, scanning for any other faces who'd been there that day. She wished she'd paid better attention to the crowd on their date. But of course, she'd only had eyes for Henry and his rugged smile, his salt-and-pepper sideburns perfectly framing his face, his tan from hours spent on his boat . . . and then, of course, she'd been focused on navigating the awkwardness of their interaction. Of course she hadn't paid attention to anything else—why would she have? She could never have guessed that a few days later Henry would be murdered and she'd be the number one suspect.

The whole date came rushing back to her as she took in the scent of the frying griddle cakes and the nutty aroma of fresh coffee, the sound of clanking silverware, and the bubbling conversation among Wolfie's clientele.

Dorothy frowned as she remembered how Henry had acted a bit strangely on that date. *So did I*, she admitted to herself. But with hindsight, had something else been going on with him? At the time, she'd assumed it was because of her. That she wasn't good enough, pretty enough, or interesting enough for him. The way he'd kept leaning his head down toward the menu, almost as if he'd been avoiding someone. That subtle head-ducking gesture was now familiar—Dorothy had been doing it all morning, hiding her face behind a newspaper while trying not to be too obvious about it.

As Dorothy made her way to the back of the restaurant to the server station, she also recalled how he'd excused himself and unceremoniously left her at the table. Maybe it had been more than awkwardness or a sudden desire to abandon their date.

"I wonder if Henry saw someone here and got spooked," Dorothy mused. She realized she sounded like every woman who'd ever been stood up, looking for a reason. But this man had ended up dead, not just out with another woman.

"Like one of his lady marks?" Blanche said. "It's certainly

possible. Everyone eats here. Maybe . . . maybe someone threatened him, and he had to leave in a hurry!"

"But he paid the bill. And he talked to the waitress, who told me so. He'd at least had time to do that." Dorothy snapped her fingers. "We need to *find that waitress.*"

Dorothy stopped a young man with jet-black hair in a waiter's uniform. "I'm looking for a waitress. Blond. I think her name is Kimberly?"

"She's in the back," he said in a melodious Dominican accent. "May I tell her what this is about? Was your food okay?"

"No problem with the food," Dorothy said. "I—I just forgot to tip her."

She felt a little guilty about fibbing, but she didn't want to scare anyone off. Sometimes you had to lie to get to the truth.

The young man disappeared, then reappeared with a blond woman Dorothy recognized.

"You were looking for me?" Kimberly said warily. "I don't remember serving you this morning."

"I forgot to tip you," Dorothy said loudly, rummaging in her purse. She held out a five-dollar bill. When Kimberly stepped forward to take it, Dorothy leaned in close. "Could I ask you a few questions?"

"I had nothing to do with the Knish Incident," Kimberly said. "I swear. I'm more of a bagel girl."

Dorothy and Blanche exchanged glances.

"No, we're not here about knishes. I wanted to know if

you remember serving me and a man here a few days ago."

Kimberly looked from Dorothy to Blanche. "We don't normally see your type come in until late night, and I'm usually off then."

Dorothy looked down at her ensemble and rolled her eyes. "I'm dressed for a Halloween party."

"In June?" Kimberly said. "Wait, are you an undercover cop or something? I told you, I had nothing to do with the Incident. We lost a lot of good knish that day."

"I was dressed more modestly, in a cream-colored blouse, and I was with a man, handsome, my age, very distinguished. He wore glasses and had a nice watch."

Kimberly stared out over the crowded dining room. "Maybe," she said. "I serve a lot of older people breakfast." She glanced pointedly at Dorothy's purse.

"Oh, for Pete's sake." Dorothy pulled a few more bills from her purse and handed them to Kimberly, who expertly tucked them into her apron pocket. "We ordered pickles," Dorothy said. "And then he left early. He paid the bill first, though."

Kimberly's eyes lit up. "I remember!" she said. "I saw him come out of the men's room, white as a sheet. Then he paid me and practically ran out of here. He didn't even want to check the bill. Most men of his age check every little thing and calculate the tip right down to the decimal point, you know what I mean?"

*White as a sheet*, Dorothy thought. Yes, someone must have

spooked him. Maybe someone had followed him into the men's room and confronted him.

"Did he say anything?" Dorothy asked. "Did you see anyone else come out of the bathroom right around then?"

"Listen, I'm pretty busy. I only remember it because he was kind of good-looking, you know, for an old geezer."

Dorothy bit her lip. Henry wasn't a geezer, not by a long shot. But now was not the time to lecture this twenty-something.

"Of course, but please try to remember—it's important. Was there anyone else hanging around him, maybe looking suspicious?"

Kimberly thought for a moment, twirling a strand of hair around her finger.

"Maybe this table of businessmen who left soon after you did? I only remember because they barely tipped and didn't finish their omelets. *Everyone* finishes their omelets here."

Dorothy vaguely remembered seeing some men in suits a few tables over. She was making progress.

"Write all this down," she told Blanche, handing her the Jackie Collins logbook.

"Anything else?" Dorothy said to the waitress. She didn't have any more dollar bills to hand out, but she scrounged in the bottom of her purse, found a few coins, and handed them over.

Kimberly glanced down with a look of disappointment but took them.

"There was one more thing that seemed kinda weird," she said. "When I saw the guy who jilted you—"

"We don't know that he *jilted* her; perhaps he was *called away* unexpectedly," Blanche interrupted. "Sometimes men just have to leave suddenly. It doesn't mean that the woman he's with isn't a perfect companion."

"Right . . ." Kimberly said slowly. "Well, anyway, he was wearing different clothes when he came out of the bathroom. He had a T-shirt on and a pair of shorts—way more casual than when he came in."

Dorothy and Blanche exchanged a look. *That's odd*, Dorothy thought.

A kitchen bell dinged nearby. "Look, I've gotta go," said Kimberly. "I have tables to cover, and anyway, that's all I know."

She turned on her heel and went back to the kitchen.

Dorothy pulled Blanche behind the server station, where empty plates clattered loudly into tubs.

"What do you make of the change of clothes?" Dorothy shouted over the din.

"The change of life?" Blanche shouted. "I wouldn't know. Hasn't happened to me yet."

"Change of *clothes*! The *outfit* change, Blanche!" Dorothy hollered.

Blanche motioned for Dorothy to follow her outside, where they could hear again.

"I think it's very suspicious," she said when they were on the street again.

"Who brings a change of clothes to lunch?" Dorothy asked. "It's strange."

"Maybe he thought he was going to get lucky, so he packed a bag," Blanche said. "Did you notice a bag at all?"

"I didn't. And why would he assume he'd get to spend the night after a lunch date? That's a long time to the next morning."

"It doesn't feel like a long time if you know what you're doing," Blanche said with a twinkle in her eye.

"Oh, please, can you be serious? We have to figure this out, for my sake—and Rose's! Not to mention poor Nettie and Jason's."

"Those two kids," Blanche said, shaking her head. "They have no idea what we're all going through for this wedding."

"Isn't that just the way, with young people? They never know how much we do for their happiness." Dorothy thought back to her own children and the sacrifices she'd made for them. The biggest one really had been staying with Stan. If she had to do it all over again, she wouldn't have stayed so long.

Dorothy rubbed the back of her hand across her sweaty cheek and came away with a muddy orange swath of bronzer and blush on her skin. It was almost noon, and the hot Miami sun beat down on Wolfie's parking lot.

Blanche was similarly melting in the heat. Blanche tried to cool herself with a silk fan, but despite her vigorous efforts, her short caramel hairdo drooped in the heat and beads of sweat glistened on her forehead.

"Let's get out of here," she said. "I could go with a tall glass of lemonade right about now."

Dorothy pulled up to the Rusty Anchor and they entered the dark, cavelike interior. The cool air was welcome after the pounding heat outside, even if it smelled like stale beer and old peanut shells.

"This is exactly what I needed! A shady escape and some lemonade," Blanche said, trailing her fingers along the beat-up baby grand piano, where she'd been known to breathily purr a tune or two. She hopped up on a barstool and promptly signaled something to the bartender that he acknowledged with a wink.

Dorothy leaned against the bar, resting her elbows on the slightly sticky surface. She wanted to give her feet a rest, but she wasn't sure she could sit down again in these jeans without cutting off circulation to all her major organs. She ordered a ginger ale and put her notebook on the wooden bar.

The bartender placed a large mint julep in front of Blanche, and she took a very long sip.

Dorothy eyed the cocktail in its tin cup. "What happened to lemonade?"

"After all this sleuthing, I need something stiffer than a frozen corpse to bring me back to life," Blanche said before adding, "oh, I'm sorry, I didn't mean to be crude about your departed beau."

"It's all right," Dorothy said with a rueful frown.

"Speaking of Henry, let's compare notes . . . Do you have yours?"

Blanche pulled out the crumpled lingerie receipt from her purse and smoothed it on the bar. Dorothy peered at Blanche's fancy cursive, jotting down her own notations about the mail bins and the collection notices in her notebook. Then she turned to a fresh page and drew numerous circles across two pages.

Inside the circles she wrote names and places such as *Hotel*, *Wolfie's*, and the names of everyone she could think of from the past week. She also left several circles blank.

"We don't know what we don't know," she said, drawing a question mark inside one of the circles.

"We sure don't," Blanche said, munching on the fresh mint garnish from her drink. "I'm not even clear on what we *do* know."

"Me neither," said Dorothy, discreetly sliding off one shoe and rubbing the sole against the side of her calf. She was already tired from running around town, and the darkness of the bar made her yearn for the comfort of her bed even though the day was still young.

"Let's make a list," she said. "Everything we do know, and what we know we don't know. It's not perfect, but it's a start. What do you think?"

"I don't know," Blanche said. "How do you know what you don't know, you know?"

# THE SUSPECTS ON THE BUS GO
# ROUND AND ROUND
## ·············18··············

*S*ophia and Rose stood on a boardwalk with a pile of cameras at their feet. They took turns snapping photos of the St. Olaf visitors posing with the vibrant cobalt ocean behind them. They had all kicked off their sensible shoes and were enjoying the feel of the powdery white sand under their toes.

Gustave stepped away from the group and leaned toward Rose.

"They are certainly making memories, ja?" he said. "This trip is one for the history books! I never thought I'd see

Cousin Hilde making angels in the sand." He gestured to an older woman who lay on the beach laughing. Next to her, a ten-year-old with light-brown hair worked intently on a lumpy sandcastle while a few of the younger men checked out the assortment of bikini-clad women on the beach. If it wasn't for the drama between the families—or the murder—this would be the perfect day, Rose thought.

Just then, a cart offering Italian ices rolled by and Jason bought treats for the whole group, handing them out one by one.

Nettie loved her lemon ice so much that she licked the paper cup, coming away with a bit of it on her nose, which Jason thoughtfully dabbed away with a handkerchief.

Rose didn't know any young people who still carried hand-kerchiefs. She had monogrammed a set of plain cotton ones for Charlie, and he'd always kept one in his pocket. He'd offered them to her when she was tearful, or when her lipstick had smeared after necking in the back of his car. Thank goodness he'd had one when they'd visited the botanical gardens in Milwaukee. Some pollen there had made her sneeze so hard that she'd blown Charlie's fedora clean off his head. He'd simply laughed and used the handkerchief on himself that day.

Rose blinked hard and looked away from the shimmering ocean to the parking lot and dabbed at her eyes with a disin-tegrating tissue. Oh, Charlie—how she missed him. She could use his love and his calm practicality now more than ever.

Gustave had followed Rose, curious about her lack of

composure. She wiped away a stray tear and cleared her throat.

"Let's hope they are all good memories, yes?" Gustave continued. Though, of course, if everyone enjoys themselves here too much, they won't want to go back to St. Olaf! I'll be all alone, a town elder with no town."

"Oh, that would never happen," said Rose. "St. Olaf is a special place. It's their home!"

"It's yours, too," Gustave said. "And you left. Permanently, only to come back a few times."

That was true, Rose thought. But it wasn't the crystal waters and golden sunshine that had lured her to Miami. It was because after Charlie died, she needed to go someplace where she wasn't faced with all the details of their lives together. Even so, she thought, she never stopped thinking about him.

"Leaving St. Olaf isn't for everyone," she said. "In fact, it's very hard. I had to adjust to everything being more expensive, for one. Not having winter feels strange, but every day I'm happy for the warmth. And I do hate not getting fresh milk right from the cow; it still pains me to buy gallons from the store. Can I tell you a secret?"

Gustave raised his bushy eyebrows.

"I keep a butter churn in my room!" Rose said. "It's hard to give up the closet space, but it's worth it. Sometimes, when the moon is full, or I've had a bad day, or the humidity is right, or the Dow is up, I go in there and churn and churn and churn. I even put the butter in those little plastic tubs in our fridge. I haven't had to buy butter in years!"

Gustave chuckled. "Oh, Rose, I see there's so much of St. Olaf still inside you. But why does your churning have to be in secret?"

"Because Blanche thinks one of the tubs is margarine! She can't know I refill it with regular butter."

Rose and Gustave erupted into belly laughs. For a moment, he looked like he had as a younger man in St. Olaf, before he'd become so stern, burdened by the responsibilities of a town elder.

"All aboard!" Sophia shouted from the steps of the bus. "Next stop, Little Havana!"

As the bus rolled past brightly colored buildings and lines of palm trees, Rose could hear excited whisperings among the St. Olaf citizens.

"Why aren't they listening to me?" Sophia complained. "I'm trying to tell them about the time I danced the rumba with Fidel, a very handsome Cuban gentleman."

"Fidel Santiago! I remember him," Rose said.

"No," Sophia said. "The other one."

"What?" Rose gasped. "When was he last in Miami? And how did you meet him?"

"A lady never tells." Sophia winked.

Rose shook her head. She never knew if Sophia was playing with her or not. "To answer your question, I suspect everyone is concerned about the paint colors. See that beautiful teal building, and that yellow one?" Rose pointed out the window. "Anyone over the age of fifteen in St. Olaf has to sign a pledge not to do that. So they must think everyone here is daring and impetuous."

"I'll never understand your kind," Sophia said. "But I love you like a daughter. Or more like a beloved pet. Speaking of daughters, I hope mine is making some progress on the case. And shouldn't you be interrogating your countrymen?"

Rose surveyed the bus full of slightly sunburned, happy St. Olafians. It was hard to know where to start—none of them looked very suspicious. She zeroed in on the ten-year-old. Though he'd been innocently making sandcastles just a few moments earlier, she knew how ruthless children could be. She thought back to Daisy, the Sunshine Cadet who'd once taken Rose's teddy bear and held him for ransom. Anyone could be a criminal, she reminded herself. No matter how innocent looking.

She carefully walked down the aisle toward the boy and his mother, who had been one of Rose's daughter's classmates in high school. Rose offered them each a stick of Juicy Fruit. The little boy said yes. Rose took a stick for herself. The act of chewing helped calm her nerves, and the flavor always made her think of carefree people on waterskis.

"So," she began, leaning in close to the boy and narrowing her eyes like Don Johnson did when confronting a suspect, "where were you five nights ago?"

Rose had interrogated her way through two-thirds of the bus. Whispers swirled around and past her as her questions stirred up even more questions and worries from the group. It was not what she wanted, but it couldn't be helped. She had to solve this murder, even if it made other people uncomfortable or made Rose look bad. She gritted her teeth and popped another stick of Juicy Fruit every time her confidence faltered.

She reached Aunt Katrina, who had rolled up the sleeves of her cotton dress and accessorized it with a neon sun visor, clearly a recent purchase from a tourist shop.

"How are you liking Miami? Do you have everything you need? Where were you on Saturday night and early Sunday morning?"

No one had seen anything so far, as the people from St. Olaf were early-to-bed types; it seemed none had ventured from their hotel rooms after their arrivals. They'd all been too busy unpacking, marveling at the little dolphin-shaped soaps in the bathrooms, brushing their teeth and getting into sensible pajamas.

Still, Rose had to ask. She didn't like the idea of Dorothy going to jail for something she didn't do. And Rose knew that the criminal justice system in Miami was different from St. Olaf's. For one, she didn't think that the Miami-Dade county jail doubled as a deli. It was just too hot here for that. But even without unreachable hunks of cheese to torture the inmates, Rose imagined that prison life was pretty rough.

"Katrina," Rose began.

"I heard what you're asking everyone," Katrina said in her heavily accented English.

"I'm just gathering information," Rose said.

Isn't that what Detective Silva had said to her? She didn't want to scare off anyone from giving her potential clues. Though she already feared that this bus trip had been one big dead end.

"Where were you on—"

"I was in my bed. Most of the time."

Rose sighed, wondering if she was going to hear about Katrina's intestinal woes or some complaint about street noise reaching her fourth-floor hotel room.

"Go on," Rose said politely, watching the vibrant store-fronts of Little Havana roll past the bus windows.

"I was hungry. I thought I'd treat myself to room service. You see, I've never stayed at a fancy hotel before." She smiled at Rose, as if to excuse the indulgence of ordering room service.

*Ordering room service isn't very midwestern*, Rose thought. She'd never done it herself. And why would she? If you always carried a hunk of Gouda in your purse, you needn't go hungry.

"But when I dialed for room service, the front desk told me, 'No room service available.'"

"Oh, I'm so sorry," Rose said. "I should have told you, the kitchen is under construction."

"Well, I didn't know that. I put on my robe and took the elevator down. I figured I'd make myself a midnight snack.

Maybe there would be bread and ham or cheese available. You know how cheese helps one sleep."

Rose nodded. She remembered giving her little ones tiny cubes of Gjetost to make them tired at bedtime. Oh, how she missed those days. Sometimes she'd give them their Gjetost a little early, so she and Charlie could have some private time.

"When I got to the lobby, the clerk at the front desk was asleep. I could hear his snoring from across the lobby!"

"Did you see anyone? Or anything suspicious?" Rose said, gripping the back of Katrina's seat, wishing the woman would speak a little faster.

"Not at first," Katrina said. "But when I went looking for the kitchen, I heard footsteps! Quick footsteps, like someone was running."

Rose felt her ears prick up like a woodland creature's, and a thrill rose up her spine. Now this was a clue! She was finally getting somewhere!

"Did you see the person running? How tall were they? What did they look like?"

"I was frightened, of course. After all, I didn't know what type of mischief was afoot in a big city hotel when outside it's darker than the inside of a cow after midnight. But I was curious," she said, clearly enjoying drawing out her story now that she had a captive listener.

It was all Rose could do not to shake the rest out of her.

"So I followed these very mysterious footsteps. I had my woolen slippers on, so whoever was making this noise couldn't have heard me. I thought they came from the hallway that leads to the cigar bar."

Rose shifted her weight from one foot to the other. "And? What happened next?"

"I saw them! A shadowy figure carrying something. Like a large sack, over their shoulder."

"Could you see any details?" Rose thought that if she could get a basic description, even just a hair color and gender, that might be enough to bring to the police.

"Well, it could have been burlap or canvas, it was hard to tell in the dark."

"I don't mean the sack! Any details about the person!" Rose urged.

Katrina shook her head. "I'm sorry. It was so dark, and they were moving quickly. I'm pretty sure it was an adult, if that helps."

Rose exhaled forcefully. Of course it was an adult! She didn't think a child would be committing crimes in the middle of the night.

*Sometimes, St. Olaf people can be so dense!*

She stopped that thought in its tracks. This was exactly what people said about her. *Simple. Gullible*, when they were being kind. *Stupid, dumb, slower than a cart with square wheels—a brainless hayseed*—but it just wasn't true.

"What time was it, exactly?" Rose asked. She'd record every detail she could and report back to her friends. Every little thing could be a clue, after all.

"I think it was after midnight. I packed my travel cuckoo clock, you see. And it smelled fresh in the lobby, like a night custodian had just cleaned the floors with Pine-Sol."

"Could you tell if they were slender or not? Muscular? Tall? Anything at all, even from a distance, would be so helpful!"

Katrina considered this question. "They looked to be about average height," she said, as if doling out top-secret information about national security. "Maybe a little taller than that. And . . ."

"And?" Rose said, hoping for just one tiny, microscopic detail she could use.

"And . . ." Katrina said. "Their build, I would say, was very . . . average."

Rose closed her eyes, trying to draw strength from the hardening lump of Juicy Fruit between her molars.

"Average height, average build. Got it," Rose said. It wasn't much, but at least it was a genuine clue. An actual eyewitness sighting that someone suspicious was running around the Cabana Sun Hotel after midnight. And possibly bringing something in—or carrying it out.

"Thank you, Aunt Katrina. You've been very helpful," Rose said.

"It was funny that they were so fast," Katrina said.

Rose was already moving to the next row of the bus to ask her standard questions. She paused, looking over her shoulder at Katrina. "Why's that funny?"

"Because," Katrina said, "they had a limp!"

# THE TRAIL GOES LIMP

## 19

*D*orothy awoke to the sound of pounding rain on the roof. In her peach-wallpapered bedroom she checked the time: nine a.m. She'd slept late, thanks to her exploits the previous day and the fact that the gloomy weather prevented the sun from brightening her room.

After a good stretch, she threw a lightweight robe over her periwinkle nightgown and padded to the kitchen, where Rose stood motionless in a floral pajama set, holding a coffee filter in her hand and a pencil between her teeth.

"Dare I ask?" Dorothy said, taking the filter from Rose and moving to the coffeemaker. She'd brew it extra strong today, she decided as she began to measure the grounds and water.

Rose sat down at the table next to a yellow legal pad half filled with handwritten notes. "I was just thinking about what Aunt Katrina said yesterday."

The coffeemaker sputtered to life, and Dorothy couldn't wait for the pot to fill with dark-brown goodness. She'd found some pieces of the puzzle, but needed a jolt of caffeine if she was going to have a chance at figuring out where they went.

"Was it about the wedding, or about the case?" Dorothy said gently. She knew both weighed heavily on Rose. She wondered if she'd get a circuitous St. Olaf story involving wooden shoes or another adventure about Petunia, Rose's childhood pet cow.

"She said she saw someone that night, running though the hotel lobby! I think she spotted our killer!"

Dorothy rushed over to the kitchen table and sat next to Rose. A cautiously optimistic feeling of hope began to unfurl in her chest.

"This is wonderful news! We have an eyewitness!" Dorothy threw an arm around Rose, shaking her gently.

"I was trying to remember if anyone we've seen this week has a limp," Rose said. "That was the most useful morsel I was able to pry out of her."

"Tell me everything, no matter how small," Dorothy said, scooting her chair closer to Rose. They compared notes, going ever each and every detail they'd observed yesterday, so engrossed that the coffee pot had long finished brewing before they thought to pour themselves a cup.

Behind the kitchen window the sky was gray and palm fronds drooped with moisture.

Sophia tottered through the kitchen door in a fuzzy robe and slippers. She made a beeline for the coffee and poured cups for the three of them.

"What's up, pussycat?" she said, craning her neck to see the notes Rose and Dorothy had been poring over.

"These are our clues, Ma," Dorothy said, taking the coffee gratefully. "I think we just might be getting somewhere." She let the mug warm her hands before taking a deep sniff of the delicious aroma, just like they did in those Folgers commercials.

"Why does it say *LIMP* in capital letters, underlined three times?" Sophia pointed to the legal pad. "What does Stan's sexual performance have to do with the case?"

Rose giggled with a mouth full of coffee, causing her to cough.

"Do we know anyone with a limp?" Dorothy said. "Think—it's important."

Dorothy waited impatiently as Sophia settled herself in the chair on the other side of Rose. She knew her mother's arthritis made her joints stiff in the morning, especially when it rained, so she bit her tongue to keep from telling her to hurry up already.

Then Sophia took a long sip of coffee and set it back down on the table. Dorothy couldn't take it anymore.

"Well?" she said. "None of us are getting any younger here, especially you!"

"Hold your horses," Sophia said sharply. "I happen to know a lot of people with limps, and I'm mentally going through the list. Do you want them alphabetically?"

"Oh, I don't think that's necessary," said Rose. "How about just their names?"

Dorothy looked up to the wooden ceiling fan. *Give me strength*, she prayed. "I should have clarified. We don't need to know everyone you've ever met with a limp. Anyone at the hotel, or in the wedding party, or anyone who might have some sort of connection to Henry."

Sophia thought for a while. "Most of the folks I know are in Shady Pines. They're not moving too fast these days."

"Maybe Blanche saw someone," Rose suggested.

Dorothy shook her head. "We need to cast a wider net and look beyond the people we've interacted with. The killer could be anyone, from anywhere. We need to canvass the hotel staff, see if they've seen anyone with a limp. Maybe it was one of the guests, or someone they've seen around."

Dorothy tuned to Rose. "Did you talk to Patricia yesterday? What did you find out from her?"

"I didn't." Rose shook her head sadly. "I meant to, but

Gustave arrived right when I was trying to find her. Then Sophia and I were stuck on the bus tour."

"Any chance you can talk to her today?" Dorothy was keenly aware that she was still the main suspect. She needed to give the police as many helpful leads as possible—or name the murderer—to get the attention off her.

Rose peered down into her coffee cup. "I have a lot of wedding details to attend to," she said. "We still don't have a ceremony venue and the bachelorette party is tonight. I'm sorry."

Dorothy patted her friend on the hand, reminding herself to be patient. "I know this wedding is important to you," she said. "But there probably won't be a wedding if we don't figure this out."

"I know," said Rose. "The bachelorette party starts at eight. I can devote a few hours to talking to Patricia, getting the word out about the bachelorette party, preparing the herring balls, and tracking down a clown—or at least a clown suit. One of us could do the clown duties, I suppose."

Dorothy and Sophia stared blankly at Rose.

"You know, a clown! A funny person with a red nose and comically large shoes?"

"Rose, we know what a clown is!" Dorothy said, crossing her arms. "We're just wondering why you'd need one in the middle of a wedding-slash-murder investigation!"

"Oh, come on, you mean to tell me neither of you had a clown at your bachelorette festivities? It's tradition!"

Sophia shook her head. "Maybe where you come from. For me, all that happened was my two girlfriends smuggled me out of my parents' house, gave me some homemade sambuca, and said I didn't have to marry my brother. I realized they were right. When I had my second engagement they did the same thing. I should have listened to them then. That no-good Augustine Bagatelli jilted me at the altar."

Dorothy covered Sophia's hand with her own. Because of her mother's tough-as-nails exterior, she often forgot the trouble her mother had had with men before meeting Dorothy's father. Though things had been rough with Stan, she wasn't the only one who'd been unlucky in love.

"I didn't have a bachelorette party," Dorothy said. "I was pregnant with Kate and certainly wasn't drinking. Plus I was still in high school."

"So neither of you had a clown?" Rose said, her voice soaked in sincere concern. "What a shame. Charlie and I had one who juggled bananas while he pedaled a unicycle. Oh, how we laughed and laughed, especially when he'd peel the banana, eat one, then slip on the peel! You'd think he'd be more careful, working so closely with fruit."

Dorothy couldn't help but laugh. Her friend was so simple, so sweet. But she had to admit, Rose had had a long and happy marriage. Maybe there was something to this clown thing. If she survived this ordeal with her freedom and ever had the chance to find love again, maybe she'd ask Rose to find her a clown for her own bachelorette someday.

"Fine," said Dorothy. "Get the clown, talk to Patricia, and we'll all meet up at the bachelorette."

Just then Blanche dragged herself into the kitchen, without the customary sashay of her hips. "Bachelorette? Oh, that sounds fun! I just wish I didn't feel as tired as a sorority girl after Mardi Gras. I think that mint julep did me in!"

"Well, you did have three of them," Dorothy pointed out. "She sang that song from *South Pacific* about washing her hair. I had to pull her off the piano."

"Was that because of Jorgen?" Sophia asked, peering over the rim of her glasses at Blanche.

"Who?" Blanche said, feigning ignorance. "I'm over that young man, whatever his name was. Besides, he could be a suspect!"

"Just because he was two-timing you with Gloria Corzon doesn't mean he's our killer," Rose said. "He's a nice boy from St. Olaf!"

"It doesn't mean he's *not* the killer," said Blanche. "Maybe it means he's a deceptive, sneaky lowlife who only happens to have the face and body of an angel."

"It's slightly suspicious," Dorothy added. "We have to consider everyone and not assume that someone is innocent, never mind our first impressions of them."

"Guilty until proven innocent," Rose said. "That's the American way."

"Turn that around, Rose," Sophia said. "Oh, never mind, you're too turned around already to tell the difference."

But that's exactly how Dorothy felt. She'd been treated as if she were already guilty by the police. She wondered if they'd find—or invent—enough circumstantial evidence to make the accusation even more solid. She had to show them the growing pile of evidence they had pointing to other people. But at exactly who?

"Wait—can I even come to the bachelorette?" Dorothy asked. "I know I'm supposed to make myself scarce. And I don't think I can wear another disguise."

"Don't you worry about that," Rose said. "Two can play at the Bryants' game. I'm not inviting any of them tonight, and they won't know a thing about it. Only the female members of the wedding party from St. Olaf. And us, of course."

"And where are you having it? The Rusty Anchor? I could wear my red dress and sing a few love songs for the bride," Blanche said.

Dorothy put her head in her hands. She didn't want to spend another evening watching Blanche warble her way through a night of free drinks and wallow in the attention of drooling, yearning men. She wanted it for herself. She could belt some Irving Berlin songs and bring a little more substance and class to the joint.

"I've found the perfect venue for it!" Sophia said. "Coconuts Disco on Ocean Drive. A hunky lifeguard I met at Haulover Beach today told me about it—it's a total hot spot. Everybody who's anybody goes there. Dwayne says that a few criminal types—the classy, organized kind, mind you—hang out at the joint. It'll be just the place to ask around about Henry or anyone who might know something about women getting ripped off by a con man."

"Good thinking, Ma. We'll spread out and canvass the crowd while we're there."

"I've got the address written down," Sophia continued. Then she peered sternly over the thick rim of her thick glasses. "But we've got to look good. Bring out your jewels, ladies. Dress flashy—I don't want to be seen there with a bunch of old biddies."

After Rose and Blanche had left to get dressed for the day, Sophia remained at the kitchen table, flipping through the yellow pages with a plate of cooling toast at her elbow. "You know, this isn't as easy as it seems. Am I looking up *Circus*? *Entertainment? Clowns Incorporated?* Am I looking for a freelance clown?"

"Maybe there's a clown association, like a union or something," Dorothy suggested.

"What do they gotta organize for? Better-fitting shoes? Affordable itty-bitty car insurance?"

Dorothy forced a smile. Her mother's attempts to be cheerful weren't helping. She'd gotten a call from the school where'd she'd started as a substitute before taking over senior English. She was informed that because of her legal troubles, she'd been placed on indefinite leave. They said they hoped she understood, and she did understand, even if *she* knew she wasn't guilty.

On top of that blow, she'd been on hold with the police department for at least ten minutes now, waiting for Detective Silva or Special Agent Crum. As she was shuffled from one desk clerk to another, she wondered if she'd be stuck in a Kafkaesque loop of waiting and holding. But though she'd been treated like a cockroach by the Bryants, at least she hadn't turned into one. Dorothy had certainly felt like a cockroach in the interrogation room.

"Here we go: *Clown, children's birthday parties.* Can you hire one of those for adults? Ah! Here's something. . . ." Sophia copied down a phone number.

Finally, the line connected and a familiar voice said: "Detective Silva."

"Hello, Detective. This is Dorothy Zbornak, from—"

"I'm very familiar with who you are," said Silva. "In fact, we've been looking into some of your recent whereabouts."

Dorothy felt a chill run down her spine. The cops were closing in—on the wrong suspect. She straightened up and pushed her shoulders back.

This was probably just an intimidation technique. She wasn't going to let them rattle her.

"Well, you won't find anything," Dorothy said. "Because

I'm innocent. I'm so innocent, in fact, that I want to help you solve this case. I've come across some information that I'm willing to share."

"Is that right?" the detective said. "Why don't you come down to the station and we'll talk."

Dorothy wasn't going back there—not voluntarily. They weren't going to put her in that little room with the terrible lighting again. Not unless they arrested her. She gulped.

"I'm happy to share it over the phone," she said. "Don't you want to hear information relevant to your case as soon as possible?"

"Of course I do," said Silva. "And why didn't you present this information any of the previous times we spoke? That would have been the time to be truthful and forthcoming."

*Do not let them rattle you*, Dorothy reminded herself. *You're an educated woman. You have rights.*

"Because I didn't have it then," Dorothy snapped. "So I'm telling you now. I should think you'd be grateful for any leads, especially since you've been barking up the wrong tree."

It sounded like the detective was opening a bag of potato chips on the other end of the line. When she spoke again, her tone was even cooler than before. "And how did you get this information? Are you meddling in my investigation?"

"I wouldn't say *meddling*—more like asking a few questions."

Now Silva was clearly munching on the potato chips. Dorothy idly wondered if they were salt and vinegar, to match Silva's sour demeanor.

"Have you heard of obstruction of justice? It's a fancy word for *meddling, interfering, and obscuring the truth*. Maybe I should pay you a visit."

"No no no," said Dorothy. "Let me tell you what I know."

"Fine," said Silva. "Let me patch in Special Agent Crum. Please hold."

"No—I don't want to—"

The chords of Inner Circle's "Bad Boys" started playing, and Dorothy wondered who selected the station's hold music. She sagged against the kitchen wall, waiting for another round of the telephone transfer-and-hold two-step.

# DANCING QUEENS

······· **20** ·······

*R*ose and her friends stood before a white art deco building lit up with purple and pink floodlights. Nettie
and half a dozen St. Olaf women oohed and ahhed at the
lights that zagged around the exterior of the club. Booming
music emanated from a set of doors behind a velvet rope.

They joined a line of people waiting to get in who were
dressed in everything from gold lamé to skintight neon to a
more punk aesthetic with spiked hair and black leather. Rose
tugged at her gold lace dress accented with pearl beading.

It was the flashiest thing she owned, but seeing the array of styles on the crowd waiting to get in, she felt more "mother of the bride" than dance-floor diva.

"I should have worn something else," she whispered to her friends. "I feel overdressed."

She pointed to a pair of women who wore thong-cut leotards over metallic tights. One sported a bouncy Afro and the other's frosted bangs were teased several inches above the metallic band tied across her forehead.

"Maybe *they're under*dressed," Blanche said. "I've never seen so much skin." She brushed at her short satin dress with a sweetheart neckline. "I personally think we look very elegant."

"Speak for yourself," Sophia piped up. "I was going for Chita Rivera, but I look more like Carmen Miranda." She wore a red dress with a flouncy hem. It was one of Blanche's tunics, but on Sophia, it was a calf-length dress. She removed the flower that Rose had pinned to her hair. "Here, take this. I don't want to attract bees. The men in there will already be looking at us like we're slabs of meat."

"Oh, I think you'll be okay," Blanche said, taking the flower and placing it in her hair. She opened a compact and pouted seductively in the mirror. "But some of us have to remain *sharp.*"

"You think you're such hot stuff, being a few decades younger than me. I tell you, a man sees a woman in a red dress and all he can think of is osso buco."

"Oscar what?" Rose said, half listening to Blanche and Sophia's conversation.

"Osso buco—you know, tender meat on the bone."

Rose coughed, hoping that Nettie hadn't heard. If only she could wrap that girl in a woolen blanket and keep her innocent until her wedding day—or at least throw on a pair of earmuffs to shelter her from Sophia's raunchy comments.

Rose tugged Dorothy to one side. "Could you please ask your mother to refrain from colorful language like that? I've got an impressionable young woman here."

"We're about to walk into a bachelorette party," Dorothy pointed out. "Don't you think it's a little late to be shielding Nettie from that kind of talk?"

Just then, the doors of the club opened and the lyrics to Donna Summer's "Bad Girls" floated out.

"I suppose you're right," Rose said as the line surged forward to the velvet ropes.

"Oh! I almost forgot," Sophia said. She pulled out a white headband with a tiny mesh veil attached and placed it on Nettie's head. "Now everyone will know you're the bride."

"You better not pay for a single drink in there!" Blanche said.

Nettie laughed while Bess carefully adjusted the mini veil and re-fluffed Nettie's zigzag waves.

"Careful!" Bess said. "I spent an hour crimping her hair. This whole look was my vision!" She gestured at Nettie like she'd just unveiled an ice sculpture. "Now twirl!"

Nettie spun around, her short white dress flaring out

around her thighs. Her lace gloves reached to her elbows, and she wore several stacks of bracelets and layers of necklaces.

"I was going for Madonna at the Video Music Awards!" Bess said.

The rest of the group was dressed up in St. Olaf style: sensible high-necked dresses. But the colors were bright, and Bess had adorned each woman with oversize brooches and even more bracelets, and had done everyone's hair in an array of curled, teased, and crimped styles straight from the pages of *Mademoiselle* and the Sears catalog.

Katrina readjusted her side ponytail tied with a Versace scarf.

"Don't lose that," Bess said. "I paid a fortune for it!"

Rose smiled. Bess had also done everyone's makeup, leaving them all just a little more glamorous. They did look great, Rose thought, even if everyone sported the same baby-blue eye shadow.

"Remember," Dorothy whispered, tugging Rose, Blanche, and Sophia close. "Don't forget to pump people for information. Be observant, take notes, and ask people questions. It'll be loud in there, so you'll have to really listen."

Rose bit her lip. "But please do it discreetly! Nettie can't know we're on a double mission here. I don't want her thinking about the murder."

Blanche nodded. "We'll do our best to blend in with the party. Maybe the drinks will help loosen people up and get them talking."

"Are you sure we can't give the investigation a rest, just for tonight?" Rose said pleadingly.

"No, we can't," Sophia said. "Because my baby girl isn't going to get framed for this. There's something fishy going on, and I intend to ask every bartender, bouncer, DJ, and dancer at this joint about Henry Pattinson, and if they know anyone with a limp."

"Don't forget to ask if anyone has a female relative who got taken in by a handsome man who was up to no good," Blanche said. "We might find someone unrelated to the wedding who had a motive to kill Henry."

The line inched forward again and they reached the bouncer, who wore a tank top and suspenders and eyed the dozen women ranging in age from early twenties to mid-eighties from beneath heavy black eyeliner. "It's so nice to see different generations spending time with each other. Are you her moms?"

"I'm her aunt, and this is my close friend Dorothy. We're here to party! Just . . . dancing and celebrating. Nothing suspicious or anything." Rose was being careful not to let on that they were simultaneously conducting a murder investigation.

"Enjoy your time with your 'close friend,'" the bouncer said, flashing a knowing smile at Dorothy and waving them into the club. They entered a vast circular space outlined in flashing lights. Dancers whirled and writhed in the dark as the DJ spun Cyndi Lauper's "Girls Just Want to Have Fun" into Salt-N-Pepa's "Push It."

"Isn't this fun?" Rose shouted over the music, a brave smile on her face. It was so loud that it hurt her ears.

"Yes!" Nettie shouted back. "Have you made any progress with the Bryants on the wedding?"

Rose pointed at her ear and shook her head, pretending that she couldn't hear Nettie. She really didn't have a good answer for that.

Nettie asked again, this time cupping her hands around Rose's ear. Rose's smile faltered as she could no longer feign ignorance, and she struggled for what to say.

"I'm still working on it!" she shouted. "Pieces are falling into place!" That wasn't a total lie, she thought. She was working on it. And she didn't say *all* the pieces were falling into place.

"The wedding is supposed to be in a few days!" Nettie cried. "We don't even have a venue, unless we do it at the Bryants' hotel. And you know they won't let us have the donkey, or any of the other St. Olaf touches."

"We will not be doing it the Bryants' way!" Rose shouted a bit louder than necessary. "And everything might be last-minute, but it's happening!"

Nettie looked at Rose, her face solemn under the shimmering disco lights. "Do you promise, Aunt Rose?"

Rose took a deep breath. Promises were something she took very seriously. When she promised she would plow Mean Old Lady Hickenlooper's pasture for her she did it, even if she never got so much as a smile in thanks. If she promised to make six dozen Swedish meatballs for the annual Christmas party at St. Olaf's Home for the Mentally Distracted, gosh darn it, she'd be there with six dozen Swedish meatballs, even if she forgot the little toothpicks to serve them.

She wanted to promise, and she wanted to fulfill it. But deep down, she wasn't confident she could make good on that promise to Nettie.

"I'm doing my best," she finally said. "Now don't worry your pretty head about this any longer. Tonight is for letting loose and having fun—now go!"

Rose pushed Nettie onto the dance floor, where Bess grabbed her hands and spun her into the writhing crowd.

Rose joined her Aunt Katrina and her elderly cousin Hilde, who hovered by the edge of action. This was supposed to be a bonding experience, Rose thought, and the clown wasn't going to arrive for another half hour. Katrina shuffled her feet but didn't really seem like she wanted to set foot on the polished dance floor. And Hilde jumped a little bit every time a dancer accidentally bumped into her.

Rose wondered if the music was too loud or too modern for her relatives. *Maybe I could get the DJ to play "Once Upon a Moonlit Fjord,"* she thought. Or better yet, the faster-paced "I Wanna Thresh with Somebody" by Winifred Houston, the first recording artist to hit number one on St. Olaf's pop *and* R&B charts. The music wasn't the problem, Rose realized, as her younger cousin Cheryl and Bess started swaying to the music.

She surveyed the crowd, wondering what was holding them back. Then it hit her—there were a lot of men in this club, and most of the couples dancing were of the same gender.

Had she brought them to one of Miami's famous gay clubs? Rose whirled around in a panic. This was a far cry from the bridal square dances they'd have in the church hall with cloudberry cordials, wedding-themed knock-knock jokes, and, of course, the juggling clowns. Maybe her guests weren't comfortable with this lifestyle. What if they were upset and word got back to Cousin Gustave?

Rose didn't remember knowing anyone from the gay community in St. Olaf when she was growing up. She supposed they must have been closeted in those days, she thought sadly.

"Are you, um, nervous about the men dancing with the men, and so on?" Rose finally forced herself to ask Katrina. "Does it make you uncomfortable?"

Cousin Hilde turned to Rose with a questioning look on her broad face.

Rose continued, "I think we're at an establishment that caters to gentleman who prefer the affections of—"

"Ach, do you mean gay? Why would I care about that?"

Rose stammered. "Well, I—I thought that maybe in St. Olaf . . ."

"Don't be so closed-minded, Rose," Katrina interjected. "We have our own gay bar in St. Olaf now! If you ever came to visit, you'd have seen it. And don't you know that we're distant cousins of Tom of Finland?"

"Oh, that's wonderful!" Rose said, wondering who the heck Tom of Finland was. "I didn't know all that."

"It's been too long since you last came home," Katrina said. "We may be from a small town, but we're not small-minded."

"I'm sorry," Rose said. "You're right. But then why isn't anyone from St. Olaf on the dance floor?"

As she gestured to the mass of dancers, they spied a dancing Dorothy being dipped by two young men dressed in skintight police uniforms.

"Now this is how a lady should be treated by law enforcement!" she yelled, elated.

Even Sophia was dancing a little bit, swaying slowly with the lifeguard she'd met at Haulover Beach. He was dressed in a red Speedo and a cut-off T-shirt that showed off his impressive abs. Blanche was at the bar, deep in conversation with a mustachioed bartender. Hopefully getting some intel, Rose thought, and not just flirting.

"It's because I don't know these dances! We were trying to watch and learn the steps, but there don't seem to be any."

It was true. The room was a riot of twisting bodies, a few disco moves, and plenty of gyration.

"I've got an idea," Rose said. She grabbed Katrina's hand and her cousin Hilde's. "Bring the others!"

They wove their way with hands clasped to find Nettie and Bess at the center of the dance floor.

"Let's make some room!" Rose wiggled her behind, gently

bumping other dancers to the side to clear a little bit of space. "Can you feel the beat?" Rose asked Katrina. "It's a little fast, but it sounds a little bit like the melody from 'Grandma in the Snow.'"

"Yes! The part where the raven sings and the grandmother thaws!"

"So," Rose said, lifting their clasped hands and pointing one foot outward. "We can do the March of the Mackerel to that song. Those steps are easy!" She grabbed a paper napkin from a passing waiter's tray and held it aloft with her other hand. "Shall we?"

Katrina nodded, and the women danced in a circle around Nettie, then moved through the crowd in a slow serpentine, their feet doing a twisting grapevine step. Soon other members of the dance floor joined the line, along with Dorothy, Blanche, and Sophia bringing up the rear.

Rose's feet—and shoulders—felt light as air as she swept through the dance floor. For the first time in what seemed like forever, Rose felt pure joy, unclouded by worry or responsibility.

After several minutes of vigorous dancing, Rose retired to the ladies' room, panting with exertion. After running her wrists under cold water from the tap, she pressed them to her cheeks. They were red from the heat of bodies pressed against her and the joy of having a wonderful night out with Nettie.

Dancing with her best friends as well as her relatives made her feel like she was having her cheesecake and eating it too. She was showing both groups that everyone could not only get along—they could have a good time together.

As Rose touched up her lipstick, two women emerged from the stalls. Rose recognized their leotards and metallic tights from the entry line. While they washed their hands, one of them whispered to the other.

"Just be careful," the blond one with the shellacked bangs said. "There's been trouble all over town. It's not safe."

Rose cocked her head to listen. This was exactly the kind of thing she should be paying attention to: criminal activity, danger in the streets, rumors of dirty dealings! Rose blotted her lipstick, buying time to hear more.

"I'll say. Big Sugar's not happy," the one with the mahogany Afro said as she reached for a paper towel.

"I heard it's gotten nasty. You don't want to cross Big Sugar," the blond said. Rose's eyes bulged, just as the blond's nervous gaze caught hers in the restroom mirror. The blond quickly looked away. "Come on, let's split."

"Wait!" Rose said, following out the door. "Who's Big Sugar?"

But it was too late. The women had disappeared into the crowd.

Rose rushed to find Dorothy, who was sitting at the bar making notes in a dog-eared paperback with a diamond necklace printed on the cover.

"You brought a book to a dance club? Maybe you do need to get out more," Rose said.

"No, silly, it's my case file." Dorothy showed Rose the lined notebook pages hidden inside.

"Then write this down—I just overheard two people talking about Big Sugar. Maybe it's one of those street gangs, or the code name for a cold-blooded assassin!"

Dorothy frowned at Rose skeptically but jotted it down. "Did they mention anything that could be tied to Henry's con game? Stolen jewels? Missing checkbooks?"

"Not exactly," Rose said. "But they said things had gotten really nasty. I'd say getting locked in a freezer is definitely nasty."

"That's true," Dorothy conceded. "But there are a lot of things going on in this city, any number of which could be considered nasty. We need to find out more about this Big Sugar person if we're going to make any connection to our case."

Just then, a tanned, shirtless bartender gingerly handed a brimming martini to the person seated next to Dorothy at the bar.

"Here you go, Miss Sugar," he said.

Rose's mouth fell open, and she met Dorothy's eyes. They turned, pretending to be casual, to see the recipient of the martini. A woman even taller than Dorothy leaned against the bar, resplendent in a shimmering white evening gown dusted in crystal beading. The woman's snow-white hair was piled into a retro bouffant that reminded Rose of cotton candy.

"Thanks, hon," the woman purred in a deep voice. "You're the only person who hasn't ticked me off today." She tossed a fifty-dollar bill onto the bar and sauntered away to a banquette table filled with men in sharp suits. They stumbled over themselves, trying to get to their feet and out of Sugar's way. She sipped her martini and extended a languid arm, holding out an old-fashioned cigarette holder. Three of the men offered her a light.

Rose pressed her lips together, trying not to squeal out loud. "Did you hear that?"

Dorothy nodded. She noted Sugar's description in her notebook, along with the date and time.

"Do you think she's a criminal mastermind? After all, ladies can be mob bosses, too. We've come a long way, baby." Rose knew that women could do anything a man could do. Look at what Sally Ride had done in aeronautics, or what Billie Jean King had done for tennis! Why couldn't women take over the world of crime as well?

Dorothy eyed the woman. "She's certainly a femme fatale. But I don't think she's our killer. First of all, she's not of average height and build. She's of above-average height, and her build is, well . . ."

Rose took stock of the gravity-defying bosom, the tiny

waist, the angular shoulders, and the hips that made Marilyn Monroe look flat as a washboard.

"Anything but average," Rose concluded. But she couldn't shake the idea that the killer could be a woman. After all, Henry had preyed on women. And Aunt Katrina hadn't been able to tell the gender of the person she'd seen running down the hallway the night of the murder. "On the other hand, she tipped *fifty dollars*! Who throws around that kind of money?"

Dorothy shrugged.

"I'll tell you who, Dorothy. A criminal mastermind or a woman of means. She could have been one of Henry's marks, and she took her revenge!"

Rose stared at the woman, trying to commit her features to memory. This was the second clue she herself had discovered, after finding out about the limp. They were going to crack this case before the wedding, gosh darn it!

"Give me that notebook," she said. She grabbed Dorothy's pencil and started sketching the woman, penning the words *BIG SUGAR* underneath. Rose had to admit that she wasn't the best artist. When she looked down she realized all she had on paper was a basic smiley face with a mole on one cheek.

As Rose filled in the swirls of hair and the impressive bosom, Sugar picked up her half-empty martini glass from the table and left her pack of gentleman callers to walk up a few steps to a dais. The DJ brought down the music.

The crowd roared, and a few men pushed to the edge of the dais, tossing bills at Sugar's feet along with a few long-stemmed roses. Sugar basked in the applause as a waiter handed her a microphone.

"Maybe that's where she gets all her Ulysseses and Benjamins," Dorothy said.

Rose squinted, surveying the men who showered Sugar with attention. "How do you know the names of her admirers?"

"I'm referring to her *cash*," Dorothy said. "I don't think she's our perp."

"Before I perform," Sugar purred, "there's an opening act, and I'm told we have a very special guest! Could Nettie please come to the stage?"

The crowd parted, and Bess pushed a blushing Nettie forward. Sugar helped the young woman to the dais, then pulled a slip of paper from the depths of her cleavage.

"It's Nettie's bachelorette tonight!" The crowd whooped and whistled. "Congratulations, hon. And in her culture, it's tradition for the lucky lady to be visited by a . . . clown." Sugar frowned down at the paper. "Is that right?"

Nettie nodded. Rose clapped and shouted: "For levity and love!"

Sugar lifted her martini glass. "To levity and love!"

Those who had drinks in their hands toasted Nettie while she grinned and took a little bow. The St. Olafians shouted blessings in their Norwegian dialect, and Hilde snapped some photos with a Polaroid camera.

Rose was so proud. She had been bashful at her own bachelorette, but Nettie was more confident, like so many women of her generation. The crowd cheered for Nettie as a clown in a harlequin suit, a red foam nose, and a curly orange wig appeared from behind the black velvet curtain to the opening notes of "Get Down Tonight" by KC and the Sunshine Band.

Despite all the wedding details still to be finalized, the difficult in-laws, the looming incarceration of her friend, and a killer on the loose, Rose was happy. This was a truly perfect moment, and nothing could spoil it.

Then the clown started unbuttoning his suit.

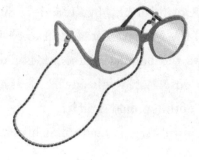

# PLOP, PLOP, FIZZ FIZZ, PLOT TWIST

## ·········· 21 ··········

*L*ate the next morning, Dorothy, Rose, Blanche, and Sophia reclined on the lanai with cool washcloths draped across their foreheads. Blanche groaned and massaged her lower back with one hand.

"I declare, I never danced so long or laughed so hard. What a wonderful night, Rose!"

"I don't need your sarcasm right now, Blanche," Rose said, flipping up the edge of her washcloth to glare at her. "It was one of the worst nights of my life."

"Oh you're exaggerating," Dorothy said. "Just because there was a little hiccup."

"A hiccup! It was a nightmare! One minute, it's all balloon animals and laughter. And then bam! A gertflufen, right there in the open! I felt like a total geronoconkin."

"It was quite a performance," Blanche tittered.

"Oh, please, it's only the human body. You've seen a naked man before," Sophia snapped.

"A naked body is fine—when you're in bed, or the shower, or the sauna. That's totally normal. What's not normal is when he still has an oversize bow tie on!"

Dorothy tried to stifle her guffaws with the washcloth. "I don't know what was funnier—the clown or your face!"

"Well, I didn't think it was funny. I'm lucky Nettie saw the humor in it. That poor girl. She's probably never even seen anything like—like *that* before!"

"Oh, I bet she has," Blanche said. "You think she and Jason just hold hands and talk about the weather? They *live* together! Big Daddy always said you should sample the milk before you buy the cow. Well, he actually said you should taste the milk of all the cows in the pasture, and your neighbor's pasture, and then decide whether you're gonna actually buy a cow or not."

Rose covered her ears with her hands and glared at Sophia. "And it's all your fault!"

She shook her damp washcloth threateningly at Sophia, who was soaking her feet in a tub of hot water and Epsom salt.

"My fault? I did the research. I made the calls. I negotiated and got you a good price. So he thew in a little something extra. What's the big deal?"

"It was more than a little something," Blanche said with a twinkle in her eye.

"How was I supposed to know he was a stripper?" Sophia grumbled. "I went through the telephone book. This wasn't a children's birthday party, so I dialed the one for *Clowns, adult*."

"Well, it may be funny to you, but Cousin Gustave stopped by this morning before the rest of you had even gotten out of bed. He lectured me at our front door, like I had done something wrong!"

"How did he even know about the clown's . . . slide whistle?"

"Hilde was taking Polaroids, remember? She went straight to Gustave and ratted me out, with pictures to boot!"

"That's just wrong," Blanche said. "Everybody knows what happens at a bachelorette party is supposed to stay among the participants. Now, why would she do something like that?"

Rose put down her washcloth, deflated. "She's always been jealous of me, ever since I outlasted everyone at the junior girls' ice fishing competition in high school. I was out there the longest, and I caught the most fish."

"It sounds like you won fair and square. Did you lord it over her or something?" Dorothy couldn't believe she was asking for more details about a St. Olaf story.

"No, I didn't. I never cared about ice fishing. I only did it because it looked fun, but in truth I hated it! The only reason I won is that I made the mistake of sitting on the ice instead of on a chair, and my bottom froze right to the lake's surface. I couldn't have moved, even though I wanted to! I just kept catching fish until finally they sent someone to check on me. But *Hilde*, she really cared about winning, and she thought I outlasted her just to spite her."

"That was probably forty years ago," Sophia said. "Why didn't she just say something to you before now?"

"Well, that wouldn't have been polite," Rose said. "You know how people are in the Midwest."

"So she holds a grudge for that many years? And I thought Sicilians were bad!"

"But that's not the worst of it," Rose continued. "I never even told you all that Cousin Gustave informed me about a new clause in the bylaws that directly affects Nettie's trust! It's an amendment that says that in order to become a full citizen of St. Olaf and be eligible for the trust, the outside party must perform an act of bravery before the wedding. And . . ." Rose picked up her legal pad and read from it. "'Such act must be witnessed by a trustworthy entity.'" She smacked the legal pad with the flat of her hand. "Yet another impossible goal to hit, just for Nettie to get what's rightfully hers. It's ridiculous!"

Dorothy took the paper, reading over the typed document. "Can he do this, just add something in?"

"He said all the elders voted on it. The ones still back in St. Olaf voted by telegram. I think he came up with it just to make it harder for them to get married."

"But why would he do that?" Dorothy's mind whirred, then clicked on a possibility. "Does he think Jason's simply after the money, and he's trying to throw up some roadblocks?"

"Jason's not after the money!" Rose said. "You've all seen how sweet he is. He loves Nettie, and he loves St. Olaf. He's jumped through every hoop wholeheartedly."

"It is a bit odd, though," Blanche said slowly. "I mean, what young man these days wants to follow these old traditions? Why is he so obsessed with all of your odd little rituals? Most young men are becoming *less* traditional these days and wouldn't put up with wearing moose antlers on Wednesdays, or what have you."

"First of all, those are ram horns, and they're for *Tuesdays* during the haymaking season."

"Is there a chance he's more interested in the money than he is in Nettie?"

"Oh, come on," Rose protested. "You're just saying that because of Jorgen. You think all young men aren't trustworthy. It's not even a lot of money. It's not like a million dollars or anything."

"But is it enough for a young man to get his start in life, especially if he doesn't want anything to do with his wealthy family?" Dorothy said.

"That is ridiculous!" Rose frowned. "Jason's completely innocent. I mean, just look at how he is with Nettie!"

"You did say you were going to investigate everyone, no matter how innocent they seemed," Dorothy said. "I'm not saying he's guilty, but . . ."

"Fine!" Rose twisted her washcloth like she was wringing a neck. "To prove my point, I won't tell him or Nettie about this new amendment until I'm sure about him. But I need to finalize a venue—preferably one we can afford. Dorothy, you can call the police station and tell them about Big Sugar."

Dorothy rolled her eyes. "For the last time. Big Sugar is a performer, not a mob boss."

"If you're going to accuse everyone, including my niece's fiancé, then Big Sugar goes on the list of suspicious individuals!" Rose smacked Dorothy with the washcloth, leaving a damp impression on her sleeve.

"Fine! But after that I'm going to focus my efforts in reality and actually try to solve this case. I have a new location to scope out—who's with me?"

"I am," said Blanche. "Now that Jorgen and I are through, I need to distract myself every moment of the day."

"I'll go, too," Sophia said. "Just give me a few more hours to get circulation in my feet. I regret doing the Running Man so much."

Dorothy and Blanche followed Rose into the living room just as the telephone rang, and Rose answered it.

*It's Nettie*, she mouthed. "What? Speak more slowly, I can't understand you." Rose pressed the receiver to her chest. "She's crying," she whispered. "I think she and Jason had a fight."

Dorothy and Blanche exchanged glances as Rose listened to Nettie on the other end of the line.

"Are you sure? But—" Then she fell silent as Nettie bawled on the other end. "And what did he say to that? *Oh, dear.*"

Rose put down the phone with a clatter. "I've got to run to the Cabana Sun Hotel right now. She said the wedding's off!"

# GREASED LIGHTNING

### 22

*R*ose paced the length of the hotel room while Nettie threw clothing into her suitcase, not even bothering to fold anything. "It's totally normal to get cold feet," Rose said. "But you two love each other."

"*I* love him," Nettie wailed, pulling dresses from the closet, making the hangers clang together. "But I think he just loves St. Olaf. Or the idea of St. Olaf. He wants a barn and a cow and even a wishing well! And I'm just the ticket for him to live the pastoral fantasy he's always dreamed of."

"Are you sure? Jason seems like he'd be happy to be any-where, as long as he's with you." Rose started folding the clothes that Nettie had haphazardly thrown into the suitcase. She couldn't help it.

"Then why is he so fixated on these traditions? There's no point to any of them, except to get the trust. I'm sorry, but it's true."

"But they're a rich celebration of our heritage," Rose began. "They all serve a purpose, in the grand scheme of things."

"Well, I don't care about them. I don't care about the trust. I think all that stuff doesn't matter. If you want to get married, get married."

Rose paused in the middle of folding one of Nettie's blouses as she realized she agreed with Nettie. She would have married Charlie even if they'd simply spat in their hands and shook on it. And even if they hadn't had their small portion of the trust, they'd have muddled along just fine. Their life together was about so much more than material things.

"Have you talked to him?" Rose said. "Really told him how you feel? I'm sure he'd put your mind at ease."

"*I tried to!*" Nettie sobbed. "But he said he had to pick up three more pounds of herring from this black-market dealer and track down a goat horn."

Rose swallowed. It was she who had instructed Jason to do those very things, and pronto. "Nettie, he's doing that because I asked—okay, I told him to," she said. "He's doing it for the wedding—for you."

"He's doing it for the *trust*." She zipped up her suitcase, not caring that a striped sock was hanging out where the zippers hadn't fully closed. Nettie yanked the suitcase off the bed and dragged it out of the room, Rose trotting behind her.

"All right," Rose said as she followed Nettie down the long hallway. "You're upset. You need to blow off some steam. Why don't you come home with me and we'll punch some pillows together."

Nettie whirled around. "Are you kidding me? That's something we did when I was like, five." She punched the elevator button. Then punched it again, extra hard.

Rose wanted to say, *You're* acting *like you're five!*

But she didn't. Instead, she rubbed Nettie's back. "Okay, we won't punch pillows. How about we punch Cousin Gustave?"

Nettie snorted, her tear-streaked face almost, but not quite, breaking into the faintest smile. The elevator doors opened, and Nettie picked up her suitcase. Rose grabbed the handle at the same time, jerking the young woman back.

"I'm going," Nettie said. "And you're not going to stop me!" She gave the suitcase a hearty tug and pulled it, with Rose attached, into the elevator with her.

"But where?" Rose said.

"The airport. I'll figure it out from there."

"I wish you'd rethink this," Rose said. "You love each other so much, and, darn it, I've worked too hard on this wedding for you to throw all that away!"

"Does the fact that my relationship is crumbling mean

nothing to you? Sorry to have wasted your time. I told you I never wanted any of this."

"I'm sorry—I didn't mean it like that!" Rose said. "We'll work it out. Let's find Jason so you can talk to him. Then if you still want to call off the wedding, I'll respect your decision."

The elevator gently came to a stop, the open door depositing them into the lobby.

"Nope," Nettie said. "I'm going straight to the Departures desk, and I'll figure it out from there. If you see Jason, you can tell him to meet me there. We can elope anywhere. If he won't do it, I'll know for sure that he's only in it for the trust."

Rose smiled sadly. Though Nettie's reasoning was harsh, it did make sense. "I'll go with you," she said. "I don't want you to have to wait alone. We can phone the hotel from the airport and leave a message for Jason. Deal?"

"Deal," Nettie said, crossing the lobby and pushing her way through the revolving doors, only to smack into the man in question, who was carrying an armload of brown paper packages.

"I got the herring!" Jason cried triumphantly.

Nettie took one look at him and burst into fresh tears. She turned away from Jason, dragging her suitcase behind her, waving frantically for a cab.

"She's still upset?" Jason said, handing the packages to Rose. "I thought this was what she wanted!"

Rose shoved the packages back into Jason's arms.

"Me too," she said. "But she's going to need to cool off. I'll give you a call."

A dark maroon jitney pulled up to the curb. The driver, a bald man with a cigar nub clamped in his jaws, popped the trunk and motioned for Nettie to throw her suitcase inside. As Rose piled into the back seat behind her, Jason started after them, his eyes widening with recognition.

"Hey, wait a minute!" Jason shouted, sprinting toward the LeSabre just as it peeled away from the curb. Rose and Nettie felt themselves sink into the plush back seat as the sedan accelerated to the next red light.

"The airport, please," Nettie said to the back of the bald man's head.

"Now, Nettie—" Rose paused. Jason was still sprinting after them, shouting something she couldn't quite make out.

The driver glanced in the rearview mirror, then pressed the gas before the traffic light even turned green.

"*Hey*, what's going on?" Rose said as the car surged ahead. Though the rearview mirror, Rose could see Jason talking to a tough-looking bunch of motorcyclists parked at the curb.

Suddenly, Jason hopped on the back of one of the motorcycles, his arms wrapped around the generous belly of a grizzled man with a long beard.

"Oh my," said Rose. "Nettie, is that one of Jason's friends?"

The roar of motorcycle engines engulfed the sedan, and

the driver veered across two lanes to turn onto the Julia Tuttle Causeway, tires screeching.

"Aunt Rose, what's happening?" Nettie warbled.

"I don't know!" Rose cried, holding on to the inside door handle, trying to keep herself upright.

"What do you want with me?" Nettie shouted at the driver, pounding him on the shoulders with her fists.

The car swerved wildly from side to side, narrowly avoiding oncoming cars. On either side of the bridge, the azure waters of the Intracoastal Waterway shimmered.

"Nettie, stop, you'll make us go off the causeway!"

"Not you," the driver tossed over his shoulder. He locked eyes with Rose in the rearview mirror, his thick brow furrowed beneath his shining bald head. "*Her*. She's been asking too many questions."

"I have?" Rose clapped a hand over her mouth.

*Oh, no*—she'd just asked another one!

*Sorry!* she mouthed to Nettie.

"What questions are you asking?" Nettie said. "What is he talking about?"

The swerving car made Rose nauseous. She rolled down her window, trying to get a breath of fresh air.

"She's been talking about Big Sugar—running her mouth. And now I'm going to shut you up for good!"

"I'm sorry—I'll be quiet! I won't stir up trouble!"

"Oh, the innocent act," the driver scoffed as he changed lanes. "I'm not falling for it."

Nettie and Rose stared at each other, wondering what on earth the man meant. "I think you've got me mixed up with someone else." Rose said. "I'm just a senior citizen trying to plan a wedding."

"Right. That's why you were casing Coconuts, asking everyone about Big Sugar. And a little bird told us that one of your associates has been singing to the cops. Tall, schoolteacher type."

"I don't have associates, I have friends!" Rose said. "And I was asking about Big Sugar—because I thought that was a new soft drink and I wanted to try it."

She was grasping at straws, trying to think of anything that could get them out of this car and away from danger.

"Nice try, Grandma," the driver spat. "I know about you and your little gang. Think you can move in on South Beach?"

"I'm not in a gang," Rose tried to explain. "I'm in a bridge club, but they don't meet that often."

"You're not fooling me. I know that you're up to more than just knitting and baking cookies. Four little old ladies just happen to be skulking around back alleys and nightclubs? Trying to blow the lid off Big Sugar so you can move in? That little one with the glasses has a blade in her purse, did you know that?" the driver said to Nettie. "I saw her using it to peel a nectarine. But my buddy Luigi said she used it to cut off a man's ear in Gainesville."

"We're not criminals!" Rose cried.

"And that foxy one with the fake Southern accent?" the

driver continued. "She used to run numbers in Jacksonville."

Rose leaned her head out the window. She thought she might throw up. This man really thought she and her girl-friends were hardcore crooks.

"But we're just old ladies!" she insisted. "Can't you see we're not a threat to anyone?!"

"That's exactly why it works so well. No one would ever suspect you. But I know the truth." The driver sneered, his raised eyebrows visible in the rearview mirror.

The sound of the motorcycles grew loud again as they surrounded the car like a swarm of metallic hornets. The driver stomped on the gas, causing the engine to whine as the car sped up. Rose and Nettie lurched from side to side in the back seat, clutching each other's hands in fear.

The motorcycles kept pace with the sedan as it sped off the causeway, until suddenly Jason appeared at Rose's window, waving frantically with one hand, the other still firmly clutching the cyclist's torso.

"Jason!" Nettie screamed. "What are you doing?"

"Hold on, Nettie," Jason said. "I'm coming for you!"

Rose's heart leapt—maybe he'd save them! Or maybe, she thought, he'd get killed trying. She watched as the motorcycle carrying Jason drifted closer to their car as they all sped down a woods-lined road and flew by a sign: BIG CYPRESS NATIONAL PRESERVE.

"He's taking us to the Everglades!" Nettie wailed. "He's going to kill us there."

A loud thump rocked the roof of the car, and a leg and arm dangled over the window nearest Rose. Tormented by visions of a being eaten by an alligator, she wept and held Nettie tightly.

"I should never have gotten you mixed up in this," Rose sobbed. "I'm awfully sorry."

Nettie shook off Rose's hug and reached around the front seat, crooking her arm around the driver's neck.

"Stop, we'll crash!" Rose shouted.

"He's going to try to kill us anyway," Nettie grunted, squeezing harder around the man's thick neck. The car slowed slightly as the driver struggled against her arms. The leg outside Rose's window dangled wildly, then found its way in along with the rest of Jason's body just as the driver shook off Nettie's arm.

Panicking, Rose whacked the driver's head with her purse, distracting him just long enough for Jason to clamber between the seats into the front of the car, even as it skidded off the road onto the sandy shoulder.

"Take the wheel!" he shouted, yanking the driver onto his lap. He pinned the driver's arms under his own as Nettie reached over the driver's seat and grabbed the steering wheel, wrenching the car back onto the road. The bumpy ride reminded Rose suddenly of the time she and Charlie had gone white-water rafting on their honeymoon in Niagara Falls, and, also, of the nights in their hotel's coin-operated vibrating bed.

"I can't reach the brake!" Nettie yelled, valiantly steering the car along the stretch of paved road, narrowly avoiding the trees.

Rose let out a gasp of relief—they could've disturbed the chipmunks, or knocked some baby birds from their nests!

Jason opened the passenger-side door and forced out the driver, who rolled over a blanket of pine needles into a ditch.

Jason hopped over the center console and stomped on the brake, bringing the car to a sudden halt.

Rose, Jason, and Nettie hugged each other and dissolved into tears of relief as the driver picked himself up and disappeared into the woods.

*We're all alive*, Rose thought, *thank goodness.*

"You saved us!" Nettie said, and planted a big kiss on Jason's cheek.

"You did, too," Jason said, still catching his breath.

"How did you know to come after us?" Nettie asked, brushing pine needles from Jason's hair, revealing a trickle of blood that trailed down his temple.

"I wanted to go with you! I thought for a second that maybe I should run up to my room and get our rings in case you'd still want to elope, but when I saw you get into that jitney, I knew something wasn't right. I recognized the man in the front seat. I knew he wasn't a cabdriver."

"Recognized him from where?"

"I'm not sure, but I think I've seen him at the cigar room before, and maybe the country club as well."

The motorcycle gang reached the car as distant sirens

pierced the air. The bearded man helped Rose out of the car and wrapped her in a leather jacket emblazoned with a shark's toothy jawbone engulfing a skull beneath the words *Land Sharks* embroidered in thick gothic lettering. The jacket was warm and comforting, and only slightly smelled of BO.

*An act of bravery*, Rose thought. Witnessed by one Rose Nylund, and the trail of police cars soon to arrive, not to mention the motorcycle escort.

# GONE, DOGGIE, GONE
......... 23 .........

*D*orothy pulled up to the neat clapboard house and lowered her sunglasses to check the address written in her notebook. After Rose had left for the hotel, Dorothy and Sophia had pored over the yellow pages, calling all the *Pattinson, H*s listed in the Miami area. They'd visited a few addresses in Coral Gables, and this was the last one on their list. Lines of yellow crime-scene tape strung across the front porch fluttered half-heartedly in the breeze. Dorothy peered up and down the street, noting that Henry's house was one of a line of modest homes abutting the bay and facing a narrow dock spanning the length of the block. Dorothy parked a few houses down, and then she, Blanche, and Sophia crept toward the house, all wearing oversize sunglasses and baseball hats.

"Hard to believe a criminal lived here," Blanche said. "It's so . . . charming! Look, he even had window boxes."

But the geraniums were fading, and the hanging ferns on Henry's porch were curled and brown due to lack of watering.

"Looks like no one except for the police has come to check on this place since he died," Dorothy said, noticing a pile of mail sticking out of the mail slot. "Even though he ripped people off, I feel bad for him."

"I know what you mean," said Sophia. "But seeming like a nice man was all part of the con."

"I suppose so," Dorothy said with a touch of sadness. What if Henry *had* been all he seemed? They might have gone on more dates. She might have had dinner on his boat. *Would it have lasted?* she wondered. Maybe not. If only he had truly been the man she'd fallen for on video. Reality was a lot messier and more disappointing.

She climbed up to the porch, the crime scene tape drooping to knee level. She could easily step over it, but maybe it was a bad idea. She was already in trouble with the police.

*But that's exactly why you need to investigate*, a voice inside her said.

Dorothy took a deep breath. Should she cross that line of tape? Her inner rule-following, law-abiding instincts screamed no. She turned back just in time to see her mother pick up the tape and duck under it.

Sophia jiggled the front door handle, which was locked. She cupped her hands around her eyes and tried to look through the front window.

"Check that mail," Blanche called from behind them. "It's a good place for clues."

Still behind the tape, Dorothy bent down and peered at the envelopes. She didn't want to disturb them just in case they were evidence. All the envelopes she could easily read were addressed to Henry Pattinson. No aliases. Nothing out of the ordinary either, like the collection notices Rose and Blanche had found at the Cabana Sun Hotel.

"It's just some utility bills and grocery store circulars," Dorothy said.

"Grab those," Sophia said. "I want the coupons."

"We're not doing that. We have to leave as little trace as possible. What if the cops come and dust for prints?" Dorothy cringed inwardly, realizing that her mother had already touched the crime-scene tape, the door handle, and the window.

"You think they're investigating that hard? Sweet cheeks, if we don't bring them some real evidence, some actual leads, they're just going to keep looking at you."

"But clearly, they've already checked this house," Dorothy said.

"You think the cops are smarter than us? The four of us are more likely to find some clues than those doughnut munchers. I bet you've read more books than that whole precinct. I've got street smarts, Blanche has an eye for men's weaknesses, and Rose . . . well, I'm sure Rose has some useful qualities somewhere."

Dorothy gritted her teeth. She hated to admit when her mother was likely to be right. She patted her pockets for the antacids she'd started carrying and popped one into her mouth. Ever since this whole thing started, her stomach had been churning. She'd already taken two this morning after one of her students had called the house, asking when she would be returning to class. She'd only been able to give him vague answers and put on a brave face. But inside, it had rocked her. This particular student had dyslexia and had benefited from meeting with Dorothy after school. They were so close to the end of the school year, and Dorothy worried how he—and all her students—would fare during finals without her. She had to clear her name, even if it meant bending—or breaking—a few rules.

Dorothy stepped over the tape, then wiped and wiped her sweaty hand on her brocade vest.

"Give me a handkerchief, Ma," she said. She took it and wiped down the door handle and the smudges on the window from Sophia's hands, then peeked in the window herself, but she couldn't see past the venetian blinds. Then she looked from right to left, checking that no nosy neighbors were around to witness her less-than-innocent-looking actions. A slight movement caught her eye in a side window of the house next door. A curtain twitched back into place, and Dorothy shoved the handkerchief into her pocket.

"Someone may have spotted us," she said, swallowing the last of the grainy, lemony antacid tablet. "Let's go around the other side."

As they looped the house, Blanche and Dorothy peered into the first-floor windows.

"Lift me up, I want to see!" Sophia said.

"The blinds are closed." Blanche sighed. "Let's try the back."

The followed a short gravel driveway to the small backyard.

"Look!" Blanche said. "That must be his car." A baby-blue Porsche was parked under a corrugated metal carport.

"That's odd," Dorothy said. "He must not have driven himself to the hotel before he was killed."

"Maybe he took the bus," Sophia said. "Have you seen the price of gas? It's darn near ninety cents a gallon!"

"Or maybe he didn't want to be seen," Blanche said. "That's a flashy car."

Dorothy peered inside the driver's side window. On the passenger seat was a wrinkled copy of *Boating World* magazine, and a handful of change sat in the front console. "No obvious clues as to why he was murdered," she said.

"What did you expect, a note?" Sophia said. "It's not like you can ask him to spell it all out for us. He's *dead*!"

"Let's try the back door," Blanche said. She trotted up to the small back porch and opened the screen door easily, but the inner door was locked.

"Wait a minute," Dorothy said. "Do you see what I see?" She pointed to a small rectangle at the bottom of the door.

"A doggie door!" Blanche said. "Do you know if Henry had a dog?"

Dorothy's heart sank down to her size elevens. He had—when they'd spoken on the phone he'd mentioned a rat terrier named after Jayne Mansfield. He'd even said he'd gotten a tiny life jacket made in her size so he could take her out with him on his boat.

*That poor dog!* she thought. Had she been locked up all along in this house for days? Dorothy prayed she'd had enough food and water. If not—the alternative was too horrible to think about.

"He did! Oh goodness, what are we going to?"

"Let's call for it," Blanche said.

"Jayne, oh, Jaynie!" Dorothy called.

Blanche whistled, and Sophia made a *pspsps* sound.

"What? That's how we did it in Sicily. That's how you call your dog, your cat, or your husband to come in at night."

"Maybe someone's taking care of that poor pooch," Blanche said.

Dorothy looked doubtful. "But it's obvious that no one's been in or out of this house for a while. We have to do something!"

Then an idea dawned on her. She looked at the doggie door, then Sophia. Then back to the doggie door.

"Ma, do you think—"

"Stop right there, I'm not crawling through that door!"

"*C'mon*," Dorothy said.

"How do you know the police didn't take the dog?" Sophia said.

"How do you know they *did*?" Blanche countered. "I thought you were an animal lover. Plus you're the smallest. I just know you can fit."

"Even if I could get into a crawling position," Sophia said, "which is undignified in a woman my age—how the heck would I ever get up again?"

"If you go inside, you might find some more clues," Dorothy pointed out. "In addition to saving a helpless animal."

Sophia let out a huff of air. "Fine. But this is the last time I get down on my knees for some dirty dog," she muttered. "I'm only doing this to keep you out of the slammer."

Blanche held Sophia's coat and Dorothy held her purse as they helped lower the octogenarian to the doormat. Sophia stuck an arm through the swinging door, holding it open as she pushed her head and shoulders through.

"Do you see anything?" Dorothy said.

"Linoleum!" Sophia's muffled voice said. She pushed a few

inches farther through the door so that only her backside and legs were visible. She wiggled forward a few more inches, exposing a border of her white slip beneath her sensible plaid skirt.

"Aha!" she yelped.

"*Ma!* Are you okay? Are you stuck?" Dorothy bent at the waist, straining to hear.

"I'm in his kitchen. He uses the same brand of olive oil as I do!" Sophia's voice emanated from somewhere beyond her hind end. "If he wasn't dead, he'd be a keeper!"

Dorothy slumped back against the wooden slats of the house. This process was tough on the nerves, she thought. Probably tough on her mother's knees as well. She felt a surge of gratitude for Sophia and all the things she was doing to try to help her clear her name.

"I'm not so sure this is a good idea," she said to Blanche. "What if she gets stuck in there?"

"Oh, she'll be fine. Wait—what was that?" The sound of a car crunching over the gravel road made them freeze in place.

Blanche peeked around the side of the house. "Someone's coming! I saw a dark sedan pass the house, and it just circled back again! Maybe someone's tailing us."

Dorothy looked worried as Sophia ventured another inch through the dog door.

"Are you sure?" Blanche craned her neck and turned around with her eyes bugged out.

"Some men are getting out of the car! They—they look

tough. Like they mean business." Blanche's lower lip trembled.

"Ma," Dorothy hissed, trying to fight the panic that rose in her throat. "Can you back up? We've got to get out of here!"

"Hurry, they're coming!" Blanche hopped up onto the porch, looking for a place to hide. She crawled underneath a wicker love seat.

"Sorry, Ma!" Dorothy pushed her mother's rear end the rest of the way into Henry's house. Once Sophia's orthopedic shoes disappeared, Dorothy grabbed a large striped umbrella from where it leaned between some beach chairs and a cooler. She opened it partway and hid behind it, just as two pairs of heavy black boots thudded up the driveway.

Dorothy's nose was inches away from a spider who'd made a temporary home in the folded-up umbrella. When it crawled closer to her face she wanted to scream and bat it away, but she held still, trying to control her breathing.

"What do we have here?" a gravelly voice said. Heavy boots moved toward the love seat. "That's quite a set of legs on that piece of furniture."

The two male voices erupted into smokers' laughs. "And what about those shoes poking out from under that umbrella? Do you think we got a Wicked Witch situation here?"

*Damnit*, Dorothy thought. They'd been discovered.

She lowered the umbrella and straightened herself up to her full height.

"We don't want any trouble," Dorothy said, recognizing

Officer Pierno and a younger Black man. They were dressed in T-shirts and jeans instead of their uniforms, but Dorothy saw the firearms in their hands and trembled.

"I think you're already in trouble," Pierno said.

The other one laughed and holstered his gun.

Blanche peered up at them from beneath the wicker love seat.

"You might as well come out," the younger man said.

Blanche bit her lip, then slowly disentangled herself from her crouched position.

The two men helped her to her feet, and she brushed off bits of dirt from her kelly-green pantsuit.

"What's going on?" Dorothy asked.

"We might ask you the same question, Ms. Zbornak," Officer Pierno said. As he holstered his gun, Dorothy flinched. She hated the sight of weapons, and seeing a gun this close made her stomach queasy.

"Relax, we're undercover," Pierno said. "And this is Officer Murphy."

"Oh, thank goodness," Blanche said. "I thought you were the killers coming to get us!"

"We've unearthed some new information and have been watching the vic's house to see if any lowlifes came around," Pierno said. "And I think Detective Silva will find it mighty interesting that you all showed up. Wouldn't you say that's strange, Murph?"

"I'd say it's downright suspicious," Officer Murphy said.

"Did you say you didn't know anything about Henry? That you'd only met him on that one date?" Pierno said, flipping open a tiny notebook.

"I did," Dorothy admitted, "but I'm trying to figure out what happened to him, because I know I certainly didn't kill him!"

"And you wouldn't have been planning on breaking and entering, would you?" Pierno asked. "Because that would be another crime to add to your file. This one being much easier to prove, of course."

"I wasn't breaking in!" Dorothy insisted.

Just then, a small cloud of curly white hair emerged from the dog door.

"What the hell?" her mother's voice rang out, this time too loud and too clear. "You shove me in there like you're microwaving yesterday's casserole? I felt like Evel Knievel getting shot out of a cannon!"

Dorothy hung her head as Sophia lifted hers and saw the two men.

"Uh-oh," she said.

Murphy and Pierno pulled Sophia from the tiny door and lifted her to her feet.

"Roping in your mother to do your dirty work. Taking advantage of an innocent old lady." Pierno tsked. "Very suspicious indeed."

"Just so we're clear," Sophia interjected. "I wasn't breaking and entering. First of all, I didn't break anything, except maybe my kneecaps. Secondly, we believe this gentleman had a dog, and that the dog could be in distress. We are simply concerned citizens engaging in an act of animal welfare."

"Is that right?" Pierno said sarcastically.

"Wouldn't you save a dog, if you could?"

"Of course," Murphy said. "Man's best friend. But, uh, where's the dog? When we first searched the house, we saw food and water bowls on the floor but no sign of a pooch."

Sophia looked around. "It probably hid, terrified you were gonna lock it up in the clink! Maybe you should go in and find it. And we'll just . . . go home and mind our own business. What do you say, officers?"

"You're all coming with me to fill out a full report. We'll send animal control to check on this theoretical dog." Officer Pierno grabbed Dorothy roughly by the upper arm and propelled her toward the sedan, which she realized was actually an unmarked police car. It even had a half-eaten doughnut on the dash.

Blanche and Sophia followed behind, spilling over with explanations, apologies, and threats to lawyer up.

"I'm taking this one down to the station," Pierno said, opening the car door and placing a hand on Dorothy's head to usher her inside. "I can't wait to see Silva's face when she hears what you've been up to."

Just then, a small white catamaran glided up to the dock

and pulled into the slip in front of Henry's house. A tall, broad-shouldered man stood on the deck, silhouetted by the bright sunlight bouncing off the water.

"What's going on here?" he called as he secured the boat to the dock with a rope. Once the catamaran was moored, he hopped onto the dock, holding something tucked under one arm.

He jogged across the street, taking in the car, the two men and three women, and the cuffs on Dorothy's wrists.

"What are you doing at my house?" he said as he stepped forward into the shadow cast by a lemon tree. Now that he wasn't backlit, Dorothy could see that the man had rugged good looks, a deep tan, and a worried expression in his eyes.

It was Henry.

# BARKING UP THE WRONG TREE

······· **24** ·······

*L*ooking at the man clutching a tiny black-and-white dog in a yellow life vest to his chest, Dorothy thought, *He looks exactly like Henry.* But then she shook her head. *But that can't be him. Henry's dead.*

She shook her head again. Maybe she was still asleep in bed and this was a dream. She preferred the one where she was dancing with Frank Sinatra to this one, where she was getting arrested.

Henry stepped forward. The little dog in his arms trembled but didn't bark or growl.

"Jayne?" Dorothy asked. The dog looked up at her at the same time as the man did. His eyes met hers and softened.

"*Dorothy?*"

"Henry? Is that really you?"

"It's me," he said. "What's—"

"I thought you were dead! Are you all right?" She started to rush forward, but Officer Pierno gently tugged her back.

"Hold up. What exactly is going on here?" Pierno pointed at Henry and flashed his badge. "Do you have ID?"

Henry placed Jayne on the ground and fumbled in his pocket for his wallet. He handed it to the cop and shifted uneasily from foot to foot as Pierno examined his driver's license, then compared the address with the house number on his mailbox.

"Why did you think I was dead? Was it because you couldn't reach me for another date?"

Dorothy opened her mouth to speak, to tell Henry the whole crazy story and ask him about one million questions. But Officer Pierno answered faster.

"Someone with your physical description was found dead. We thought it was you. The resemblance is uncanny," Pierno said, walking in a slow circle around Henry, taking in every detail. "But we found something very interesting when we ran the victim's prints."

Though he remained standing, Henry's entire being appeared to collapse. His face fell and his shoulders slumped. Jayne started whining and scrabbling at his shins.

Henry absently lifted her up and buried his face in her fur. When he raised his head again, his eyes were full of tears.

"Was it someone who looked like me exactly? But with a pierced ear, and a mole right here?" He touched his temple with a trembling finger.

A very bad feeling pooled in Dorothy's gut.

"Yes," Pierno said. "The prints came up with a long list of petty priors for a Morty Pattinson. But the name didn't match the first ID made at the scene—the only ID we *could* make." Pierno glared at Dorothy.

Henry nodded and staggered to his front porch. He sat heavily on the wooden porch swing with Jayne beside him. He put his head in his hands and let out the saddest sigh that Dorothy had ever heard.

"That's my brother. We're twins—identical."

Dorothy gulped, locking eyes with Sophia and Blanche, then the cops. The Girls looked as surprised as she felt. Dozens of questions swirled in her head, but all she wanted to do was comfort Henry. He looked so sad and broken on that swing, his little dog curled up next to him.

"Oh, Henry, I'm so sorry. What a shock. What can we do for you?" Dorothy turned to the cops and her mother. "Can we get him some tea or something? A blanket? And can you take these cuffs off?"

Officer Pierno looked at Dorothy, then back at Henry, then back to Dorothy.

"Let's uncuff her," Murphy said. "She's obviously not a threat."

"I need to feed Jayne," Henry said. "I need to call my mother. She lives in Hoboken and probably doesn't know. Damnit, Morty!"

Henry erupted into fresh sobs, his head hidden again in his hands. Dorothy hadn't seen a man cry very often in her life, and his grief was so raw and painful. She wanted to wrap her arms around him and help. She jangled the cuffs at her wrists, feeling helpless.

Sophia sidled over to Henry. "Give me your keys, sweetheart. I'll feed the dog and get her some water." Henry moved slowly and handed his keys to Sophia as if in a dream.

*"Pspsps,"* Sophia said, and Jayne trotted right after her. She and Blanche disappeared inside the house.

"Henry, I'm so sorry for your loss. I didn't know you had a twin!" Dorothy replayed their conversations in her head. He had mentioned a brother at one point, and something about him wanting to borrow his boat.

"I wasn't . . . I wasn't very proud of him," Henry said, his voice hoarse. "He had his flaws, and my whole life I had to get him out of scrapes. I didn't want you to think the worst of me, considering he and I have so much in common, being twins." Henry rose to his feet again. "Why are you here, Dorothy? And in cuffs? Can someone tell me what happened?"

"Yes, am I officially cleared now?" Dorothy asked. "Especially since Henry is alive? Obviously, I didn't kill him!"

Pierno reluctantly removed Dorothy's cuffs.

"Watch her," he said to Murphy. "I'm going to call this in."

Pierno went to his car and spoke on his radio for a few minutes, then returned with a notebook and a small tape recorder. "Why don't you start at the beginning?"

The five of them, plus Jayne, moved to Henry's living room, a neat, masculine space with a woven blue rug, photos of boats on the walls, and a leather couch and a few overstuffed armchairs. A small TV set with antennas sat in the corner, next to an eight-track stereo system.

Jayne settled herself at Henry's feet as he explained that his brother had always been the wild one, often chasing get-rich-quick schemes, and willing to bend the rules when it suited him. He'd given their poor mother plenty of heartache growing up in New Jersey, and when he wanted to move down to Florida, Henry helped him get set up with an apartment.

He even loaned him his Porsche until Morty found a job and could get on his feet.

"But when Morty bought us matching Breitling watches to celebrate some business success, I suspected that he was up to his old tricks," Henry said sadly. "He couldn't help himself. Why work when in a day he could make a week or a month's pay with one of his schemes? It was frustrating."

Officer Pierno made occasional notes as the tape recorder whirred on the coffee table.

"I stopped lending him my car. I stopped giving him money, hoping that would help force him back on track. It was hard, you know?" Henry rubbed at his five o'clock shadow. "He was my brother. I loved him."

Then Henry sat silently for a long time. The kettle whistled, and Sophia disappeared into the kitchen. When she came back, she gave Henry a cup of tea and patted his shoulder.

"There, there," she said.

"Was he involved in conning women? Taking them out, then running off with their money?" Murphy asked.

Henry grimaced. "I hate to say it, but that sounds like him. He always had a lot of girlfriends, and they always wanted to help him. He was like a lost puppy dog to them, wasn't he, Jayne?"

He scratched behind Jayne's pointy ears. "But he was suddenly making more money. I don't know if it was from conning women, but he was always up to something. I knew it probably wasn't all legal, but I told myself that if I didn't know for sure, I could pretend he'd gone legit—or at least that he was trying to."

"So, when did you last see him alive? We'd like to retrace his steps and figure out what happened," Pierno said.

"It was the day of our date," Henry said, looking at Dorothy. "I didn't see him at breakfast, so I left a note for my brother and headed out to meet you. I'm sorry I had to leave you in the lurch like that. I tried calling your house later on, but the line was always busy."

Dorothy nodded. Rose had been on the phone all day, making wedding arrangements for Nettie. "Please don't apologize, Henry. I was angry at the time; however, now it's clear that other things were going on. But that's the reason why they think I'm your killer. They think we quarreled and that I was getting revenge on you."

"I'm so sorry you got mixed up in this. I always told Morty that not only was he hurting me with his behavior, he was putting himself in danger. But he always had one more scheme, one more idea that would put him over the top. And he'd asked me to help him with one last score. He wanted me to take him, and some package, on my boat to the Caymans. I wouldn't do it. I said no. He stopped speaking to me for a while after that. Now I wonder if I'd helped him with that, would he have gotten mixed up in this other business?"

"You can't think like that, honey," Sophia said. "People make their own choices. You tried to help him."

"Then he started working for a sugar company, making deliveries all over town to bakeries, restaurants, that sort of thing. But when I'd ask him about his work, he always got cagey. I wasn't sure that's what he was actually doing."

The word *sugar* rang a bell in Dorothy's mind. Big Sugar, Rose's pet theory. But that was just Rose leaping to conclusions about that singer named Sugar. Still, it was probably just a coincidence.

"Did he ever say the words *Big Sugar*?" Dorothy asked.

Henry's eyes snapped up. "Yeah, that was his nickname for his job, but I think it had another name."

"Big Sugar refers to the sugar *industry*," Pierno said. "It's big business down here. It's not a single company."

"Morty said Big Sugar had him running all over town.

Sometimes he'd mention someone called the General, saying he owed him a paycheck or wanted him to work nights."

As he talked, Dorothy flipped through her notebook, past the terrible drawing of Sugar and back a few more pages to when she and Rose had compared notes, after Rose and Blanche had tried to speak with the Bryants. She found the list of addresses that they'd been sending letters to. General Sugar Co. was on the list.

"So do you think he was making a sugar delivery when he was killed?" Dorothy said.

"Pipe down, lady. I'm the one asking questions here," Pierno said, crossing his arms. After a pause, he looked toward Henry. "So, do you think he was making a delivery when he was killed?"

Sophia smirked into her teacup.

"Maybe," Henry said. "When I saw him the night before our date, he was stressed. Like, really stressed. He wanted me to get the boat ready because he said some guys might be after him, and he'd need to lay low for a couple days. I was furious that he was getting involved with dangerous people. But he's my brother, so of course I offered to take him out on my boat with me and cruise around until things cooled off. I fueled it up, patched a few leaks, and stocked it with enough food and water to last a week. We were going to set sail after my date with Dorothy."

"So why didn't you leave together?"

Henry shifted in his seat. "We were supposed to. At the

last minute, Morty said he had one last job to do—one that would put him square with some people he owed money to, with enough left over to start a small legit business in Curaçao. He had an idea to create these foam things you can put in the pool. Like an inner tube or raft, but you don't have to inflate them. He was going to call them pool noodles," Henry said sadly.

Dorothy had a mental image of a swimming pool filled with egg noodles, carrots, and celery, like a giant bowl of soup. She shuddered. Pool noodles would never take off.

"The day we were supposed to leave he came and found me at Wolfie's," he said, turning to Dorothy. "I spotted him during our date. I tried to avoid him, but he looked scared."

Dorothy nodded. That checked with his odd behavior, seemingly trying to hide his face, and the times where he seemed like he wasn't paying attention.

Dorothy cleared her throat. "Morty had a note in his pocket, mentioning our date and the wedding."

Henry nodded. "He must have grabbed that from my day planner when he came to find me."

"I thought he was going to come up to our table," Henry said. He looked apologetically at Dorothy. "I didn't want you to meet him at all—let alone in that state. So I met him in the men's room. He said he was doing one last job for the General, then would meet me at the boat. He told me that if he didn't show by midnight to shove off by myself and head for open water without him. He told me to call a bait shop in the Everglades and ask for John Donson. He'd leave word that he was okay and where I should pick him up. I waited for him until midnight, and he never showed. I had a terrible feeling, but Morty was always running late. So I waited a few more hours.

"Finally I shoved off. I called that bait shop every day, multiple times, whenever I could dock and get to a pay phone. No word from him at all. That terrible feeling just got worse, you know? So I said *Screw it* and decided to come back and find him myself. I'd even thought about reporting him missing, but I didn't know exactly who the General was. No offense, but he could have someone on the inside, you know?"

Murphy shrugged and nodded at Henry knowingly.

Pierno lightly smacked him with his detective notebook. "We don't have any dirty cops on the force."

Murphy hurried to shake his head vigorously, for Pierno's benefit this time.

Dorothy tapped her forehead as pieces started to fall into place. "If Morty met you at the restaurant, that explains why the waitress thought that you had changed clothes," she said. "She must have seen Morty leaving the bathroom after you paid the bill."

Henry looked from Dorothy to the cops, his eyebrows knitted together in grief and confusion.

"So now I'm back," Henry said. "And here you all are. So what happened to Morty?"

# JAILHOUSE CROCK

## 25

*D*orothy, Blanche, and Sophia staggered out of Detective Silva's office. They'd voluntarily followed the police to the station and given lengthy statements. Henry had also come voluntarily and was still in another room, answering questions with Murphy and Pierno.

"Do you think they'll get to the bottom of it?" Sophia said. She took off her glasses and cleaned them on the edge of her cardigan.

"They better," Dorothy said. "We've told them everything

we know, and I assume Henry is doing the same." As they turned to go, Silva came back out of her office.

"Ms. Zbornak?" she said sternly. "Though I appreciate your cooperation today, you're still a person of interest."

"What?" Dorothy said. "Henry is alive! So I obviously didn't kill anyone!"

"Not from where I sit. We still don't yet know who killed Morty," Silva said, pointing the end of a pencil at Dorothy. "And the original motive still applies; you could have gotten conned and been angry. With a case of mistaken identity, anything's possible."

"But I had no idea that Morty even existed until today!"

"Exactly," Silva said. "He could have been posing as Henry, especially since they look so much alike."

Dorothy slumped against the cold tile of the precinct wall. It was starting all over again! She couldn't take it. At this point, just turn her into a cockroach already.

"If you have more questions for my daughter you can direct them to her lawyer! *Capisce?*" Sophia shouted so loudly that the whole precinct heard. "I'm going to get you that Matlock man to represent you, pussycat. Even if I have to empty my savings! Even if I have to sell myself on the street! Blanche, maybe I can borrow some of your outfits."

"That won't be necessary, Ma," Dorothy said before Blanche could unleash the retort forming on her lips. "But thank you." She'd hire a lawyer if she needed to. Whatever it took to clear her name. She'd also explain to her mother the difference between real-life lawyers and those who played them on TV.

As they exited the interview room, another door opened and deposited Rose, Jason, and Nettie into the hall. The six of them stared at each other, surrounded by the ringing phones and the bustle of the police station.

"What are you doing here?" Dorothy asked.

Rose looked a little worse for wear, with mascara streaks down her face. Jason held an ice pack to his head and had the beginnings of a black eye. Nettie's hair was completely disheveled, but she had a huge grin on her face.

"You should have seen it! Aunt Rose and I got kidnapped, and Jason saved us!"

"You helped! The way you wrestled that guy from the back seat was like a scene out of *Charlie's Angels*!" Jason said, throwing his free arm around Nettie. She leaned her head on his shoulder, making him cry, "Ouch!"

"Oops, sorry, baby," she said, rubbing his shoulder gently. "And Aunt Rose helped, too! She socked the perp with her purse."

Rose blushed, looking down at her dinged-up pocketbook, which appeared to be leaking some sort of watery fluid.

"Oh, it was nothing. Just a good wallop. I don't think it would have had the same impact if I hadn't had a jar of pickled onions in there."

"But are you all right? And who kidnapped you?" Blanche cried, taking in Rose's disheveled outfit and pickle-juice-stained lap.

"Let me at him!" Sophia said with narrowed eyes. "I want to hit him with *my* purse, too. Maybe a little lower than his head, though."

"He got away," Jason said. "But the police have his car and a full description."

"Do you have any idea who he is?" Blanche said.

"I'm not exactly sure, but I may have seen him around the hotel. I don't know his name, but I think I once heard Chip refer to him as the General."

Wheels turned in Dorothy's head. The name General reminded her of something Henry had said back at his house. If only she'd been taking notes! Too bad she'd been handcuffed much of the time. Should she go back and tell Silva to look into this General person? She should be able to trust that by sharing this knowledge she would be looked at in a more favorable light, and that maybe the police would be able to track down this General. But she was exhausted, all out of trust at the moment.

"Let's get out of here," she said to her friends. "I have some questions for all of you."

The six of them piled into Dorothy's car, with Nettie on Jason's lap. On the drive back to Richmond Street both parties shared their stories, interrupting each other and spilling over with details, questions, and gasps of surprise. When they stumbled into the living room, the older women kicked off their shoes and collapsed onto the furniture.

Nettie and Jason busied themselves in the kitchen, emerging with cups of coffee and a tray of cookies.

"Those are for the wedding!" Rose said.

"We're eating them *now*," Nettie said. "You all have been through a terrible ordeal. Butter and sugar helps."

"That's it!" Dorothy said. "Jason, this General person—do you know if he's in the sugar business, perhaps?"

Jason's eyes went wide. "You know, I think he is! Let me call Chip. He's always schmoozing for business opportunities. He might know."

Jason disappeared into the kitchen. Dorothy leaned her neck back on the couch. Her head felt like an Olympic pool full of so-called pool noodles, each one a piece of new information, sliding around each other and slipping through her fingers as soon as she tried to grasp them. Henry, Morty, Big Sugar—how did it all fit together? They had almost all the pieces, but they weren't adding up to answers.

Dorothy helped herself to a cookie. It was tiny and round, dusted with powdered sugar.

"Rose, this is the best cookie I've ever eaten," she said.

Rose's exhausted face brightened. "Thank you, Dorothy. At least I can do something right."

Jason emerged from the kitchen. "I called Chip, and he doesn't know. He's going to drive over to the club and ask around."

"Wonderful," said Rose. "Now why don't you all get some rest? We have everything all set for the wedding in two days—well, except for the venue, and the dress, and some herring-related matters. And I need to telephone the Bryants and inform them that we will be having a St. Olaf wedding, which they're welcome to attend."

"No, Aunt Rose, please," Nettie said. "You've done so much and gotten kidnapped along the way! You need to rest."

"And I'll tell my parents myself," Jason said. "It's only right that I do it. I'm not scared of them anymore, or what they'll say."

"Good for you!" Blanche said. "Nice to see you standing up for yourself."

"And, Aunt Rose, if it doesn't work out—if the wedding doesn't cross every *T* or dot every *I* like the town elders want, that's okay with us."

"We don't care about the trust," Jason said. "We just want to get married."

"Please tell me you're *not* going to try to elope again!" Rose cried.

"No," said Nettie, "we want to celebrate with everyone who came down to be with us. But if there's no herring, ceremonial plate, or spinning of the groom—"

"Or if the donkey is incapacitated, or the officiant forgets the exact words to the Binding of the Pinkie Fingers, we'll be okay," Jason finished. Rose smiled, and Dorothy saw at least ten years disappear from her face.

"You know what? I'm okay with it, too," she said. "I have one last idea for a venue, and I'd like your opinions. I also have something that might work for Nettie's wedding dress, but it already has the feet sewn in."

As Rose huddled with Jason and Nettie, Sophia softly snored on one of the coral rattan armchairs. Blanche covered her with a crocheted blanket.

A few moments later the phone rang.

Dorothy answered it, hearing a familiar voice on the other end. Special Agent Crum cleared his throat. "I'm calling to tell you that we haven't located the man who kidnapped your friends, so we're sending a unit to watch your house tonight."

"Should we be worried?" Dorothy said, instinctively clutching her cardigan tighter around herself like a protective shield.

"I don't think you're in any real danger, but it's better if you all stay home with the doors and windows locked. If any of you need to leave the house, don't go alone."

"Okay," Dorothy said. "Did you figure out who Morty's killer is?"

"Not yet." Crum sighed. "But we're close. In the meantime, stay safe."

After hanging up the phone, Dorothy looked over the living room full of people she loved. She wanted to keep them safe and wouldn't let any of them leave tonight, deciding that they'd make up the foldaway bed for Nettie and Jason. Dorothy vowed to stay up all night and keep watch, telephone at the ready. But first, she needed something.

She dug through the hall closet, removing raincoats, umbrellas, several badminton rackets, and a clarinet of mysterious origin until she found what she was looking for. Dorothy had really wanted the fondue pot when she bought Little League raffle tickets last spring, but she had figured she'd hold on to the baseball bat she'd won instead and give it to some neighborhood kid. Holding it now, she tested its weight in her hands.

If whoever killed Monty or tried to kidnap Rose and Nettie showed up at their house, they would have to contend with her.

# ANY WAY YOU SLICE IT

········26········

After an early dinner of frozen pizza, everyone started to get ready for bed. Rose loaned Nettie a cornflower-blue nightgown and gave Jason a pair of Charlie's old pajamas that she'd kept in the bottom drawer of her dresser. Jason made a series of phone calls, first to his parents, then to Patricia and Chip, filling them in on everything.

"My family wasn't as mad as I thought they'd be! I think the fact that Nettie got kidnapped and I almost died rescuing her made them go a little easier on me." He laughed. "I might have played up my injuries a bit."

"You leapt from a moving motorcycle onto a speeding car!" Nettie said proudly. "You should brag about that for the next hundred years!"

"I agree," said Rose. She tousled Nettie's hair. It was so nice having the two of them sleep over. She wanted to keep them there with her in her home forever. Maybe her roommates wouldn't like the idea, but it would sure be fun, she thought.

"What if they stayed here indefinitely? It would be like one big sleepover party," she whispered to Blanche.

"Well, it would certainly be cozy," Blanche said. "And I wouldn't mind having a man around the house again. But they're young. They want their own place, not someplace with you three little old ladies and me."

The doorbell rang, startling Sophia awake.

"*Who's there? What's there?*" she shouted. Then she barked and growled for a second before looking around the living room and realizing where she was. "Oh. I dreamed I was getting shoved through that doggie door again. Except I was a white poodle. And on the other side was a spaniel, but he was also Christopher Plummer, and then we—"

"Spare us the gory details, Ma," Dorothy said as Rose answered the door.

It was a rain-spattered Patricia and Chip, holding a giant white bakery box between them and smiling.

"A peace offering," Patricia said, handing the box to Rose. "You've been through so much, and we thought you could use some cheesecake. Jason said it was your favorite."

"How lovely," Rose said, taking the box. "Come in out of the rain. I apologize, we're already in our pajamas."

"We came straight from the hotel," Patricia said, removing her khaki trench coat and shaking the rain from her somehow still-perfect hair. "Jason told us all about your ordeal, and we just feel terrible!"

"Are you ladies all right?" Chip asked, entering the foyer in a cloud of woodsy cologne. He carefully wiped his feet on the doormat. Rose noticed his expensive loafers were soaked, and she was surprised to see he was actually wearing thick socks with them tonight. "Do you need anything? I could run out to the store for you."

Rose had always thought Chip was a little obnoxious, but his kind efforts to help softened her up. "You can serve up that cheesecake for us!"

After getting silverware and paper plates from the kitchen, Chip cut the cake and handed out generous slices to everyone. Patricia sat down next to Jason, right on the floor. She hugged her brother tightly and kissed the side of his head.

"I was so scared when I heard what happened!" she said. "Are you sure you don't have a concussion?"

"I'm fine," he said, shaking off his older sister's attentions.

Patricia turned to Nettie. "You take care of him for me, all right?"

"I won't take my eyes off him," Nettie promised. "You should have seen him wrestle the kidnapper!"

"Speaking of that guy," Jason said. "Chip, did you have any luck asking around about him?"

Chip cleared his throat and shook his head. "I thought he sounded familiar, but no dice."

"But isn't he that General guy? The one who hangs around the cigar bar?" Jason pressed.

Chip pushed his wet hair back from his eyes. "It sounded like him at first, especially when you said he was bald—but the General drives a Ferrari, not a sedan. And he's a businessman, not a criminal lowlife. It wasn't him." He clapped Jason on the arm. "Sorry, man, wish I could be of more help."

Sophia yawned, and Patricia checked her diamond-studded watch. "It's getting late, and we should let you sleep," she said. "And I forgot—Mom and Dad wanted me to tell you in person: They are willing to scale back the wedding. I convinced them that something small and intimate would be more appropriate, considering everything that's happened."

"Thanks, sis," Jason said. "That's a relief."

Rose let out a long, happy sigh and beamed at Nettie. Family rifts had been mended, and everyone was safe and sound, wrapped in blankets, tummies full. She could finally relax with her slice of cheesecake, even if store-bought wasn't as good as homemade.

# STILL WATERS

······· *27* ·······

*R*ose was threading paper garlands the following afternoon when the doorbell rang, followed by a series
of loud knocks. She rushed to the front door and peered
through the peephole. She wasn't going to open the door
to just anyone, as Dorothy had instructed. It was only the
mailman, Rose saw with relief.

They'd spent the morning with Nettie, Sophia, and
Dorothy, driving around Miami looking for a wedding dress
for Nettie. She had liked some off-the-rack dresses that didn't

fit, but the ones that did fit, she didn't like.

Jason had gone off with his groomsmen to pick up their suits and collect the flowers from the florist that the Bryants had chosen—and paid for.

By four p.m., all of them were exhausted and more than a little cranky. But everyone was careful not to snap at each other, considering what they all had been through. Every time the phone rang, Dorothy jumped up to answer it. Rose could tell she was hoping it might be the police calling with an update—or maybe Henry. But the next call was from Cousin Gustave.

Rose steeled herself. She wasn't sure she could handle another stern talking-to from her cousin, or some new St. Olaf–mandated cowpat to jump over.

"I'm so glad you're safe, Rose," Gustave said. "We all are."

Rose's shoulders relaxed slightly.

"I wanted you to know that I spoke with the town elders and told them how hard you've worked to make this a true St. Olaf wedding. No matter how the ceremony goes tomorrow, I'll make sure Nettie gets her trust."

Rose's mouth hung open and her eyes watered. The town elders finally recognized her efforts, and Nettie would be taken care of. A huge grin spread across her face.

"Rose? Did you hear me?" Gustave said.

"Yes!" Rose laughed. Then she bit her lip, remembering how difficult it had been to get to this point. "Gustave, why did you make it so hard for me? I almost thought there was some reason you didn't want this wedding to actually happen."

Gustave cleared his throat. "I suppose because I was jealous that you've been able to build a life outside of St. Olaf. This is the first time I've ever left the state, and well, I suppose I didn't believe you could really do it. I am sorry to say I was wrong."

Rose gulped, her damp eyes now filling with tears. She never thought in a million years that she'd hear Cousin Gustave say he was wrong.

"So it didn't have anything to do with trying to keep the money from the trust?"

"Of course not," Gustave said. "When did you become so suspicious of everyone?"

She didn't need to think hard about it. Ever since the day she found a corpse in her cheesecake, she'd grown a little less naive and trusting. Right then and there, Rose made a vow to herself that she wouldn't let everything that happened stop her from thinking the best about people.

After they hung up, Katrina rang. She'd attempted to take the bus to Bal Harbour but ended up at the Vizcaya Museum on the opposite side of town and needed instructions on how to get back to the Cabana Sun Hotel. Rose handed the phone to Sophia, who patiently explained the route to her.

Rose was glad to see the St. Olafians venturing out and exploring this colorful city without her to hold their hands.

Maybe they'd see how wonderful Miami was, despite the unexpected freezer corpses and attempted kidnappings. Maybe they'd come back someday, she thought. She knew their photos and memories would last a lifetime.

The phone rang one more time. Dorothy answered, then turned to Rose. "I was hoping it was the police, telling us they found the killer. But it's for you."

Rose picked up the receiver. *It's Chip*, she mouthed. Dorothy went back to her crossword puzzle, which she had been filling out in ink.

"How are you all doing? All safe and sound at home?" Chip asked.

"Yes," Rose said, wishing he'd get to the point. She had about a hundred more herring balls to make.

"Great! I was told to call you and invite you to a rehearsal dinner. I know it's last minute, but the Corzons have offered the use of their boat, and my in-laws thought it would be a nice chance for the families to get together before the wedding tomorrow."

"How nice!" Rose said, perking up. "What time?" The frostiness around her heart regarding the Bryants had thawed a bit after they'd given up fighting over the wedding, but she realized there'd been a few icicles left. As Rose jotted down the rehearsal dinner details from Chip, the rest of the icicles melted clean off.

That evening, the four older women and the soon-to-be-wed couple strode down to the Venetian Marina. Nettie wore a white sundress that fluttered in the breeze, and Rose sported a sailor dress that she hadn't worn since Fleet Week in 1977, when she'd accidentally gotten an anchor tattoo on her lower back.

Storm clouds had rolled in, making the sky prematurely dark as they strode past rows of docked pleasure craft.

"I hope we don't get rain." Dorothy frowned, just as a distant rumble of thunder sounded.

"They say rain's good luck," Jason noted, chucking Nettie under the chin.

Nettie grinned. "That's on the wedding day. But I'm not hung up on that stuff. I'm happy no matter what."

"I hope the boat has a roof!" Rose said. "I'd hate to have to cancel this lovely gesture from the Bryants."

"The Corzons' boat has a big awning, and an interior cabin, if I remember correctly," Jason said. "Speaking of, I don't see it yet."

A whistle pierced the twilight, and soon Chip appeared striding down the pier with an uneven gait, dressed sharply in crisp khakis and a pink polo shirt. Rose wondered if it was because he'd already had a cocktail or two, or if his croquet injury was bothering him. She was about to ask Dorothy if she noticed anything strange about the way he was walking, but Chip had already reached them and was gesturing impatiently.

"Are you all right?" he said. "I thought you were coming at seven thirty?"

"Oh, I'm sorry," Rose said, smacking herself on the head. "I could've sworn you said eight. I should have written it down."

"Did we miss the boat?" Sophia said. "That happened to my sister Lydia, and I never saw her again."

"I never knew I had an aunt Lydia!" Dorothy said. "What happened to her?"

"We lost her somewhere between Genoa and Ellis Island," Sophia said. "I don't think she really wanted to come to America. Last I heard, she married a Merchant Marine named Ralph."

"Don't worry," Chip said. "They had to vacate the slip, but they're not far out. I stayed behind to bring you out in the dinghy."

He led the group farther down the pier, where a set of wooden stairs led to a platform at water level. A bright orange inflatable boat was tied to a post and bobbed gently in the water.

"Will we all fit in that?" Blanche asked dubiously.

"Of course," Chip said. "It's quite seaworthy." He took Blanche's hand and gently helped her into the boat, then did the same with Sophia, Dorothy, and Rose.

"What a gentleman," Rose said. Jason's side of the family really wasn't so bad, once you got to know them.

"Shouldn't we put on life vests?" Dorothy asked. She was

wedged between Sophia and Blanche on one of the bench seats.

"We're not going far," Chip said. "The boat's just there." He pointed to some lights a little farther out on the bay.

He yanked the cord on the outboard motor, causing it to roar to life. The dinghy veered away from the pier, and everyone's hair blew back in the wind.

The lights from small craft on the bay glistened like stars against the dark blue of the water. Distant strains of "Margaritaville" from a waterfront restaurant faded away as the motor churned. Rose huddled close to Nettie for warmth. As they drew farther out, the dinghy began skipping over the waves, jerking everyone from side to side. Rose had to hold on to Nettie with one hand and a rope on the other, just to stay in her seat. She craned her neck to the row behind her to see Blanche, Dorothy, and Sophia bouncing like rag dolls in the back.

"Could you slow down a bit?" Rose shouted.

Clearly Chip hadn't heard her. She shouted again. Flecks of water began splashing Rose in the face. The hairdo she'd worked hard on with hot rollers and Elnett was already wrecked, and she'd look a mess once they reached the rehearsal dinner.

"For goodness' sake, Chip—can you *please* slow down?!"

Chip glanced at Rose, set his face in a hard line, and pushed the throttle down all the way. The boat zoomed ahead even faster than before. A sick, uneasy feeling enveloped Rose like a fog as they bounced uncomfortably over the waves. Why was he boating so recklessly? This clearly wasn't good for their joints—not even for the people under sixty.

"When will we get to the boat?" Sophia asked. "I haven't experienced this much turbulence since Dorothy's marriage."

"That's—a—low—blow, Ma!" Dorothy shouted, staccato over the waves.

"Almost there, ladies!" Chip called over his shoulder.

Rose peered ahead. She didn't see any lights, or any boat. In fact, it seemed like Chip was taking them out to a deserted space in the middle of the bay.

Alarm bells started clanging in her head: *Anyone could be a criminal. Anyone.*

Rose casually leaned toward Nettie. "I don't think he's taking us to the Corzons' boat."

Nettie turned to Rose, her eyes wide.

Nettie leaned and whispered in Jason's ear as Rose turned to her three friends behind her. She silently mouthed the word *danger*.

"What?" Sophia said. "I can't hear you over this motor!"

Suddenly, Jason stood up and grabbed Chip's collar. "What are you *doing*?" he screamed. "There's no boat here!"

Chip rolled his eyes and slowed the motor.

He looked at Jason, then sucker punched him.

Nettie screamed as Jason went overboard. Chip revved

the engine again, leaving Jason sputtering in the frothy wake.

"I *knew* I didn't like you! That's my fiancé!" Nettie lunged at Chip, scratching at his face with her fingernails. "You can suck eggs!"

Rose screamed, trying to pull Nettie off him. He was clearly violent—unhinged even, and she didn't want Nettie to get hurt. They rocked back and forth as Chip tried to pry Nettie's hands off his neck.

"Get off me, you tacky little hillbilly!" Chip yelled, once he'd torn one of Nettie's hands from his neck. "I did you a favor getting rid of that hideous wedding dress that looked like a tea cozy!"

Nettie gasped. "That was *you*? Hit him with your purse, Aunt Rose!" Nettie screamed.

But Rose had only brought her evening bag, a tiny satin affair that wouldn't hurt a fly.

Rose turned to her friends. "What do we do?" They were frozen in shock, arms wrapped around each other.

Rose tried to stand up to reach the motor and slow the dinghy down. Her legs wobbled like she was trying to stand on a Jell-O salad, and she fell to the dinghy floor, where a few inches of water sloshed around her, soaking her dress. She struggled to a sitting position just in time to see Chip toss Nettie overboard.

# THICKER THAN WATER

## ·············28············

*D*orothy watched in horror as Rose scrabbled over the edge of the dinghy, reaching for Nettie just as the young woman disappeared under the surface.

Dorothy grabbed at the back of Rose's dress, yanking her toward her.

"You're not going overboard, too!" Dorothy yelled as Rose sagged against her legs.

"What in heaven is going on?" said Blanche. "He's just going to drop us all into the watery deep?"

"That seems to be his plan," Dorothy said, scanning the waves for Nettie. After a moment she reappeared a few yards behind them, her hair plastered to her head and sputtering for breath.

"Look!" Sophia said. "I think I see Jason back there, too!"

Dorothy squinted into the night. Darkness had fallen, but she could see the fabric of Jason's shirt as he swam toward them, even though the distance between him and the boat grew wider with every second.

"Talk about a horrible brother-in-law," Sophia said.

"How can you joke at a time like this? I'm too young to die!" Blanche wailed.

Dorothy rose to her feet, taking a few steps toward Chip. He made a sudden, exaggerated martial arts move with his arms, causing Dorothy to rear back.

"I'm not going to attack you," Dorothy shouted. "Let's just talk it over. We won't do anything to hurt you!"

"It's too late for that," Chip yelled, his voice skipping into a higher register. "You and your meddling have ruined everything!"

"You mean our investigation?" Dorothy said. "We were just trying to clear my name. We had no idea it had anything to do with you!"

"You stupid old woman," Chip spat. "It has *everything* to do with me."

Dorothy's mind went still for a split second. "Why did you kill Morty?" Dorothy asked calmly. Chip was certainly acting like a killer, but she still didn't have all the pieces. Only the desperation of a cornered man would make sense of his current behavior.

"I'm not saying anything! You shut up!" He pointed a shaking finger in Dorothy's face.

Dorothy noticed that Chip's eyes bulged from his sockets and that they were tinged with red. *He might be on something*, she thought. He was certainly acting hopped up and erratic, and she'd need to try to calm him down if any of them were to have a chance of getting out of this alive.

"It's okay," she said, putting on her best teacher voice: clear, low, and calm. The voice that quieted a riotous class-room in thirty seconds flat. The tone she used when getting problem students to open up to her. The voice she used on the administration when advocating for extra credit for the kids who needed it. "If you're going to throw us overboard, you might as well tell me what's bothering you."

Chip looked at her, then back to the darkness ahead.

"Who am I gonna tell at the bottom of the bay?" Dorothy continued, meeting Chip's wild eyes. "Seriously."

Chip leaned forward, so close to Dorothy that she could smell his rancid breath. "I had it all figured out. The General was going to make me his second-in-command. No more bowing and scraping to the Bryants, taking orders from my own wife. He knew I was smart—it was all my idea!"

"What was your idea?" Dorothy said, slow and even, trying to draw him out.

"To use the two biggest industries in Miami—sugar production and the tourist industry—as our fronts. I knew that if we could make deliveries in and out of hotels, restaurants, you name it, we could make our moves all over the city and no one would look twice."

"Uh-huh." Dorothy nodded, trying to force a gentle smile. "That's a brilliant idea, actually."

"I know," Chip said. "And then Morty had to mess it all up. He started skimming off every delivery, stealing our product, thinking me and the General wouldn't notice."

"So you're a drug dealer?" Sophia asked. "What was it—snow, hash, toot, liquid heaven, jelly beans?"

"I'm not a drug dealer! We were moving stuff you didn't want people looking at too closely—anything that fell off a boat, so to speak." He rubbed at his nose vigorously for a moment. "Okay, yes, some drugs, too, here and there, sure."

"You had an impressive operation," Dorothy said, trying to butter him up. "And Morty got greedy."

"That's right," Chip said. "And no one would even be the wiser if the General had followed through."

"So you killed him," Dorothy said flatly.

Chip turned down the motor, causing the dinghy to slow. "I caught him in the act, trying to sneak off with a load of product. We scuffled, and he pulled a knife. I didn't have a weapon on me, so I banged him on the head with a fire extinguisher and shoved him in the freezer. He stabbed my foot with the knife before I could get the door shut. I freaked, not knowing if he was dead or just knocked out, so I jammed the door and ran off to call the General."

Chip's hands shook as he cut the motor. The dinghy bobbed in the waves as fat raindrops began to fall. "I'm not supposed to get my hands dirty—not like that. That was part of our deal. The General said he'd take care of it, take him somewhere else."

"So Morty wasn't supposed to be found at the hotel," Dorothy said.

"Exactly," Chip cried. "You don't crap where you eat, you know? I'm trying to build the business. I didn't want cops crawling all over the place, not to mention the bad publicity. The General was supposed to finish Morty off where no one would ever find him. Later he told me he got tied up with another job. Now I wonder if he was hanging me out to dry."

The rain pounded harder, stinging Dorothy's face. She'd gotten him to open up, but here they were in the middle of the bay. She looked around for any other boats, but there was no one around to help them. She prayed Jason and Nettie were okay, but even if they were, they were dozens of yards away at best. Dorothy snuck a glance back at her mother and friends. Rose was sobbing, looking out behind them for Nettie and Jason. Sophia was fiddling with her purse handle and saying the holy rosary, and Blanche wept into her scarf.

"The whole operation was so easy. Of course, it made things tough when the Cabana's kitchen was under construction, but we operated in hotels all over town." He looked at Sophia for a long while. "We were about to expand into old folks' homes, can you believe that? The General said it was genius."

"It was," Dorothy said, trying to keep him talking to prolong the time between now and their likely watery demise. "But we won't tell anyone. If you just take us back to shore, we swear not to tell anyone anything."

Chip laughed, an echoing, high-pitched sound. "You think I'm stupid, just like the Bryants. Well, I'm not, Grandma. Since you're the biggest and the strongest, I'll get rid of you first."

He loomed over Dorothy, reaching toward her neck.

Dorothy juked from left to right, trying to avoid his grasping hands and making the boat rock from side to side. Chip grunted and lunged at her, pushing her toward the edge of the dinghy.

"Get your hands off my daughter!" Sophia yelled, standing up on the bench seat and bringing her purse down hard on Chip's head. For a moment, he remained stock-still, his eyes unfocusing and rolling back in his head.

"Grab him!" Blanche shouted.

Dorothy clutched his waist, pulling him down onto the dinghy floor. "Roll him over!" She pushed on his stomach. The water in the bottom of the boat had gotten deeper with the rain, and bubbles emanated from his mouth.

Blanche stepped over the seat but lost her balance, falling on top of Chip. She tied his hands tightly behind his back with her scarf, double- then triple-knotting it. Together, Blanche and Dorothy propped him up against the side of the dinghy.

"Does anyone have anything else we can tie him with?"

Rose seemed to shake out of her stupor and grabbed the loose end of a rope from the keel. "Try this!"

Blanche and Dorothy secured the heavy rope around Chip's legs.

"We need more," Dorothy said. "What if he wakes up?"

"I have an idea!" said Blanche. She reached under her dress and started shimmying. After a moment, she swung a pair of pantyhose in the air. "These are silk, you know."

"Hand 'em over," Dorothy said with a snap, then wrapped the pantyhose around Chip's midriff, pinning his arms in place. Dorothy pulled her own pantyhose off, regretting that she'd worn the control-top ones when the operation started proving difficult. Rose removed her white stockings and then helped Sophia roll down her thick compression hose.

"At least buy me dinner first!" Sophia grumbled.

The last of the sunset had disappeared behind the horizon, and goose bumps covered Dorothy's arms and legs. Chip awoke, and once he discovered that he was trussed up in lingerie like a Cornish game hen he started to wriggle and squirm, grunting like an animal.

Dorothy wasn't quite sure how to work the outboard motor, but she yanked the cord like she'd seen Chip do. She steered the dinghy in a tight circle, trying to approximate where they'd come from. It was hard to see in the dark, but a line of distant lights indicated the shore.

"We have to find Nettie and Jason!" cried Rose, perched at the front of the dinghy like a figurehead, peering into the night.

# SHAKE IT OFF

······· **29** ·······

*B*ack at home, Rose hugged Dorothy tightly as they watched the sun rise through their kitchen window. After the excitement of narrowly cheating death, finally rescuing Nettie and Jason, making it to shore, and watching Chip get taken away in cuffs, neither one of them could sleep. After being fully checked out by paramedics, Sophia and Blanche had gone straight to sleep, but Dorothy and Rose spent the entire night talking, putting together the last missing pieces

317

of the puzzle as they ripped seams and hand-stitched a very special garment together.

Rose's hands still shook as she thought of what might have been. Chip could have killed them all. Perhaps Chip hadn't meant to go that far, but he'd ended Morty's life all the same, Rose thought.

She couldn't believe he'd even brought them cheesecake the night before he planned to kill them! She shook her head. He'd gotten in so deep with one murder that he felt the only way out was to commit six more.

And poor Patricia, she thought. Working her tail off for her family—meanwhile her husband was using their business to help run a criminal enterprise right under her nose. Talk about sleeping with the enemy. After the arrest, Jason and Nettie left to pick up Patricia themselves to tell her the news, and they all spent the night at the Bryants'.

That was a sleepover Rose was glad to miss.

She didn't want to see Patricia's world crumble before her eyes, or deal with any more pain and heartbreak. Seeing Nettie and Jason get shoved overboard had been almost too much to bear. Thank goodness they were young and strong and able to tread water. She'd almost lost her own life, as well as those of her friends. Rose wiped her eyes.

It was time to brush herself off and put the horrible ordeal behind her. After all, she had a donkey to wrangle and a wedding to attend.

# ALL YOU NEED IS LOVE
# (AND CHEESECAKE)

············ **30** ············

*T*he day of the wedding had finally arrived, with a few rain clouds and a last-minute shipment of dried herring delivered by FedEx. Dorothy stood among the guests in wedding finery who lined the walkway to the front door of 6151 Richmond Street. All had eager smiles on their faces, despite the light rain that began to fall on their heads.

A string quartet, shielded from the rain by a couple of beach umbrellas, began to play the opening notes of Journey's "Don't Stop Believin'," and a hush fell over the crowd. Shortly, the little Petrosini boy picked his way across the lawn, throwing fistfuls of flowers from a handheld basket, a look of grave solemnity on his face. Next came the maid of honor, Bess, in a poofy pink dress with a drop waist, beaming on the arm of Jorgen, resplendent in his traditional Norwegian bunad, accessorized with a fading black eye, courtesy of Mr. Corzon.

The hush turned to laughter and scattered applause when a donkey stepped onto the lawn braying triumphantly and carrying Jason, whose feet almost reached the ground. Jason wore a well-cut dark suit over a traditional bunad vest in orange, white, and green, the colors of the Miami flag. He shook his dark hair out of his eyes and smiled bashfully as he clutched the donkey's mane, trying to keep his balance.

At the end of the aisle, Jason gracelessly dismounted his ride at a makeshift altar constructed with tables borrowed from the Cabana Sun Hotel and draped in Rose's heirloom lace tablecloths. Stepping in front of a garden trellis strewn with colorful paper garlands, flowers, and palm fronds, Jason handed the reins to Sophia, who led the donkey to one side and fed it an apple from her purse.

Finally Nettie appeared, escorted by a beaming Gustave and Rose. She clutched a vivid bouquet of roses and peonies as she made her way down the aisle, her sparkling eyes locked on her groom. She glowed in her tea-length, high-necked ivory lace dress and stepped through the grass in traditional wooden clogs hand-carved by Gustave as an early wedding gift.

A ruggedly handsome gray-haired minister from the

Bryants' congregation in Palm Beach cleared his throat as the bride and groom came to stand still before him with clasped hands. Dorothy knew that the minister had been paid a hefty bribe by Mr. Bryant to incorporate various St. Olaf elements into the service, and she hoped he'd follow through, for Rose's sake.

"I should get his phone number," Blanche whispered to Dorothy. "In case I have any sins to confess in the near future." She stared at the minister for a moment longer. "I think I just might."

"Shh," said Dorothy as the ceremony began.

First Jorgen presented a tray bearing two pairs of folded stiped pajamas to the minister, who waved his hands vaguely over them. "May these pajamas keep your marital bed as warm as your hearts," he intoned. He then proceeded with a traditional wedding ceremony, pausing occasionally to consult Rose's handwritten instructions. In all, he dutifully rang a bell, yodeled, and flawlessly performed Sigmund's Soul Search by staring deep into both Jason's and Nettie's eyes for a full minute each, making sure the youngsters were unblinkingly committed to the wedded life. Occasionally Rose would demurely raise a hand and correct his pronunciation of certain Norwegian words.

Several hymns were sung by the guests and personal vows were exchanged between Nettie and Jason, causing Dorothy to dab at her eyes with a tissue. Their hopeful earnestness was so far from the cynicism she'd occasionally had about romance because of her experience with Stan; seeing this couple with so much love between and around them made her optimistic that sometimes relationships could be different. After all, they'd had to overcome feuding in-laws, a sabotaged wedding dress, a kidnapping, and even a murder to get to this point. Maybe there was hope for anyone to find a love like that.

At the end of the ceremony, the couple kissed while Rose blew hard on the goat horn, making Sophia cover her ears. When Nettie and Jason turned to face their cheering guests as a married couple, everyone gently pelted them with unin-flated balloons in the St. Olaf tradition.

Nettie tossed her bouquet high in the air, and it was caught by a tall woman in a demure pink suit who held it triumphantly above her snow-white bouffant. She brought the bouquet to her nose and inhaled the scent of the flowers, then winked in the direction of the best man. Jorgen's eyes widened and he stood a little straighter.

"Miss Sugar?" Dorothy said. "I never thought we'd see her again."

"She begged me for an invite at the bachelorette party," Sophia said, shrugging. "After the clown performance, she said this was a wedding she just had to attend!"

Dorothy laughed, then took her mother's arm and followed the wedding party into the living room. The donkey remained in the front yard, where it grazed on dandelions while a few children petted its furry sides.

The living room was draped in more paper garlands and

overflowed with flowers on every surface. The coral sofa had been pushed to one side to make room for a makeshift dance floor. The DJ from Coconuts spun records in a corner, and an expensive, multitiered wedding cake the Bryants had ordered perched on a table next to Rose's homemade cookies.

Gustave and Katrina carried trays of herring balls, offering them to guests as Nettie's side of the family mingled happily with Jason's. Rose had ended up inviting everyone from both lists, even though having that many people at the house was likely a fire hazard. Mr. and Mrs. Corzon slowly danced together in one corner of the living room while the bellhops from the Cabana Sun Hotel sampled herring balls from the buffet.

Rose rushed by, trying to shoo a green parrot out the open front door.

"Jason wanted a bird to fly over Nettie's head," Rose said. "I didn't think he'd bring it inside."

"It was a wonderful ceremony," Dorothy said, catching her friend's arm as the bird landed across the room on Jorgen's shoulder. He let it sit there as he poured a glass of champagne for Miss Sugar, entranced by her statuesque beauty.

Dorothy noticed that the Bryants shook hands with everyone, but their eyes were haunted beneath their smiles. They were putting on a brave face for Jason's sake, but soon word would get out about their son-in-law and the dirty dealings at their hotel. Sophia stood next to Patricia, talking her through her marital betrayal and offering pearls of Sicilian wisdom gleaned from Sophia's own hard knocks in life.

"I guess no family is perfect," Rose said. "Everyone has their problems, no matter what they want it to look like from the outside."

"I'll say," Dorothy said. She thought of Henry and his brother. Rose and her St. Olaf cousins. Herself and her mother. And all the hurt feelings and love underneath it all.

Nettie sidled up to the two women, and Dorothy noticed the flush of joy in Nettie's complexion, which nicely set off the string of Rose's pearls around her neck.

"You look beautiful," Dorothy said. "We're so happy you wanted to have the wedding here."

"I'm so lucky Aunt Rose kept her wedding dress all these years!" Nettie cried. "Thank you both for making the alterations. And for saving the day—again."

She twirled, releasing the faint scent of mothballs. Rose kissed her on the cheek.

"I couldn't have done it without my friends," Rose said, smiling at Dorothy.

Dorothy surveyed the room, made zany and festive by their overnight efforts. After a week of false accusations, multiple suspects, a frozen corpse, mistaken identity, and attempted murder, they'd finally made it to this glorious day. Blanche and Sophia joined Dorothy and Rose, and they all wrapped their arms around one another. They'd survived, thanks to their friendship.

They watched Jason and Nettie slow dance in their living

room, and Dorothy realized that love—among friends, family, and between a loving couple—truly conquered all.

As the party rocked on into the evening, Dorothy stepped out onto the lanai to get some air. She was filled with joy at Nettie's happiness, but she felt an ache in her heart. She'd longed to dance with someone at the reception, to have someone look at her—even for a moment—the way Jason looked at Nettie.

But just as Dorothy sat down and got comfortable on the chaise longue, Detective Silva knocked on the sliding door. She was dressed in a pale blue pussy-bow blouse under a structured gray pantsuit and held a small gift-wrapped box in her hands.

"I came to tell you that you're officially off the hook for Henry Pattinson's murder—I mean Morty's—oh, you get my point," she said, sitting next to Dorothy on one of the white wrought-iron chairs.

"Thank you, but I gathered that when you took my statement at the marina," Dorothy said curtly. Her feet hurt, and she had little patience left for the policewoman who'd made her life more difficult with her accusations.

"I get that you're angry with me," Detective Silva said. "But I was just doing my job. You have no idea how tough I have to be, leading this squad. There was pressure from top brass to get a quick conviction since the murder happened in a tourist area. And for a while, you were our strongest lead." She handed the box to Dorothy.

"Wedding gifts go in the living room," Dorothy said, waving it away.

"It's for you," Detective Silva said. "A small token of my appreciation for helping solve the case. If it wasn't for you and your friends, we wouldn't have looked into Chip or his connection to the General. We knew something was up with Big Sugar, but if you hadn't gotten Chip to crack on that boat, we'd never have made the connection."

"Well, we *were* pretty brave," Dorothy admitted with a nod and slight smile. "And resourceful." She unwrapped the small box, opening it to find four small golden medallions nestled in velvet inside.

"These are civilian medals of honor," Detective Silva said while Dorothy turned one of the medallions over in her hands. "There will be an official ceremony in a few weeks for you and your friends."

Dorothy tucked the medal back in the box and looked up with a smile. "Thank you," she said. "I'd rather not have been a suspect, or nearly drowned in Biscayne Bay, but it's nice to be recognized."

"No hard feelings?" Detective Silva asked. She offered her hand to Dorothy.

"No hard feelings," Dorothy said, taking her hand and shaking it warmly.

"Maybe keep that in your purse," Detective Silva said as she stood to leave. "Just in case you get into any other scrapes with the law." As the detective stepped back into the house to leave, Dorothy rested her head in her hands and sighed, once again alone at a wedding. No partner, no boyfriend, no date. Maybe she was too old to find love again. Maybe it was just too late for her.

She heard the sliding door open again. She looked up with irritation, about to ask Detective Silva what she wanted now, when she realized who the tall figure was joining her on the lanai. *Henry*.

Henry sat down next to her on the chaise, smelling of Stetson cologne and herring balls, which he carried on a little plate. "Would you like some?" he asked. "Your friend Rose pushed them on me."

Dorothy smiled and set the plate to one side. "It's good to see you," she said.

"I wasn't sure if I was still invited. Honestly . . ." He trailed off into a deep sigh, conveying the depth of his grief from the past few days.

"You don't have to say anything," Dorothy said. "I'm just sorry for your loss."

"I like you, Dorothy, I really do," Henry said. "But with everything that's happened, I'm just not feeling very romantically minded. I'm sorry."

"I completely understand," Dorothy said. "I'm still recovering myself."

"I'm going to sail to Curaçao. Scatter Morty's ashes in those turquoise waters. It's what he would have wanted."

Dorothy squeezed his hand. "You're a good brother."

"I'm not sure how long I'll be gone, or when I'll feel like coming back. But when I do, would it be okay if I gave you a call?"

Dorothy smiled. "I'd like that," she said.

Henry gave her a polite peck on the cheek, then walked off into the night.

Even though she knew it was all for the best, seeing Henry walk away made Dorothy feel hollowed out and lonely all over again. Though she'd cleared her name and they'd all saved the wedding, she couldn't help but feel a little bit deflated knowing that she'd ended up exactly where she'd expected: sitting alone surrounded by the sights and sounds of a joyous wedding party. Maybe she'd just have to get used to that feeling, she thought.

She rearranged her features into a close approximation of a smile. As she stood up to rejoin the party, she noticed Blanche, Rose, and her own mother peeking at her from behind a potted hibiscus and giggling.

"What are you three doing?" Dorothy intoned. "Can't a woman have a few minutes of privacy?"

"Not in this house," Sophia said, creeping out from behind the hibiscus. "Come on inside."

She waved Dorothy into the kitchen, where Rose and Blanche were already waiting for them at the breakfast table. Rose held out a platter of mini cheesecakes drizzled in lingonberry sauce. Each woman took one, along with a cocktail napkin emblazoned with HAPPY 60TH! and an image of some birthday balloons. They'd already run out of the wedding-themed ones.

Dorothy took a bite of the cheesecake. It was creamy and comforting, the graham-cracker crust perfectly crumbly. It reminded her of all the cheesecakes shared with her girlfriends at the kitchen table in their pajamas, at restaurants for their birthdays, and celebrating holidays together. After a few bites, she felt a teeny bit better than she had a moment ago.

"So what did he say?" Blanche said, wiping a touch of lingonberry sauce from her lips. "And was that a kiss I saw?"

"He seemed very gentlemanly," Rose added. "I'm sorry I was so tough on you about dating. You never know where you'll find love. Or with who."

"Are you going to see him again?" Sophia asked.

Dorothy put her cheesecake down and lifted her hands like a shield. "That's none of your business. Suffice to say that I'm still open to finding love."

Rose and Blanche squealed, and Sophia gave Dorothy a knowing look.

"I'm glad to hear that, pussycat. But the next time you meet a man, let's run a background check on him and his whole family."

"I have no problem with that," Dorothy said, and laughed. Rose put down her plate of cheesecake and grasped Dorothy's hands in her own.

"Of course," Rose said, her eyes sparkling, "if there's any trouble with Dorothy's next date, at least we know the four of us are pretty good at this crime-solving thing."

# ACKNOWLEDGMENTS

To my husband, Nick Courage, for his love and encouragement, and for talking with me about his grandmother Rose, a true Golden Girl.

To my parents, who have helped me so much over the years and instilled a love for reading, writing, and good cheesecake.

To Adrienne, Maria, and Danny for sharing helpful details about Miami in the 1980s. Thank you also to the Henry family.

To editor extraordinaire Adam Wilson, the wonderful Cassidy Leyendecker, cover designer Amanda Hudson at Faceout Studio, art director Amy C. King, and the copy editors and proofreaders, such as Meredith Jones and Guy Cunningham, who helped polish this book to a golden shine.

To my amazing friend and agent Andrea Somberg and the team at Harvey Klinger Literary Agency.

To my golden girlfriends Emily Erstling, Abby Wilson, Emily Askin, Lindsay Patross, Annie Colvin, Moira McGuinley, Allison Carey, Danielle Chiotti, Melissa Bramowitz, Bronwyn Rowntree, Tamar Krishnamurti, Bess Newman, Alisa Drooker, Michelle Elsner, Janine Jelks-Seale, T. Kamara, Katie Glosser, and Katie Kurtzman.

To Ryan Labay, Susan Hans O'Connor, and Robin Carroll, thank you for being a friend.

To the writers, producers, cast, and crew of *The Golden Girls* for inspiring me and making life funnier and sweeter for me and so many others.

# ST. OLAF'S KISS CHEESECAKE RECIPE

**For the crust:**
2 cups graham crackers
(12 full-size crackers)
½ cup slivered almonds
½ cup melted butter
⅓ cup sugar

**For the filling:**
32 oz. (four 8-oz. packages)
cream cheese
1 cup sugar
1 T. all-purpose flour
1 t. vanilla
4 whole eggs
1 egg yolk
½ cup cream

**For the drizzle:**
1 jar of ligonberries
sugar to taste
water as needed

Spray or butter a 10-inch springform pan.

**Crust**

Crush graham crackers and slivered almonds in food processor.

Add melted butter and sugar. Process to combine.

Press evenly onto bottom and up the sides of the pan.

**Filling**

Bring all ingredients to room temperature. Preheat oven to 400 degrees.

Beat cream cheese, sugar, all-purpose flour, and vanilla. Then gradually beat in whole eggs, egg yolk, and cream.

Pour into pan and bake 15 minutes at 400 degrees.

Lower oven temperature to 250 degrees and bake 1 hour.

Remove cheesecake from oven and cool on wire rack.

Refrigerate a few hours or overnight.

**Lingonberry Drizzle**

Slowly heat lingonberries in saucepan over low heat.

Add water one tablespoon at a time to thin the sauce to desired consistency and add one teaspoon of sugar at a time to desired sweetness.

Gently spoon the sauce in the middle of the cooled cheesecake and refrigerate to set.

Serve by dipping knife in water and wiping the blade between slices.

*Recipe developed by Sandra Ekstrom and Rachel Ekstrom Courage*